Forbidden

R.D. Power

Written 2008-2009

Edited by Anna Genoese
Cover design by Rebecca Swift
Formatted by Polgarus Studio

ISBN 978-0-9917983-8-4

The author is not a representative of nor endorsed by any of the trademarks used or discussed in this book, which is a work of fiction and not meant to imply or represent reality.

Dedicated to:

My sister, Kathy Lalonde

PROLOGUE

The jury members filed into the courtroom and took their seats. Kyle Summers was instructed to stand. Awaiting the verdict, he shook so hard, he had to support himself by leaning on the table in front of him. His future—his life—came down to this decision. From what he'd been through in the last few months, including repeated attempts on his life, he had become so cynical he was almost certain the verdict would be guilty, which meant the rest of his life in prison for helping terrorists murder sixty-one Americans. His legs gave out, and he fell onto the chair. His lawyer helped him to his feet. The foreman read the verdict:

"On the count of providing material support or resources to designated foreign terrorist organizations …"

CHAPTER ONE

Context

Kyle Summers was damaged. Psychologically. He hadn't been born that way, but his parents had made sure of it. He'd had the misfortune to be born to parents who resented his very existence, parents who never wanted to be parents, but who were too Catholic to abort the child.

Carl Summers and Elizabeth Cox met at Caltech. She was pursuing her bachelor's degree in economics; he was a brilliant graduate student of physics studying quantum mechanics under Nobel laureate Richard Feynman.

Attracted by Carl's obvious economic potential, Liz estimated her expected utility as the wife of a professor at an elite university and elected to marry him. But her assumption that, all else equal, a brilliant Caltech PhD would land a post at a top school failed to account for man's imperfect reasoning skills. It turned out that Carl's y gene conferred a distinct disadvantage in a physical sciences academia already glutted with them and under pressure from activists to balance the body types. The only offer of employment he got upon completing his doctorate was from the University of Saskatchewan.

To say that Liz was put out about this turn of affairs would be like saying Hitler was a meany: it was true, but failed to capture the profundity of the matter. Recalculating her expected utility, she decided to cut her losses and substitute a better catch for Carl. But fate intervened: her contraceptive sponge had failed her. So, the bitter woman followed her husband to Saskatoon.

A hard twenty-three-hour labor did little to endear the neonate to Liz, as he'd had the audacity to survive the birth. Unwanted from the start, Kyle was left to himself for the most part. His cries for food brought a bottle of baby formula; his cries for attention brought a slamming door and loud music. The cranky baby put more pressure on the marriage. Carl blamed the baby for his wife becoming as frigid as a Saskatoon winter.

To preclude going mad, Liz enrolled in the graduate program in economics at the university. That kept her occupied for the next five years. Every day, Kyle was deposited in daycare from eight in the morning till six at night, and put to bed at seven.

Meanwhile, Carl had been making a name for himself in the nascent field of quantum computing. He had got an offer from the University of Chicago for a professorship the year before, but his wife had another year to go for her PhD, so he turned it down. When Chicago renewed its offer the next year, Carl immediately accepted. He told his wife with a smile that they could leave Saskatoon for Chicago. She then apprised him that she'd be taking an assistant professorship at Chico State in sunny California.

That spawned a shouting match that marked the end of the marriage.

*

Six-year-old Kyle stood in the doorway, unnoticed as usual, as his parents bellowed at each other. Upset at the proceedings, he watched and whimpered until the argument got around to him. Then he suffered a mental breakdown.

"You take the little bugger!" said his mother.

"You're his mother, you take him!" returned his father.

It went on like this for a few minutes before Carl noticed his son sitting on the floor, rocking back and forth with a look of vacancy in his teary eyes. Evidently feeling guilty about this, Carl picked him up and said to his wife, "I'll take him, you miserable bitch."

She packed her bags and left for good. A month later, father and son moved to Chicago.

The incident exacted a lasting psychological toll on the wretched lad. He'd known he was unloved and unwanted before, but now he became convinced he was unlovable and worthless. He seemed to be sick all the time and ate very little; he was often depressed, anxious and intractable; he became unresponsive to his father or anyone else, sitting alone in his room whenever home and standing at the fence by himself in the Chicago schoolyard; he became aggressive when bothered.

One February day in the schoolyard, things came to a head when two boys started shoving him around. Little Kyle went wild, punching, kicking and biting his opponents until they ran away screaming with Kyle throwing rocks at them. The vice-principal insisted Kyle get professional help.

Carl enlisted the help of a child psychologist at the University of Chicago, which was the first break Kyle had got since birth. The woman worked with Kyle for three years to help him overcome the emotional damage inflicted by his parents. Recognizing his great intellect, she got him into a program for gifted students. She suggested to Carl that he get Kyle involved in sports to help him develop socially.

Carl tried karate, hoping the discipline its advocates preached would help control his son's violent outbursts. Kyle took to that sport and worked hard to excel. The psychologist also strongly recommended that Carl spend time with his son. He complied by allowing Kyle to hang around the physics department after school. Kyle could read, observe, or use a computer, but was to keep quiet. Carl even let his son sit in on his evening quantum physics classes. Students in his courses at first thought the boy sitting in the back row was a child prodigy, until his father introduced his son.

"The young lad in the back is my son, who prefers to sit here *quietly* than to stay in daycare. You won't notice him after a couple of classes."

Ironically, he *was* a prodigy, who began to understand the material his third time through, and had it mastered by his fifth time through at age twelve. He started sitting in on other physics classes.

By the time he turned fourteen, Kyle had achieved normality for the most part. Low self-esteem and a conviction he was unlovable were the chief persistent issues from the neglect and rejection he'd suffered as a child. He was terrified of girls and couldn't even talk to a pretty one. Not that girls wanted anything to do with a boy who was the epitome of the geeky teenager. His tightly-curled, brown hair looked like a cockeyed bird's nest; his buck teeth protruded through his lips; his green-grey eyes were appealing, but hidden behind thick glasses; his crooked nose, broken from a karate kick, would have to stay that way until his growth spurt ended. Pimples festooned his face and spangled his shoulders. Still, accepted as a peer in university physics classes and having achieved his black belt in *shorin-ryu* karate, he felt happy.

The University of Chicago admitted the fourteen-year-old into its physics program the next September. He worked on his father's research project: basic quantum computer design.

In his senior year, his father died of cancer. Never close to his father, Kyle put the loss behind him quickly, but he was left alone in the world. He worked every waking hour to crowd out his loneliness.

At age seventeen, Kyle completed his bachelor's degree, his thesis presenting his radical ideas for overcoming a key roadblock to creating a quantum computer: the tendency of a quantum computer to decay from a quantum state into an incoherent state as it interacts with the external world—a phenomenon known as decoherence. He continued in the PhD program the next fall, intending to advance toward his goal of building a quantum computer.

Unbeknownst to Kyle, during his first three years of graduate study, someone was putting his ideas to good use. Dr. Richard Hugel had a research specialty in superconductor-based quantum computing, and was making enough progress to persuade some venture capitalists to bankroll his new firm, Hugel Quantum Corp. Rick had read Kyle's thesis and saw at once that his mission to build the world's first quantum computer would be much more likely to meet with success with Kyle's ideas for controlling decoherence. He tried to recruit Kyle, but was shocked and insulted when Kyle refused. Kyle was dubious that Rick's model would prove viable and chose instead to stay in school and pursue his own theories.

Kyle assumed the copyright on his thesis would protect his ideas for building a quantum computer. He found out different near the end of his third year when he discovered Hugel Quantum Corp. had built and patented a component based on the method for controlling decoherence described in his thesis. Eager to express his disenchantment, he showed up at the modern building housing the company in Chicago and began screaming at Rick. Rick suggested he settle down, and explained what copyright does and doesn't cover, but concluded by re-extending his invitation to join his firm.

"Work for a thief? Go to hell," responded Kyle. "You can't get away with stealing my ideas."

"Read copyright law. I have every right to turn your ideas into reality. If you were too naïve to know that, then tough luck. There's nothing you can do about it." Rick cared not that the smaller man held him in disesteem until the smaller man held him in a rear grab and demonstrated a little of what it takes to earn a third degree black belt in karate. Only the intercession of Rick's small staff saved Rick from serious injury.

Kyle stormed out, went home, and learned from a quick look on the Internet that Rick was correct. What Rick did may have been immoral, but was perfectly legal. It left Kyle in a quandary. How was he to build his quantum computer prototype with an important component already appropriated by the competition?

The episode also raised another conundrum. He was ready to write his dissertation, which would detail his ingenious ideas for building his quantum computer, but he now knew that if he did, anyone could take the ideas and build his computer. The obvious deduction was he could not write his dissertation—at least, not until he could build his machine and patent it—so out of the PhD program he dropped.

To bring his computer to fruition, he needed at least ten million dollars, he figured. He was willing to risk his entire fortune, but that still left him $9,999,137 short. Investors would be needed, but he had no idea how to find them and nothing to show them except for the component owned by his competition, which the most likely investors were already backing, so he took a job as a lab technician at the university to pay the bills and cast about for investors.

To make matters worse, he now had legal trouble. Rick had filed assault charges against him. There was method to Rick's madness here. His scientists had hit obstacles that were beginning to look insurmountable. Investors were getting antsy with the lack of progress. He needed a breakthrough and he felt sure Kyle could provide it.

Rick's lawyer phoned Kyle with an offer. The assault charges would be dropped if he would agree to join Hugel Quantum Corp. The lawyer interpreted the stream of execrations flowing out of the earpiece as a no. He sweetened the pot: join Hugel and you get credit for your ideas and five percent of the company. Kyle rejected the offer because he didn't trust Rick, and because he continued to believe that the Hugel model was foredoomed to failure.

The assault case went forward until it became clear that Kyle would not change his mind. His threat to make sure everyone would learn in the trial that Hugel Quantum Corp. had purloined the only promising piece of technology it owned convinced Rick to withdraw the charge. No sense making investors more nervous.

*

Fortune seemed to smile on Kyle at that juncture, for the day after the charges were withdrawn, he met the answer to his prayers. Amy Janssen was a young venture capitalist looking for promising investments. She'd been keeping a close eye on the Hugel situation for her employer, Comptech Venture Partners. She found out the company had used Kyle's ideas for protecting quantum information from decoherence, which had turned out to be its only breakthrough to date. She also knew Hugel was desperate to hire Kyle. Clearly this Kyle Summers was a hot property.

On Kyle's lunch break, Amy walked up to him in a courtyard and introduced herself. Women were as complicated to Kyle as quantum mechanics was to everyone else. Pretty women turned this genius into a nervous moron. And this woman was *pretty*. She had appealing, soft brown eyes, full lips, prominent cheeks, and a voluptuous body—but her lustrous dark red hair down to the middle of her back was her best asset. They shook hands, Amy smiling warmly at him and Kyle looking at the ground anxiously. She invited him to lunch, saying she had a business proposal. He was too nervous to respond.

Seeing the effect she was having on the nerd, she smiled at her power over him. "I work for Comptech Venture Partners. We're a venture capital firm looking for good investments. We've been studying the quantum computer research industry for a few years now, and we've learned something very important: you are considered to be the up and coming star in the field. Let me tell you, it's unusual for a venture capital company to invest in an individual, but we want to get our greedy little mitts on you before the competition does," she said with a vivid smile.

He returned a timorous smile.

She went on: "I know you need money to make your computer. I think we can really help each other." She put her hand on his arm, and he took a deep breath. With another smile, she said, "Let's have lunch and talk about it." He nodded, and they went into a local bistro. They were shown to a small, round table by the window.

Once seated, she said, "So, Kyle, I hear you're a genius." Kyle shrugged as his eyes darted to hers and back down. Her short skirt drew Kyle's focus away from the floor to her comely legs, as she sat with her right leg crossed over her left. She rocked it rhythmically to keep his attention. As his eyes dragged themselves away from her thighs on the way to her eyes, they got held up on her plenteous breasts, which were confined in a tight sweater. When his eyes had their fill there, they headed back to the floor, detouring along her legs. Amy continued, "Nothing impresses me more than a man who has a knack for ingenious breakthroughs. Those are the kind of men who make something of themselves and of anyone lucky enough to be associated with them." Kyle blushed and smiled. He glanced at her eyes, then her legs before returning his gaze to the floor. "I'm new at this, but I've discovered I have a real talent for discovering talent. I'm convinced we can create a cutting edge company in no time. Are you interested?"

"Sounds great, but there must be a catch."

"No catch other than the question of ownership. My firm will require a substantial part of the firm in return for our investment. You're the best, I know, but even you have to admit that this is a long shot. The technology is only in its infancy, after all. To be perfectly honest, we don't actually expect you or any one person or firm to invent a quantum computer. We do think you can invent some important and ultimately lucrative components for a quantum computer."

"Are you aware that Hugel Quantum Corp. has already stolen one of my components?"

"I'm aware they used your ideas to build it, yes. Please, Kyle, don't be shy; look me in the eyes." He did as she asked, but couldn't keep his eyes on hers for long. She resumed: "Legally they did nothing wrong, but it was unethical to proceed without your permission. I have to be honest with you, Kyle, and I hope this helps earn your trust: Comptech Venture Partners is also backing Hugel Quantum Corp."

"But we can't both succeed; our models are too different."

"As I said, we think the quantum computer will come about from innovations from various companies and individuals. We backed them almost from the start—and don't get angry about this—mainly because we thought their method of controlling decoherence had great promise." Kyle's cast his eyes upward. "We know now it was your design. That's precisely why I'm here today. You're a proven commodity, and we're betting you'll come up with more breakthroughs. And, believe it or not, it's good news that we own a big stake of Hugel. It will be a lot easier to come to an agreement to share the technology if we need to."

"It's so galling that they have to agree to share my technology."

"I know they took your ideas, but the law is on their side, since they own the patent. But let's not let that sidetrack us now; it's too far in the future. We'll work that out, trust me." With another friendly smile, she placed her hand on his arm and squeezed lightly. Evidently thrilled with her touch, his breathing quickened. "We would start with seed money of maybe two hundred and fifty thousand dollars, and can go up to several million if the early work looks promising. What do you say, Kyle?"

"How much of my company would your firm demand?"

"We'll negotiate, but forty-nine percent is standard for start-ups."

"Half the company?"

"As I mentioned, this is a risky business, and the partners demand a lot for the risk. Our partners are patient investors. They know they won't see any return for years—but, again, that patience comes with a high price."

"I'll need to check this out with a lawyer."

"Of course. Here's my card. Have your lawyer call me."

"Sounds like we might be able to come to an agreement," said Kyle. "It seems almost too good to be true. Good luck is in the habit of ignoring me."

"Not anymore." They shook hands. "This firm will be our baby. I'll be spending a lot of time with you to nurse you through the challenges of each stage of the company life cycle." He smiled again, this time holding her gaze for a few seconds.

*

Kyle incorporated Summers Quantum Computers the next week, and signed the Comptech contract two weeks after that. With the seed money, he bought secondhand machinery to enable him to begin the process of building computer components. He rented a small, dilapidated factory building in Evanston, Illinois, just northwest of Chicago, and he hired two research assistants.

Amy, spending much of her time at Summers Quantum Computers, became the de facto office manager. Apparently seeing her initial role primarily as cheerleader, she continually expressed her absolute confidence he would succeed and told him how much she adored his genius.

Kyle's infatuation with her soon became love. Because he felt unworthy of any woman, one he considered a goddess in particular, he kept his feelings to himself. But as his awkward grins became beaming smiles and as his shy glances became longing gazes, she evidently recognized her hold over him and used it to wield subtle control.

He yearned to spend time with her and would interrupt what he was doing whenever she was in the office to be with her. When she criticized him for ignoring his responsibilities and interfering with hers, he apologized and thenceforth spent time with her only when invited. He spent sixteen hours a day on his research, more now to please her than to create the prototype.

It took almost a year before he got up the nerve to ask her out in his unique way. He stood outside the office she used when onsite and paced for almost ten minutes. Then he knocked and opened the door when invited in. He stood at the door visibly shaking and unable to utter a syllable.

"You want something?" she said with a friendly smile.

"Uh, yes. Uh, I know you probably don't want to and, um, I would never blame you because you're so perfect and I'm so flawed, so feel free to say no and … I mean, would you possibly want … No, never mind."

"Are you trying to ask me out?"

He nodded sheepishly.

*

She had known it would come to this sooner or later and had decided how to react, but worried about how he would take it. She considered him homely—his buckteeth were gross, his complexion poor, his hair out of control, his horn-rimmed glasses hideous, his wardrobe appalling—and often winced at his social ineptness, but she was fully aware of the bright future this man had. Wanting to keep this diamond in the rough hidden from the world, she had made no attempt to polish him.

She answered, "I'd really like to date you, Kyle, but technically it's a conflict of interest for me. You're a client."

Clearly embarrassed and upset, he apologized before rushing back to his work station at the back of the building.

"Ah, shit," she said to herself as she followed him. "Kyle, we need to talk," she said.

Wiping away some tears, he said, "No, we don't. I didn't know I was a mere client to you."

"No, you must know you're much more than that."

"What am I then? A meal ticket?"

"Of course not."

"It's because I'm ugly, isn't it?"

"I don't think you're ugly."

"Is there really any need for you to be here so much? Are you worried I'm not working?"

"Kyle, you're being ridiculous now. My job is to help your company through its growing pains to maximize your chances of success. I need to be here for that."

"Why?" She had no ready answer for that. He continued, "I don't want you looking over my shoulder every step of the way. I want you to leave."

Shocked at this turn of events, she struggled to recover from a potentially disastrous ending to her assigned role at Summers Quantum Computers—which was, in a nutshell, to keep an eye on him and make sure he worked hard.

"Please, Kyle, settle down. I didn't mean to hurt you. You have to know I think the world of you. I admire you more than anyone I've ever met. As I said, I do want to go out with you. I just meant we have to be really careful because it puts me in a very awkward situation. You understand that, don't you?"

"I guess."

"Tell you what. Let's take it really slow. We'll start with seeing each other once a week socially, all right?" He nodded with his bucktoothy smile. "But I need to be able to do my job.

I need to spend a lot of time here, if only to reassure my bosses that I'm on top of the situation. All right?" Another nod with a smile.

*

The couple dated weekly for several months. Kyle took some steps to better himself as their relationship matured. He was preparing to pop the question. He got braces to rein in his salient teeth; he got his nose straightened; he got treatment for his acne; he bought some new clothes for their fancy dates. Still, she never once invited him in for a nightcap.

By month eight, he became a little insistent on going further than a kiss outside her door. She invited him in, but only to talk. "I know it might be frustrating for you to hear, but I'm that very rare lady who wants to keep her virginity for her husband."

At first, his face fell. Then his eyes opened wide. Maybe she was trying to hint at what he what he wanted more than anything on Earth! He told himself, *I know she would only say yes because she figures I'll be rich, but what more can someone like me expect?* He sat there silently for a minute screwing up his courage. Then he stuttered, "Uh, does that mean you want to … uh, you know, get married or something?"

*

Her eyes popped open in shock. She hadn't meant to imply that, but now realized that was an obvious inference. She just about yelped, "No!" but controlled herself. If she rejected him, he might eject her from his life. His prospects were too bright to risk it. His research on the quantum computer was going very well.

"God, Kyle, that was unexpected. I'm so surprised that I honestly don't know what to answer. May I have some time to consider your proposal?" Disappointed, he nodded slowly. "Don't be angry," she said.

Then she rallied as she overcame her shock. "I'm hesitant only because this is—and I'm definitely not saying no—this is absolutely a conflict of interest. I would have to quit my job before accepting your proposal, and where would that leave your company's venture funding? You're so close now. I'll tell you what. As soon as you succeed in creating and selling the world's first quantum computer, I will marry you!"

In ecstasy, he kissed his goddess.

The last major stumbling block to completing and testing his prototype was that his arch rival owned one of the key components. Kyle reminded Amy of her promise to deal with this issue, and she assured him she was working on it. But when she came to him with a proposed resolution, he rejected it out of hand.

"Kyle," she said with evident angst, "we've worked out a way to get your component: a merger with Hugel."

"What? No way!"

"I knew you'd object, but our lawyers have been working on this for some time, and they feel this is the best solution."

"I won't go along with it. It's my technology! It's blackmail!"

"You have to be realistic. I know this is a sensitive subject and, frankly, I think what Hugel did was despicable, but it was perfectly legal. That's why he has you over a barrel." She went to him, took him in her arms and kissed him. "This is the only way. In fact, continued funding by Comptech depends on it, but … listen to me, please. Comptech knows full well that you're close. They also know that Hugel is spinning his wheels getting nowhere. He's desperate for a deal, and I've used that to your advantage. He's agreed to a twenty percent stake in your firm in return for sharing the patents."

"Twenty percent! He did nothing to earn that. Nothing other than steal. That twenty percent could be worth billions some day, and he stole his way into it."

"Kyle, please. As infuriating as it is, that is beside the point. He owns it, and every court in the country will back him. Listen! Comptech has agreed to split the twenty percent. That leaves you with forty-one percent, Comptech with thirty-nine percent, and Hugel with twenty."

"Jesus Christ! This is so unfair. Maybe I can come up with another way to control decoherence, or at least a variation of my idea different enough to get a new patent."

"No, Kyle. It's a lot bigger than you. My company is insistent on this."

"It might take a year or two, but I think I can work my way around it. Comptech won't have to give up ten percent to that asshole."

"No, you don't understand. Our partners have invested a bundle on Hugel and want some return soon. They will not stand for Hugel going out of business; they won't permit a lengthy delay to get around a problem that only you have."

"If Comptech was foolish enough to back Hugel, they deserve to lose their investment. If they're foolish enough to drop me, let them. I'll find other investors. It shouldn't be hard at this stage. Tell them to go to hell."

"After everything I've done for you, you'd do that to me?"

"Not you. Them."

"I'm still their representative, Kyle. And, anyway, that strategy wouldn't get you your component back. Worst case scenario, they'll put your component up for sale on the open market, and another competitor will grab it. You have absolutely no choice on this. If you look at this without emotion, you know this is the only way to go."

He was so incensed, he had turned deep red by this time. "No! I won't do it!"

"We'll get to use all of Hugel's modern machinery. It's already paid for. That should speed up the process."

"I said no and that's final."

Doing her best to hide her consternation, Amy tried, "How about this: you give me ten percent, which will be ours if and when we get married, and I'll tell Hugel it's ten percent or nothing for him." Judging by his expression, she knew he remained unpersuaded. She needed to seal the deal. "Kyle, I'm ready to quit Comptech. I'm ready to accept your proposal. Are you ready to start the new company with me as your wife to be?"

His fury evaporated at once and he smiled. "Yes." He hugged her. "When can we get married?"

"I stand by my original pledge. The minute you build and sell your first computer, we'll set the date. In the meantime, let's pick out my engagement ring."

CHAPTER TWO

Twenty Months Later

"A small company named Qubit Inc. of Evanston, Illinois, startled the high tech world today by announcing it would soon be ready to sell the world's first fully operational quantum computer," said the TV news commentator. "The announcement was so unexpected, the first reaction from high tech analysts was one of disbelief. None of the major university labs or multinational computer companies that are spending millions pursuing this research is close to a working prototype.

"Anticipating this reaction, the genius behind the machine, Dr. Richard Hugel, brought along one of his computers and took it through its paces. As dubious scientists, investors, and bureaucrats watched the demonstration, their jaws seemed to drop in unison. He used the computer to solve in mere seconds a complex problem that would have had the most advanced supercomputer chugging away for months. Reactions after the demonstration ranged from excited amazement to deep concern …"

Deep concern took precedence with the competition. The nation's leading computer, chip, and memory manufacturers augured a bleak future when this new technology rendered theirs obsolete, so they did what any huge conglomerate does when faced with worrisome competition: they ran crying to the government. They hired expensive lobbyists to cajole, threaten, and bribe—the legal kind for re-election purposes—congressmen and senators.

The lobbyists began by orchestrating a campaign by employees and shareholders to besiege their members of Congress with petitions to prevent the sale of quantum computers. Congress did what it always does when faced with such tempests: it established a committee to hear the petitions to justify what the honorable members already knew would be the outcome.

At the hearing, the lobbyists presented a wealth of cogent arguments against the new technology, but the central points that had the lawmakers nodding were three: there currently existed no capacity to defend the nation's computers—including those at the CIA, FBI, NSA, NSC, Homeland Security, and Pentagon—against intrusion by the users of quantum computers, foreign or domestic; enemies of the United States ranging from hostile nations to terrorists organizations could use this technology to design weapons of unimaginable destruction; and America's economy would face destabilization as the new technology put millions out of work and caused the stock markets to teeter under the weight of bellwether companies facing bankruptcy.

The last argument resonated most with representatives and senators from states with millions of voters who depended on the digital computing industry for their dividends, paychecks, or pensions. The lobbyists were careful to keep the issue out of the media as much as possible. The hearings were blacked out.

Qubit Inc. was invited to testify at the hearing and given two hours, compared with forty-seven hours for petitioners, to present their arguments. The fledgling company had no political pull, no understanding of what it was up against, and no money to hire the experts that might have been able to fight the enactment of the law.

The company sent its president, Rick Hugel, to argue its case. A well-spoken and charismatic man, who had always excelled in public fora, he spoke with a confidence bordering on hubris, but he was out of his league in the cutthroat world of national politics. Focusing on America's history of leading the pack in technology, he argued that quantum computers were simply the latest example of how American genius would keep the nation number one in the world. But he could not effectively counter the fear tactics employed by the politically savvy lobbyists.

Shy of negative media coverage from an outright ban, the House inserted a little-noticed measure into the middle of an omnibus bill that stipulated an undefined "delay" in the introduction of this new technology until its effects could be better understood. A pittance was set aside to fund research into the societal and economic effects of quantum computing. The bill also made it illegal for the American inventors of the technology to go offshore and manufacture it, a measure that would almost certainly fail a test in court, but with appeals would effectually delay the computer's introduction for years. The bill became law with all the alacrity millions of dollars in political contributions could buy.

Other than a few small publications in the computer industry, the independent ones of which condemned it, the media missed or ignored the new law, focused as they were on the latest earth-shattering sex scandal gathering force in Washington.

After receiving the government's edict, the three Qubit principals met to discuss the fallout. The meeting was tense.

"You said you'd handle the politics. You kept me out of it because you're the face of Qubit, because you're the persuasive one, because you're the expert on politics. Well, you blew it!" exclaimed Kyle to Rick.

"Kyle, that's uncalled for," rebuked Amy. "His presentation was exceptional."

"Except it didn't work!"

"We were unprepared for the onslaught," conceded Rick.

"No kidding. It was your responsibility to be prepared."

"It's just a temporary setback," suggested Rick.

"A temporary setback," barked Kyle. "It's a multi-billion-dollar annihilation!"

"Calm down, Kyle," scolded Amy.

Remaining worked up, Kyle bleated, "By the time we're permitted to enter the market, our competitors will have already caught up or passed us. Until that time, we won't be allowed to enter the market."

"Don't be so cynical," advised Rick.

"You're so goddamn naïve, you drive me bonkers. This is why you blew it, Rick. They shut us down because we beat them. If they allowed us to get to market, they'd eventually be done and they knew it. Time and again, I warned you two of this, but you dismissed me every time. I suggested we just go to market so they wouldn't have the chance to shut us down, but you two insisted on a public spectacle, so you could bask in the spotlight."

"It was an incredible amount of free publicity that yielded almost two dozen immediate orders for our computer and a hundred more potential buyers," pointed out Amy.

"The idea was fine; your timing was the problem. We were still months away from setting up our manufacturing capabilities."

"Without those orders, our lenders would not have given us the money we needed to set up our manufacturing."

"So, as I suggested at the time, approach a few potential investors and let them know about the breakthrough. Don't let the whole world know. Your premature public unveiling gave our competitors the advance warning they needed to muster their forces and crush us. And, while I'm being so cynical, here's my next prediction: the specs of our computer, which the government has, will somehow find their way into our competitors' hands before we can capture the market. Open your eyes. We're fucked."

"The consensus is that the studies they're funding will show that America has no choice but to pursue this technology. We'll be to market in a few years for sure," said Amy.

"A few years! We don't have the money to survive a few days. We have a debt of over eight million dollars. I still don't know how that happened."

"Comptech's investments usually top out at ten million dollars, and we passed that last year," explained Amy. "We've been operating mainly on bank loans since then."

"With bank loans of eight million, this so-called delay is as good as a death sentence. As you're well aware, the banks are calling in their loans and Comptech is pressuring us to declare bankruptcy."

"Maybe we should consider it," said Rick.

"What?" said Kyle. "Have you lost your mind?"

"Comptech says they could auction off the technology for millions," said Amy.

"The technology is my computer and it's worth *billions*! I've spent ten years on this and I refuse to give it up."

"What do you suggest?" asked Amy.

"I suggest we ignore the law and ship our computers," replied Kyle.

"But they'll stop us," pointed out Rick.

"Yes, they will, but the genie will be out of the bottle."

"We'll go to jail," said Amy.

"There's no provision for a jail sentence in the legislation," answered Kyle. "I say we fill all the orders we have now."

"They'll just come here, shut us down, then they'll go and seize the computers from our customers," opined Rick.

"Maybe, but two of our computers are going to Canada. I'm getting those out right away. I called our customers, and they're readying the sites for installation. That will cover our debts, and give us some cash to survive. Unless our storm troopers are going to invade Canada, the genie will be out, and then there'll be no sense in seizing the computers from our

American customers. If they shut us down anyway, I'll open a factory in Toronto."

"They told us we can't operate overseas," said Rick.

"I'm Canadian, too, remember? I'll renounce my American citizenship if I have to. They cannot dictate what I can or can't do as a citizen and resident of Canada."

"What about us?" said Amy.

"We'll be married, so you can come with me and eventually get your citizenship."

Amy glanced at Rick and said to Kyle, "You know I'm not marrying you until we succeed. You've told me that's what drives you, and I'm sticking to it."

"We'll succeed in Canada. As for Rick," added Kyle, "well, you're the one who screwed up."

"Kyle, that is not acceptable," said Amy. "Rick owns ten percent of the firm."

"Only because he stole my ideas. If Qubit succeeded, we all succeeded, but it failed and it's his fault!" He turned to address Rick. "There'll be a new ownership structure in Canada. We'll need new investors and it's coming out of your share, you bloodsucker."

Now agitated, Rick hollered, "You won't get away with this, asshole!"

"How do you plan to stop me?"

"I'll take you to court!"

"Calm down, both of you," suggested Amy. "Set up Qubit in Canada and include Rick, and as soon as we succeed, I'll marry you as promised."

"Tell you what. Marry me now and I'll include Rick."

"I don't like your pressure tactics. You're using marriage as a bargaining chip."

"Oh, look who's talking!" shrieked Kyle.

"Don't scream at me!"

Kyle lowered his head. Over the last two years Amy's subtle control had evolved into more or less complete dominance. Knowing he was unworthy of her and afraid of losing her, Kyle had let it happen.

She went on, "You disgust me when you get in one of your stubborn moods. Get out and don't come back until you can be reasonable." Kyle looked at her sadly. "Leave now," she demanded.

He walked out, leaving Amy and Rick to discuss the awful situation.

At dawn the next day, Kyle pulled his old car up to the small loading dock, and crammed one large box in the trunk, one in the back seat, and one on the front passenger seat. He stopped at his building and brought one box up to his apartment. Then he drove northeast to Detroit. Saying at the border he was a computer salesman with appointments in Toronto and Kingston, he crossed into Ontario. While driving up the 401 highway to Toronto, he called his customer and told him to expect him by mid-afternoon—and called Amy to tell her what he was doing. She wasn't in, but he left a message.

Four hours later, he parked in front of the physics building at the University of Toronto. He unloaded one of the boxes and met Dr. Lan Mao, who fortunately did not spot the delivery vehicle. The two spent the afternoon and evening setting up the computer and testing it. A thrilled Dr. Mao promised the five million dollar payment would be wired to the company's bank account within the week.

At dawn the next morning, Kyle left for Kingston, Ontario. There he met Dr. Natalya Fuhrman at Queen's University's Department of Physics, and went through the same process. At 4:30 PM, he left for home. Ten and a half hours later, he arrived home, exhausted but pleased to have completed his mission without incident.

When he went into the office later that day, he learned Amy and Rick had left town the day before for meetings with regulators. They returned two days later, but reported no progress.

Kyle called his twenty American customers to set delivery and setup dates for the computer. Aware of the injunction against the sale, most reacted with surprise. He presented the decision as red tape that the company was cutting through. Still, all but two of the twenty customers said they would wait for a green light from their solicitors. Kyle set up delivery dates with those two customers for late the next week.

Meanwhile, the work on fabricating Qubit computers continued. When Kyle placed another completed unit in the locked storage room, he discovered that three computers were missing. Kyle confronted Amy and Rick. "Three computers are on the missing list. Where are they?"

"You took them," answered Rick.

"Jesus Christ! Do you think I'm asking you what happened to the computers I took? You're playing stupid by being stupid."

"Are you sure we can't account for—"

"We had thirty-six computers. I took three. That leaves thirty-three. But there are only thirty here."

"Someone must have stolen them," said Amy. "One of our employees, probably."

"As you're well aware, our computers are worth five million bucks apiece, so we have them locked up in a secure room, and have security guards around the clock. Only the three of us have keys. The lock can't be jimmied and it isn't busted. One or both of you took them."

"Are you actually accusing me of stealing from my own company?" Amy said, her voice rising with each syllable. "What would I have to gain? You're including me in your future plans, remember?"

"But not Rick," he said, as he looked over to Rick.

"It isn't enough you're trying to cheat Rick out of his rightful portion of the company?" Amy said. "You have to accuse him of stealing?"

Kyle kept his glare on Rick.

"Call the cops," challenged Rick. "I have nothing to hide."

"You know damn well we can't do that. The government will be in here seizing everything if they find out even one computer is gone."

"If they find out you sold two computers to Canada," Rick pointed out.

"The ten million dollars from those sales went directly into the company's bank account. We can pay off all our creditors now, and stay in business for a while. So I gave our company a temporary reprieve. What did you do with the money you got, asshole?"

"Kyle!" chided Amy. "It's outrageous to accuse Rick of stealing. Not that I'd blame him if he did; by trying to deal him out, you practically forced him to do it."

"So you're telling me that he didn't do it, but I forced him to do it?"

"Do not put words in my mouth. The bottom line is since you have no proof and you're not willing to go to the police, you have to drop it."

"Sure. I mean, it's only fifteen million dollars. Chump change. What am I worried for?" said Kyle, as he glared at Rick. "This isn't over," Kyle warned Rick as he walked out of his office.

*

Early the next morning, a truck and two sedans pulled into the Qubit parking lot. The man in charge got out of one of the cars and walked with his partner into the tiny factory. Holding out his badge, he identified himself as Special Agent Ebbling of the FBI and asked the receptionist at the front to get Dr. Hugel. She informed him the gentleman was out for the morning. He then asked for Ms Janssen and was told she was not yet in the office.

"So who's in charge now?" said the agent.

"That would be Mr. Summers."

"Call him here right away then."

She paged for him over the intercom. Two minutes later, a bespectacled man in blue jeans, a lumberjack shirt, and ratty boots sauntered to the front. "You rang, Gladys?" Kyle said.

"Special Agent Ebbling, FBI," said the man as he brandished his badge. Kyle frowned, but put his hand out for a shake, which the agent ignored.

Kyle withdrew his hand and decided to return the insult. "Here I thought special meant you were exceptional, but I see now you're the other kind of special." Ebbling glared at him. Kyle asked, "What do you want?"

"We're here to shut you down."

"On what basis?" said Kyle, with considerable volume.

"On the basis of national security," Ebbling replied as he handed Kyle a warrant authorizing the agents to seize all assets of Qubit Inc.

"This is theft, pure and simple!" screamed Kyle. "You can't come into a place of business in the United States and steal everything we own."

"We can and we will. The government can seize and keep all assets of any individual or organization engaged in any act of domestic or international terrorism against the United States."

"Terrorism? What the hell are you talking about?"

"I strongly advise you to stand aside or it will be my distinct pleasure to arrest you."

Kyle stepped to the receptionist's desk, picked up the phone, and dialed.

Agent Ebbling disconnected the phone. "Who do you think you're phoning?"

"None of your business. I can phone whomever I damn well please."

Ebbling produced a piece of paper and handed it to Kyle, saying, "This is a National Security Letter. It allows us to seize all data and documents pertaining to any sales or attempted sales of your computer."

"Where's the warrant?"

"We don't need one. That's the beauty of National Security Letters."

"What? How the hell does that work? Just type up a letter and you can take whatever you want?"

"You got it," said Agent Ebbling. He told his partner to get the team started.

"Well, fuck that and fuck you. I'm calling CNN, ABC, the *New York Times*—"

The special agent chuckled and said, "Oh, I forgot to add that the order forbids you from telling anyone about the order."

"You can't get away with this! This is not China. This is America."

"Oh, clam up," said Agent Ebbling, as several agents walked in.

Kyle began dialing again, but Ebbling knocked the phone out of his hands. Kyle then pushed the agent out of the way to get to his phone. Before he knew it, he was on the ground with Ebbling's knee on his back. Ebbling's partner put handcuffs on him and started reading him his rights.

While they dragged him out to one of the sedans, Kyle said, "You won't get away with this, you goddamn Nazis!"

He was put in the back of one of the sedans and sped off to the Chicago field office.

The FBI team spread out into the computer assembly area, telling the eleven workers to stand aside and go home for the day, buttressing their command with badges held aloft. Most employees left directly, the duller ones happy to have the day off and oblivious to the implication for their continued employment with Qubit. Others, concerned about their jobs, asked for information, but were escorted off the premises without answers.

Amy arrived at that point and protested, but was warned to cooperate or share Kyle's fate. She provided the key for the storage room.

The truck backed into the lone loading dock, and the FBI team proceeded to load the thirty computers already boxed and two more partial units on the short assembly line. They also took components from the clean room. The company's three digital computers used for management were taken, as were the contents of paper files relating to the technology. Machinery to build the computers was also taken. Company bank accounts were frozen.

At the FBI field office, Kyle was confronted with evidence he'd tried to sell Qubit computers. He said, in effect, "So what?" Asked whether he or anyone at the firm had delivered any computers, he gave a firm no. The legislation having specified no penalty for attempting to sell the computers, Kyle was released later that morning, with no charges laid against him—yet.

Kyle, Rick, and Amy met with an attorney that afternoon, and learned there was nothing they could do to get their computers back in the foreseeable future. The lawyer explained, "They used Section 806 of the Patriot Act, which allows the government to seize your assets without notice."

"On what basis?" asked Kyle.

"On the basis that there is probable cause to believe that the assets were involved in terrorism."

"Terrorism? How the hell do they figure that?"

"They found out you were trying to sell your computers despite the injunction, so they shut you down."

"And how is that terrorism?" said Kyle.

"It's not, but now they think your computers are out there, and apparently someone has been rooting around in secret CIA files. Those files are protected with encryption methods that cannot be broken—even with supercomputers—but someone did it. They think it must have been done with one of your computers. They're going through your records to track down who might be in possession of your computers."

"And how can hacking into a computer be considered terrorism?"

"They haven't told me much. It's possible the hackers have already used the information against our country, but I doubt it, since you're not under arrest. I think they're waiting for the other shoe to drop. They probably have good reason to believe that someone is plotting an attack against our interests. The government thinks your computer made it possible, and that's all they need under Section 806 to seize your assets."

"There *might* be an attack? That's all they need to take everything we own? Unbelievable. What proof do they have that it was one of our computers?"

"It's just circumstantial so far, but from what I understand, only your computer is capable of this. You three are suspects and can expect to be questioned soon. They'll study the documents they seized and start a full-fledged investigation, I'm sure. Have you already sold some computers?" asked the lawyer. Kyle, Amy and Rick looked at each other. "I need to know the truth."

"Kyle sold two to Canadian customers," admitted Rick.

"That was stupid," asserted the lawyer.

"What the hell do you know?" snapped Kyle. "As far as I'm concerned, it's the government that broke the law by presuming to prevent us from conducting a legal business in or outside of the United States. It can't possibly be constitutional. If we just accepted it and gave up, it would mean bankruptcy. I did what I had to do to save my company, so don't give me this shit that I'm stupid."

"Someone is using your computer to check out top-secret American government information, so they've concluded you're helping to plan a terrorist act—which, under the Patriot Act, gives them the right to seize everything. Chances are slim you'll ever get the quantum computers back, although I'm optimistic about the digital ones."

Kyle chuckled bitterly and said, "Oh, well, that's different. As long as they give us back three thousand dollars worth of obsolete computers, I don't care if they keep the other *hundred and sixty million dollars* worth of our cutting edge computers. They've stolen all our assets! Isn't that illegal?"

"You can go to court, but under Section 806, the government is only required to prove that the assets were involved in terrorism by a preponderance of the evidence. It's a civil proceeding, so you're not entitled to be represented by an attorney at public expense. It will cost you hundreds of thousands to fight them. And they'll stretch it out; they won't even declare forfeiture for several months. In the meantime, you have to make do without your computers."

"So they're trying to bankrupt us," concluded Amy.

"You got it. They believe you're involved in terrorism and will be merciless."

"Can't we put political pressure on the government? They can't treat American citizens like this!" exclaimed Kyle.

"I think we can take the seizure to the court of public opinion, but know that they'll portray you as terrorists, and the public tends to believe their government when it comes to terrorism. And since they served you with a National Security Letter that forbids you from telling anyone about the seizure of your financial information, we have to be careful about what we say."

"Can they actually get away with that gag order?"

"National Security Letters aren't supposed to apply to firms like yours, but the FBI takes advantage of them whenever it thinks it can get away with it. I'm sure we can fight that successfully."

"I can't figure out if your knack is focusing on the positive or the trivial. If you were a doctor, you'd be telling me my father came out of the accident without any visible scratches, and leave aside the trifle that he is no longer breathing. I don't give a shit about our financial records," said Kyle. "I want our goddamn computers and machinery back!"

"What do you recommend?" said Rick.

"I'll start working on the fight against the forfeiture, if you want. I don't think we can do anything else for now."

They gave him the go-ahead. After he left, Kyle turned to Rick and said, "Who did you sell those three computers to, Rick?"

"I didn't sell any computers," he claimed. "We do know you sold two to Canadians, though."

"Do you honestly think University of Toronto or Queen's University physicists are hacking into CIA files?" replied Kyle.

"And who are they renting computer time to?" challenged Rick. Kyle hadn't thought of that and could not answer.

Amy said, "We have a more immediate problem. What do we do next? We have no more computers or computer parts, and no machinery. We can't build more. We have to lay off all our staff." The other two agreed, and Amy carried out the disagreeable task.

*

The next week, Amy called Kyle to her office for a meeting. She opened with, "We haven't had the chance to tell you about an exciting development."

"You haven't had the chance? What about walking two hundred feet down the hall to where I am sixteen hours a day? Since you were obviously afraid to tell me, I can't wait to hear this."

Rick swallowed and said, "Digital Technology Computers has made an incredibly generous offer to buy us out."

"What? They can piss right off!"

"You see?" said Amy, "This is why we didn't tell you earlier. Your knee-jerk reaction was so predictable."

"Before you get the full effect of my reaction, tell me what the offer is."

"One hundred million dollars! That's forty-one million for you," Amy said.

"Thanks, I can do the math."

"Don't talk down to me, Kyle," she ordered. He lowered his eyes. "We've been negotiating with them since they called last Friday."

"Without my knowledge."

"That's right. We knew you'd disapprove."

"I do, and I'll stop any further negotiations."

"You own only forty-one percent of this firm, Kyle. Comptech is on our side. You can't stop us."

"I'm sorry, Amy, but I can stop you. I am the only one in the world who knows how to engineer this computer. I've been very careful about what I've documented; the patents don't specify everything. You taught me a valuable lesson when you stole my ideas, Rick. Thank you for that. If you sell out, I will not share my knowledge with DTC!"

"You'll have no choice!" screamed Amy.

"We're sitting on a goldmine here. To sell out for a hundred million dollars would be the worst deal of all time. All we need to sell is twenty computers for that. We already have that many orders. In a few years, we can buy what's left over of DTC."

"We have twenty orders, but no computers, and we can't build any more. You have to be more realistic and less greedy," advised Amy, "or you'll end up with nothing."

"This is so ironic," countered Kyle. "The black knights who led the charge against us are suddenly our white knights. Those bastards lobby to protect their antiquated asses with one face while trying to buy us out with their other face. They're working to make us desperate enough to take a penny on the dollar for what this firm will be worth a few years out. I will never agree to their blackmail!"

Amy decided to play again her ace in the hole. "Kyle, if you don't sell, we don't get married."

She was his queen, but this was the one issue that he would defy her on in the belief that it was the right thing to do for their future together. Unable to look her in the eyes, he said, "I'm sorry, Amy, but whether you realize it or not, I'm doing this for us. I won't sell, and if you two do, they don't get my design," and he walked out.

Amy looked at Rick in astonishment. She and Rick went ahead and invited DTC representatives to Qubit as part of their due diligence assessment prior to buying out the firm. They hoped Kyle would come around to their conclusion that the buyout was their best remaining option. If not, they and Comptech would sell their fifty-nine percent to DTC—then Kyle would be their problem.

CHAPTER THREE

Takeover Target

Erin Wilson, representing DTC, stood outside the home of Qubit Inc., and shook her head. "Can you believe that this is the first company to make a viable quantum computer?" she said to her colleague, Allen Levinson. "What a dump. No wonder they suggested they would come to us."

Erin was a tall, svelte woman of twenty-six. Her silken, light brown hair was combed straight back and fell down to her shoulders. Her large eyes were penetrating and defiant, yet exquisite. In dim light, they appeared charcoal grey, but the daylight revealed them in all their grey-blue splendor. Her bottom lip was a little fuller than her top lip, lending a *humph!* to her *You don't actually think you have a chance for me?* expression. Her pert nose and even the high arch of her brow promised audacity. This unapproachable face she presented to the world to keep men—who reverted from respectful businessmen to predators the minute she showed her luminous smile—at bay.

Today, though, she was to meet Rick Hugel. Erin was not one to worship anyone, but if that were ever to be the case, it would be Rick Hugel. Her background research for this assignment convinced her that this was a great man. He beat the rest of the world in inventing a marketable quantum computer, an incredible accomplishment that evinced his genius and presaged a future of limitless success—assuming the company could get around its legal troubles. As if his genius and success weren't enough, he was as handsome as any leading man in Hollywood. He stood six-foot-three, and had a muscular body, handsome face, blond hair, and a charismatic personality that had all the women panting. She had pushed her boss hard for this assignment and was relishing it.

Erin and Allen walked in the front door to an empty reception desk. "Hello?" she called. Getting no response, she and Allen walked down the hall past two closed doors and into a large rectangular room with several abandoned work stations. "Hello?" she repeated.

Up came a shaggy head from behind a partition at the far end of the room. "What do you want?" asked Kyle.

"Real professional," muttered Allen to Erin, with a sarcastic smirk. "You'd think a company as close to drowning as this would take an offer of a lifeline more seriously."

"We have an appointment with Dr. Hugel," said Erin.

"First door on the left down the hall," shouted the unkempt nerd as he disappeared behind the partition.

They turned and walked down the hall and knocked on the door. "Just a minute," said the occupant. A moment later the door opened, and Erin stood transfixed by the handsome face of Rick Hugel. His pictures did him an injustice, she thought.

"Nice to meet you," he said, while extending a hand to Erin, who seized it and shook. "Ms Wilson, I presume?"

"Yes. Please call me Erin." Her radiant smile got away from her.

"And call me Rick. And you're Mr. Levinson?" he said, shaking his hand.

"We had a little trouble finding the building, then your office," noted Allen who was also staring longingly at Rick.

"Oh, sorry. We had to lay all our employees off once we were informed that we couldn't sell our computer. There's just me, Amy Janssen, and Kyle Summers."

"I think we just met Summers," said Allen with a discernable sneer. Erin elbowed him.

"Yeah, he's our engineer," Rick said. "A necessary evil to turn ideas into reality, I'm afraid."

"So you come up with the ideas, Summers engineers them, and Ms Janssen is the CFO?" asked Erin.

"That's right."

"If I may say so, sir, what you've achieved is remarkable," complimented Erin. "That you beat everyone else to the punch, my firm included, with scant resources other than pure brainpower and moxie is so impressive."

"Thank you, Erin," he said. "So how do you want to proceed? How do we form an alliance with Digital Technology Computers for our mutual benefit?"

"To be frank, Rick—"

"No, I'd prefer to be Rick," he said, with a smirk that meant she was supposed to laugh, Erin inferred. She forced a laugh. Allen cast his eyes upward.

Erin resumed: "I'm not sure alliance is the best word for it. If we like what we see, we'd be taking over Qubit, but it would certainly be mutually beneficial. We'd agree to keep the current owners on—in fact, in your case, we'd insist on it—and in return your legacy lives on."

"Great," replied Rick. "We're at your service. What can I do for you, Erin?"

"Why don't you start by opening your books, so we can determine the financial shape of the company?" she said.

"You'll need to speak to Amy on that account, if you'll pardon the pun."

Erin put on another chuckle. "Okay. Where is she?"

"She'll be here any time. You can wait in her office if you want."

"Allen is our forensic accountant. He'll be poring over your finances."

"Well, I better not offer him any coffee, then."

Erin, who hated puns, nevertheless tittered again and said, "Maybe Allen can work with Amy when she arrives, and I can work with you on the technical aspects of your computer."

Allen frowned at her.

"This way, Allen."

"Anywhere you lead, I'll follow," said Allen suggestively. That earned him a smirk from Erin and a scowl from Rick.

"Not your type," muttered Erin with a smile.

"Guess not." Allen sighed.

Rick led Allen to Amy's office and invited him to take a seat.

He and Erin walked down the hall toward the assembly room. Amy walked in as they reached the end of the hall. Rick waved and said to Erin, "There's Amy. I'll introduce you two after we see Kyle." Amy returned the wave. Rick proceeded: "I have a previous engagement out of the office this morning, but I've set aside some time this afternoon for us to talk. In the meantime, Kyle can show you what we've built."

"I understood the government seized all your computers."

"Kyle has one stashed somewhere, which he can access remotely from here. A word of warning about Kyle: he's taken our setback rather hard, I'm afraid. He's outraged and depressed."

Erin wanted to see the Qubit computer in action, but was uncomfortable about dealing with an upset techie. She said, "If he just turns your ideas into hardware under your direction, what does he really know about the technology itself? I was really looking forward to learning from the guru in this field. Can't you show me the computer?"

"We'll speak after lunch. For now, Kyle can really help you. He's a good engineer and has picked up a great deal from me. In fact, to hear him talk, you'd think he designed the whole thing."

They reached Kyle's work station. She winced at his disheveled appearance: his unruly hair, unshaven mug, thick glasses sitting askew on his nose, and a lumberjack shirt, faded jeans, and old work boots.

"Kyle, this is Erin Wilson. She's here from DTC to—"

"What? I told you I'm not interested in selling out." He turned to Erin and said, "You wasted your time, lady. Qubit is not for sale. So go away."

"Kyle!" scolded Rick. "Don't be so disrespectful." He turned to Erin and said, "I'm sorry, Erin. As I mentioned,

Kyle's upset about the government's decision. He's taking it out on anyone who comes near him."

"Whereas Rick here, who hasn't a clue what it took to build my computer, seems to be acting as if everything's hunky-dory. Well, Rick, this woman has come to offer a pittance for our house in the shadow of Chernobyl after the meltdown she caused made it all but worthless, and you sit here in your wondrous trance chanting, 'Isn't that mushroom cloud beautiful?'"

"Can't you just hear her out?"

"No!"

"We're offering you the chance to salvage something out of what you've accomplished," said Erin.

"Aren't you generous? Go straight to hell."

"Rick, can I please just deal with you?"

"There will be no deal with this company!" Kyle declared. "DTC was at the front of the line begging Congress to enact the law against quantum computing, against us. You bastards knew you were beaten, so you ran to big brother to shut down the competition, and you succeeded. Then you have the temerity to frame your proffered heist as a helping hand? I'll die before your shitty firm makes one red cent off us."

Erin stood there in shock. She hadn't expected any resistance to a one hundred million dollar offer to a firm on the verge of extinction. Suddenly, the success of her assignment was looking dubious. But failure was unacceptable. Recovering her composure, she turned to Rick for help. "Does this man speak for Qubit, Dr. Hugel?"

"Let's see what Amy thinks, shall we, Kyle?" said Rick. "Amy!" he shouted. She stuck her head out of her doorway.

"Amy, we need you here right away." Amy and Allen walked to Kyle's work station.

When Amy walked in, Kyle straightened his glasses and his hand went to his hair in an unsuccessful attempt to groom himself. Erin stood there agog, witnessing the transformation. His fierce eyes softened and began to gleam, his sour grin became a bright smile, and his breathing quickened. He looked like a different man. Erin mused, *You'd think he was staring at Aphrodite*. Amy smiled back at him and walked over to Erin.

"Where are your manners, Kyle? Aren't you going to introduce me?"

"Uh, yes, this is, um—"

"Erin Wilson," she finished. "Pleased to meet you."

"Likewise. I trust Kyle is being completely cooperative and telling you everything you need to know about our technology?"

"Well, not really, no."

"He's refused to cooperate at all," chimed in Rick.

"Kyle," said Amy softly, "this woman is here on behalf of a company that could be our salvation. What is your problem?"

"You know what my problem is. We discussed this the other day."

"And tell me, what harm could it possibly do to hear them out?"

"None. The problem will be when they want to hear us out, to find out how the computer works, then deal us out."

"We represent a venerated firm," objected Erin. "We do not steal."

"No, you just use your political and economic power to drive down the value of the assets, then pay bottom dollar for them. Legalized theft."

Amy pointed out, "You yourself made a compelling case that our firm is on the brink. This is one potential solution. Nothing says we have to take their offer, so what harm could it possibly do to hear them out? Just play along for now, okay?"

He nodded in submission. Amy returned to her office to discuss finances with Allen.

Kyle's visage resumed its disgusted aspect. He glared at Rick who smiled again, and said, "I'll see you after lunch, Erin," as he walked off.

Kyle turned his glare to Erin. She attempted to get him on her side. "You lit up when she came in. She must be an amazing woman."

"Yes she is, and no, I'm not cooperating with you."

"But you agreed when Ms Janssen … Can you at least show me the computer? Please?"

Kyle rolled his chair aside. "It's on. Use it," he said.

"Where is the actual computer?"

"Well hidden."

"I'd really like to see it."

"Not possible. This work station is connected to it. Use it."

She moved another chair in front of the keyboard and sat. "I wouldn't know where to start. I don't recognize this user interface."

"Do you know anything about computers?"

"I have a Master's in Computer Science."

"From where? Sheboygan Computer and Interior Decorating Institute?"

"From Dartmouth."

"Come on then, Ms Wilson, Ivy League Master of Computer Science. Use it."

"What programs do you have?"

"You don't have to learn new programming languages, if that's what you mean. Our software platform supports SQL, AMPL, and … You look confused."

"Not at all. So you can access the Internet through it."

"Of course."

"What else can you do with it?"

"Only the limited imagination of software programmers like you can limit this computer. This technology is light years beyond what your multi-million dollar research effort has managed."

"Right now this technology is worthless since it can't be sold. Right? Right?" He nodded. "You need the resources— more to the point—the political clout of my company if your breakthrough is to survive."

"The same political clout that killed the breakthrough can resuscitate it? But only if DTC reaps the profits?"

Erin thought, *Uh oh.*

Kyle went on, "What a goddamn nerve you have, lady. I'll show you nothing."

"Fine. I'll just deal with Dr. Hugel," she said as she walked away. "I'd rather deal with Genghis Khan than you," she added under her breath. She jutted her head into Amy's office and told her Kyle refused to help. Amy apologized and said she'd have another talk with him. Erin returned, "Listen, Amy, can I just work with Rick? He's the person I really want to hear from."

"Okay by me. He's out till after noon, though."

"And if I may be so bold, Amy, if we end up taking over Qubit, I'll insist that we drop Summers."

Amy flashed a look of concern. Erin, who said this in hopes she wouldn't have to cross paths again with Kyle, was surprised at Amy's reaction. She continued, "Really, Amy, we have a thousand techies like him, but without the attitude."

"Not like him, you don't. But if you can get what you need from Rick, all the better."

That afternoon, Rick volunteered few specifics about the workings of the computer. At one point, Erin got a tad testy, contending that he was trying to keep her in the dark. He proceeded to give her an elementary account of the theory behind the computer.

"Okay. As you know, today's computers are digital, meaning they're built around the binary system; all bits of information are encoded zero or one. But quantum computers aren't limited to zero or one. 'Qubits,' as they're called, can be a zero or a one, can be simultaneously both zero and one, or be somewhere in between."

"But how is that possible?"

"The quantum world doesn't work like the world we live and breathe in. We can't apply our logic to it. To answer your question, no one really knows how an atom can be in two places at once."

"An atom?"

"Qubits represent atoms and subatomic particles that work together to act as a processor and computer memory."

"But how does it work?"

"I'm not delving into quantum mechanics here. I'm trying to explain what the computer can do. The key is these simultaneous multiple states, which has a special term in the field: superposition of qubits. Because of this, a quantum computer has the potential to be millions of times more powerful than the most powerful supercomputer in the world. It's like parallelism; you know, getting a lot of computers to work on a single problem at the same time. Parallelism means a quantum computer can work on a million computations at once, instead of one like today's computers."

Rick's exposition was none too edifying. He never got beyond the generalities Erin already knew about from what she'd read about the technology on the Internet and from texts of Rick's presentations to government regulators. Any time she asked him to get more technical, he seemed unwilling to do so.

At the end of the work day, Rick suggested, "Let me take you to dinner and we'll continue this."

"Uh," she said, taken aback, "I have too much to do tonight. Can we pick this up in the morning?"

"I'm afraid I'm booked until late tomorrow afternoon. Can I take you to dinner then?"

"Will I get more detailed answers to my questions?" He nodded. "Okay, but it's a business meeting," she asserted. He nodded with a smile.

The next morning, Allen asked Erin for help going through the extensive paper files of the company relating to administration. Hoping to find something in writing to answer her many unanswered questions, she acquiesced. She found very little, not even basic information such as how many computers were built. This was a key question for her.

She mentioned to her partner, "Rick could not or would not answer how many computers they had or have, and nothing I see here answers it either. Have you found anything?" He shook his head. She continued, "They're hiding something important. Would you mind asking Summers?"

"Yes, I would. He's an unwholesome thing, and I intend to keep my distance."

"He's not that bad."

"He has all the charm of a cranky badger."

"True, but maybe he just needs a little polishing."

"He needs a little sandblasting," said Allen.

"So you leave it to the woman?"

"We both know you're tougher than me. After Amy goes out to lunch, you keep Summers occupied for a few minutes, and I'll look around the building for the computer Summers is hooked up to and whatever else I can find."

After Amy left, Erin walked back to Kyle's cubicle. He was eating a tuna sandwich. "In a better mood today?" she said with a half-smile.

"I was."

"It's nice to see you, too."

"Here to blight my afternoon?"

"It'll be quick if you would just answer a couple of questions."

"No. Go away. I would be left unbothered."

"Listen, I know we got off on the wrong foot yesterday, and I'd like to apologize." He kept eating and staring at his computer monitor. Erin said, "Please, at least tell me how many computers you built all together."

"None of your business."

"Excuse me, but it is my business. It's critical to know since each one is worth a potential five million dollars."

"Since this is not your company and it's not going to be, it is *not* your business. Where's gay boy, anyway?"

"God, you're an ass," she snapped without thinking.

She was about to apologize for her unprofessional outburst when he said, "Don't tell Allen that; he'll think I'm the receiver."

"Don't worry, he's not interested in you."

"He senses that there's not a gay bone in my body—and there never will be. So what's he looking for?"

"You're just trying to change the subject."

"Which is precisely what you just tried to do."

This guy is irritatingly sharp, she thought to herself.

Kyle raised his head and yelled, "Look around to your heart's content, Allen. There's nothing to find." Turning back to Erin, he said, "Now, what weren't we talking about?"

"Why are you being so obstinate? You're a smart guy. Surely you must realize we are your only chance to bring your computer to market."

"Realize this!" he said. "I put everything I had into this for the last ten years. All my money, all my time, all my knowledge, all my brains, my soul, everything! And it finally paid off. We were poised to go to market. We had hundreds of investors begging to buy a piece of us. We had more than twenty orders at five million bucks a pop. We're the next IBM, everyone said. Nothing could stop us from making billions. Billions! And I had the promise of Amy's hand when we succeeded.

"But something did stop us: the damn government at the behest of your company and others. A bunch of paranoid fascists absolutely destroyed us with a half-page declaration denying us permission to sell our computer with some vague reference to national security. And now I have no Amy, no money, no prospects. All I have left is my computer. Then you march in here, the person representing the cabal that ruined me, and demand my computer, too, as if you're doing me some big favor, then you have the audacity to get all huffy when I tell you to go to hell. So try, just try to get anything out of me."

"We can help to get the government's decision overturned. We really want you on board with this, but if we have to, we can do it without your cooperation. We both know Rick is the genius behind Qubit."

Kyle laughed.

"What's so funny?" asked Erin.

"I'll let you figure out what it might be. I can't wait to see you back here, cap in hand, apologizing and begging for help because you finally realized your mistake. Then I'll send you packing, having failed in your mission."

Dismissing his bluster, she shook her head at him and walked away, but something in the way he delivered his last statement concerned her: confident because genuine. "Find anything?" she asked Allen.

"No," he said. "Just a bunch of junk."

Erin went back to work reading documents until Rick arrived at 5:30. They went out to dinner. During their meal, Rick seemed much more intent on sharing himself with her than on sharing important details about Qubit. As tempting as the handsome man was, she resisted his various hints. On the way home in Rick's car after dinner, he asked if she'd like a nightcap in his apartment. That was a step too far over the line.

She answered, "Rick, *please*. I'm not here to be the latest notch on your belt. I'm here to do a job—an important job for my firm, a life and death one for yours. You have to take this seriously. Once I finish this assignment, I'll be happy to have dinner with you again. Until then, this is strictly business."

She asked to set up an appointment with him for the next morning, but he told her he was going to be out all day again and wouldn't return until mid-afternoon the following day. She became uneasy again at what was by now clearly an attempt to avoid her questions.

After she and Allen spent the next day and a half examining files, she went to Amy with a few questions. Getting no satisfactory answer to any, she said, "Amy, I'm detecting a clear pattern. Rick is always out, you never have answers to my questions, and Kyle is too rude to answer them. We need to see better cooperation if we're going to recommend going forward."

"I'm sorry, Erin," Amy responded. "I'm not trying to be difficult, but my job concerned finances alone, and I've given you everything I have."

"How many Qubit computers are in existence? Surely as CFO you must know that."

"Thirty-something. I'll call Kyle in here right now, and we'll get an exact answer." She picked up her phone and asked him to come to her office. He appeared two minutes later with a bright smile that dimmed considerably upon encountering Erin. "Kyle, how many computers have we made?" said Amy.

"That's confidential."

"Kyle, tell her." He looked at her as if considering whether to disobey her, but she repeated, "Kyle!"

"The FBI raided us and stole thirty-six computers. They also took the parts for two more."

"Is that every one that was built? What about the one you're hooked into?" said Erin.

He looked at Amy as if to implore her to stop the inquisition. A glare put him in his place, and he said, "I took that one offsite before the FBI raided us."

"Offsite?"

"It's in his apartment," revealed Amy. Kyle sighed out of exasperation. "And he sold two in Canada," Amy admitted. Kyle grimaced and looked down.

"I thought you were forbidden to sell any," said Erin, obviously disconcerted.

"Which would've bankrupted us immediately if we'd listened," Kyle answered. "We owed our creditors and employees most of the ten million we earned from the sales. We're living on the few bucks we have left over."

"But if the government finds out—" Erin started to say.

"I'll tell them to fuck themselves. I have Canadian citizenship, too. The U.S. government has no right to tell me I can't sell my product to Canadian customers."

"Whether you agree with the law or not, you're not free to break it. This raises the question of what legal trouble your firm may be in."

"Guess that means you'll be going. Bye."

"Have you sold any others?" asked Erin.

"No," answered Kyle.

"Then why does this letter to the FBI signed by you, Kyle, state the FBI confiscated thirty computers and parts for two more? You told me they took thirty-six computers."

"Where the hell did you get that letter?" challenged Kyle.

"Allen found a copy somewhere on the premises," replied Erin. "Did they take thirty or thirty-six?"

"There were only thirty on the premises when the FBI raided us," answered Amy.

"But you had built thirty-six, right?" Amy nodded. "Thirty confiscated, plus two sold to the Canadians, plus the one in Kyle's apartment makes thirty-three. What happened to the other three?"

"Well … they seem to have disappeared," responded Amy.

"Disappeared?" said Erin. "Oh, please."

"Okay, Amy, this is where this had to lead, so you can take it from here," Kyle said.

"They were stolen," said Amy.

"Did you report it to the police?"

"No. As Kyle argued, we weren't even supposed to have them—we told the FBI they got them all—so we couldn't report the theft."

"That's a loss of fifteen million dollars. And worse, it raises the threat that someone else might reverse-engineer this technology. You seem pretty unconcerned about it." She looked at Amy, who smiled, and at Kyle who turned his head and sighed.

"Erin, I'm sorry about our intransigence," said Amy, now clearly worried that DTC would give up on them. "We really have nothing to hide from you. We're just very embarrassed about the theft. Tell us what you need from us, and we'll be cooperative."

"I'll have to tell my bosses about this latest development. I'm sure I'll need to convince them not to give up on Qubit. To do that, I need to be convinced that taking over Qubit won't land DTC in a world of trouble. Can you do that?"

"I'm sure we can," answered Amy.

"We are not selling out—" started Kyle before Amy jumped in with, "Enough, Kyle. Erin's been very patient with us so far, and we need to show some goodwill. Once DTC makes a formal offer, all the owners will have their say."

"It's almost two o'clock," said Erin. "Can we meet back here in an hour?"

Kyle responded, "I have a doctor's appointment at three and a dinner date with Amy this evening. Can't this wait till Monday?"

"No, it can't," replied Erin, emboldened by Amy's zeal to reach a deal.

"Why don't you join Kyle and me for a drink and dinner, and we can talk shop?" Erin nodded. Amy looked at Kyle and said, "Don't you give me your wounded puppy dog look. I'm just being nice. We'll meet at Eddie's at seven."

Kyle shook his head and walked out.

Erin had another idea and discussed it with Amy before leaving to transmit the latest intelligence to her office and getting the go-ahead to proceed.

That evening, Erin showed up at 7:10 and saw Kyle sitting at a table on the left. She went to the table and sat across from him. She was surprised to see how good he could look when he tried. Just a few simple steps—taking a shower, getting his hair cut short, shaving, dressing nicely, and ditching his dreadful glasses—changed a seemingly revolting man into someone she would have considered attractive had he a better disposition. She said hi. He returned a nod and turned his head aside to look at the door for Amy's entrance.

"You wearing contacts?" she asked, trying to start a conversation.

He pulled protective eyeglasses out of his pocket and said, "I invested half my paltry savings in laser eye surgery this afternoon. I'm supposed to be wearing these for a day or so." He put them on and smiled.

"Well, I was going to say you look much better without the nerd glasses," she complimented, in an attempt to build better rapport with the intractable man. She meant it, too; his eyes were arresting.

He took them off.

"That's better. I'm not even ashamed to be seen with you," she added, with a smile to underscore that she was joking.

He returned, "That's the nicest thing any woman has ever said to me. In fact, if you said you *were* ashamed to be seen with me, that would still qualify as the nicest." He turned his head back to the door.

"So, maybe if we get to know a little about each other, we won't be at odds all the time," she said. "I'm from Dover, Delaware. I have a sister and a brother; I'm the eldest—"

"Uh-huh, and when did you lose your first tooth?"

"Come on, Kyle. Try being civil for once. Where are you from?" No answer. "Kyle?"

"Saskatoon."

"So you really are Canadian?"

"An American who knows Saskatoon is in Canada. Impressive."

"What brought you to Chicago?" He yawned. "I asked what brought you to Chicago."

"I heard."

"Well?"

"My father."

"You moved here as a child." He lifted his eyes to the sky. "I hear you graduated from the University of Chicago when you were seventeen."

"Yup," he answered, as he leaned his chin on his hand and closed his eyes.

"And you went to grad school there, but no PhD?"

"Nope."

"Why?"

"What difference does it make to you?" he snapped, eyes now glowering.

"I'm just trying to be friendly."

"I'm trying to be rude: shut the hell up. I win."

She tried a few more times to start a conversation, but he ignored her. A half-hour, two beers, and no Amy later, he became more somber than usual. Finally at 7:44 his phone rang. He took the call and his face fell.

He looked at Erin and said, "Amy apologizes, but something's come up and she won't be able to make it." His eyes began to water, which Erin noticed. "My eyes are a bit sore from the surgery," he explained. He took a small bottle out of his jacket pocket and put some drops in his eyes.

Erin knew what had come up with Amy. She and Allen had met with Amy and Rick from three PM to seven PM to discuss fundamental information on Qubit without Kyle's interference. Allen remained with Amy and Rick, ironing out the final details while Erin joined Kyle at the pub in hopes of gaining further information from him.

Erin said, "Let me buy you a drink to drown your pain." As he was about to decline, she asked a passing waitress for two shooters and two beers. He got up to leave, but she said, "I can't drink them by myself. Just stay until they're gone." He sat reluctantly. Since her attempts to get him to open up by being nice weren't working, she decided to try goading him. "May I ask what you see in her?"

"Amy? Isn't it obvious? Her gorgeous face, her amazing hair, her perfect body, her brains—"

"You're talking about Amy Janssen?" Erin said, as the waitress came with the drinks.

"No, Amy Eisenhower." He lifted the shot glass from the table, downed the shot, and lowered the glass. He repeated the procedure with the beer, although he managed only half.

"The Amy Janssen I know isn't particularly brainy. She's attractive, but far from gorgeous. I've seen her type before. She uses her looks to live off whatever sap flows her way and makes it seem like she's doing him the favor. You've swelled her head with false conceit of her perfection, and you've become her slave. The trophy you covet isn't worth winning. I guess love really is blind."

"You're the one who's blind. My computer wouldn't exist without her. Not only did she invest in my computer on behalf of her former company, she made me believe in myself. Every time I was ready to give up, she pushed me and pushed me until I did it, until I made the crucial breakthrough to create the quantum computer."

"You?"

"Yes, me. Not that anyone ever even patted me on the back for it, so I'll do it." He patted himself on the back and said, "Congratulations on inventing the computer, me. Keep up the good work. Have a drink to celebrate." He drained the rest of his beer.

Erin thought it was most likely the booze talking. Rick had mentioned that Kyle liked to take all the credit, but it was worth checking out. She said, "Why, then, does your company represent Rick as the inventor?"

"Put your best face forward, as Amy would put it."

"I can't believe the inventor of anything so impressive would let someone else take the credit. Does she control you that much?"

"You don't understand. I did it all for her; to please her, to have her for my own. She said I needed something to aim for, so she wouldn't marry me until I succeeded."

Erin remained incredulous, but wanted to keep him talking. She gave him her shooter and beer. "You succeeded. Where's your ring?"

"Don't mock me. She said I haven't succeeded since we can't sell the damn computer."

"I guess you'd do pretty much anything to marry her?" He made no response, but drank the second shooter and chased it with some beer. She continued, "I mean, you must be desperate enough to do *anything* to keep your invention alive—anything to get Amy."

"You trying to insinuate something?"

"To tell you the truth, I wonder if those three missing computers somehow found their way to market."

Now drunk, he said, "That makes two of us." He drank more beer.

"What do you mean?"

"Nothing."

"Do you suspect Amy or Rick of selling them?"

"Not Amy," he said. Before she could press him, he said, "I don't want to talk about this anymore." He tipped his glass back, but got only drops.

"You think Rick sold them?"

"Shut up about that!" he said. "We're out of beer. I want more. I think I'll stay a while and get shitfaced. Wench!" he shouted to Erin. "Beer me!" To his astonishment she obeyed his command, appearing a minute later with a glass of beer and a wry smile. As he reached out for it, she tipped the glass and poured the frosty beer onto his lap. "Oh, Christ, that's cold," he said.

"Will there be anything else, milord?" she said.

"That will be all, thank you."

She chuckled and left. He followed a minute later, passing her at the entrance. "You know the number for a cab?" she asked.

"What am I, a fucking phone book? Dial 411," he said as he meandered toward his car.

"I'll have to dial 911 if I let you drive in that condition," she said as she followed him. "Give me your keys." He took them out of his pocket and held them up above his head. She tickled his armpit, which brought his arm down, and she grabbed them. He reached out to get them back, but she put them down her shirt. He went to dig them out, but she said, "Don't you dare!" He tried again, and she slapped him. He looked at her in shock and tried once more. She slapped him again.

"Ouch," he screamed. "Give me my keys!"

"You're drunk, and you've just had laser surgery. You'll kill yourself if you try to drive."

"So what?"

"I don't want you killing yourself—or anyone else." She was a little tipsy from two drinks, but not impaired. "I'll drive. Where's your car?"

He pointed at an ancient Dodge Aspen. She laughed at it. It had been white, but now it was rust.

"Hey, it may be a shitbox, but it runs like a ... shitbox."

They got in. She turned the ignition and coughed at the blue exhaust when it finally caught. "Where to?" she said. He pointed her to his apartment building a few blocks away. As she parked, she said, "Can I call a cab from your place? I still don't have a phone number."

"Yeah, come on."

They walked into his apartment, and Kyle handed her the phone book.

While Erin talked to the dispatcher, Kyle went to his room to change out of his wet clothes. She used the opportunity to look for the quantum computer stashed in his apartment. She found it in the hall closet, still in the box. It couldn't have been the one he was connecting to, she knew. When he emerged from the bedroom, she was sitting on his couch.

She said, "They said it would take fifteen minutes to get a cab here."

"Did you find the computer?" he asked. She cast him a confused look. "I figured it out while I was changing. That's why you showed up tonight. That's why you tried to get me drunk. That's why you spilled beer on me. That's why you left right after you spilled beer on me and waited at the door for me to leave. That's why you insisted on driving me home. You couldn't give a shit if I wrapped myself around a tree. You wanted to see the quantum computer."

Knowing he was too sharp to fall for a lie, she came clean. "You caught me, Sherlock. Of course I want to see the machine. My company told me to get a good look at it when I told them you still had one. But it's still in the box, which raises a very interesting question: where is the computer you connected to?"

"Beyond your reach at the physics department, University of Toronto, so you wasted your whole evening."

"Not if you set up the one in your closet."

"I can't set up a quantum computer in an apartment, for God's sake. The site needs to be specially prepared. You know nothing about this technology, do you?"

"Which is why I keep asking you and Rick to show me. Let me see the computer."

"You can leave now," he said as he opened the door to the hallway.

She left and waited in the front entrance for the taxi.

CHAPTER FOUR

Surprise

When Allen told Erin the next morning that he learned Kyle owned the largest share of Qubit, she concluded that the company was indeed using Rick as a front man, and that Kyle was the brains behind the quantum computer. This was a most unwelcome development. She would need Kyle's cooperation, but getting that could prove impossible.

Erin went to Amy early Monday morning to settle the issue. She let on she had more information than she did to see what would come of it. "Amy, I know Rick is only the figurehead of your company, yet you and he insist on keeping up the charade." Amy blanched noticeably at this assertion, telling Erin she was on the right track. "The other night, you told Allen that Kyle is the largest shareowner of the firm, and Kyle told me much more about the technology than Rick did, than Rick could, I'm sure," Erin fibbed. Amy opened her mouth to object, but Erin cut her off, "Don't! I'm on to you. Kyle made the breakthrough and built the computer. I'm guessing you use

Rick as the front man because he's so attractive and persuasive. Right?"

"Okay, Erin, you figured it out." Her fears having been confirmed, Erin struggled to cover up her dismay. Amy went on, "Kyle is … Kyle is Kyle. He's impulsive, blunt, insolent, weak, and repulsive." Erin frowned at this, wondering at the low opinion Amy harbored of the man who idolized her and who had achieved so much for her sake. "We knew Kyle couldn't be seen as the face of Qubit if we were to succeed with investors. Rick is Kyle's opposite. He's charming, convincing, and beautiful, and he has a PhD in physics. Kyle only has his bachelor's. Who would you choose for front man?"

"Your strategy worked with the media because Rick's surface knowledge sufficed with them, but sending him in to explain this to the regulators was a serious mistake, wasn't it?"

"And if we sent in Kyle, he'd have screamed at them."

"Maybe so, but he could have fully explained the technology and what it could and couldn't do. He might've been able to allay their objections. Anyway, I'll give you one last chance. I need to hear from the real genius behind Qubit. I need you to use your influence with Kyle to make him cooperate with me. I need in-depth knowledge on how the computer works, on what it can do, and his take on the dangers it poses that so concerned the regulators. If you refuse, I will recommend against investing in Qubit."

Amy picked up her phone barked, "Kyle, come here," and hung up. "Just tell me what strings to pull, and my puppet will tell you everything."

Erin looked at her and thought, *What a despicable woman!*

Kyle walked in, scowled at Erin, and waited for Amy's command. "Kyle," she began in the imperious tone she reserved for him, "apparently you told Erin that you are the one who invented and built the computer." Kyle lowered his eyes at her tone of rebuke. "Now that Erin knows, she's made the reasonable demand that you tell her everything she wants to know about our computer."

"No, Amy. She'll just steal our technology."

"Kyle, you want us to get married, right?"

"It's everything I want."

"Well, it'll never happen unless we salvage something out of this disastrous situation we find ourselves in. Erin knows damn well we're desperate—"

"Because you told her!"

"You're falling in my esteem every second you persist in arguing against me. You spend the day with Erin telling her everything—and I mean *everything*—or we're through. Do you understand?" He nodded. "Good. Take Erin to your office. Erin, if he causes any trouble, let me know right away."

"I will," Erin said, as she followed Kyle to his cubicle. As he sat at his computer, she noticed his face was mottled; she saw only hatred in his eyes. "Can we please be adults about this and do our jobs?" she suggested. He stood and paid a mock deferential obeisance. She smirked and said, "I'll get out of your hair forever once we're done."

After a few minutes of composing himself with eyes shut, he turned to her and said, "What do you want to know?"

"First how the technology works, then how you engineered it, then what it can do, then what precisely the regulators objected to, then what you did about it."

"How much do you know about quantum mechanics?"

"Just what Rick told me."

"Nothing, then." He gave her a quick course on the theory behind the computer. Then he applied it to explain the engineering. "Qubits use properties of photons and electrons, and atoms and ions. As I've said, photons don't interact well, but they travel easily, which makes them good for transmitting quantum information. Electrons, atoms, and ions are the opposite in this respect: they don't travel well, but readily interact, which makes them good for storing and processing quantum information." He went on to explain how each can be applied to quantum computing, then to explain the rudiments of the engineering. "So, qubits consist of controlled particles and the devices to control them, that is, to trap particles and switch them from one state to another. There are different devices that can accomplish this. I started out using superconducting electronics ..."

After he finished explaining the engineering behind the machine she looked at him in awe. "That's really incredible," she opined. "On a shoestring budget you did it before anyone else. How?" He shrugged. "I mean you don't even have a PhD." He glared at her. "It's not an insult," she protested. "What you've accomplished would be amazing for a hundred PhDs."

"I dropped out before getting my PhD."

"Why?"

"Copyright versus patent law. Rick used my undergraduate thesis to build one of the key components of my machine. It had explicit instructions on how to engineer the part. I had no idea someone could use my ideas and steal it from under my nose—legally, apparently—so I couldn't submit a doctoral dissertation for fear of someone stealing all my ideas."

"Rick stole your ideas, yet you started a business with him?"

"The bastard owned the patent. It would've taken years to find another way to address the problem of decoherence—if there is another way. The venture capital company backing me insisted we join forces. There was no choice."

"Tell me what this machine can do."

Kyle gave the same basic account as Rick gave, focusing on the incredible computing speed and what that implied. "It makes your company's supercomputer look like a five-dollar calculator."

"Which is why the government shut you down?"

"They shut us down because your firm and others sold them a tale of woe. The legislators used its potential to break secret codes as their excuse."

"But isn't that a real problem for the government?" Kyle shrugged. She proceeded, "Is top-secret information safe with your computer around?"

"Since quantum computers can factor large numbers, they can easily decode and encode secret information. Current methods of encryption are nothing for quantum computers. No information accessible through the Internet would be safe."

"But top-secret government networks are protected from the Internet by more than encryption. What about the firewalls?"

"They don't teach hacking at Dartmouth, do they? There are ways through any firewall. The CIA needs to communicate with the outside world through email. Their people need to get access to the CIA internal network when they're traveling.

Satellite offices need to communicate with the main office. That's all done through the World Wide Web. Quantum computers are very efficient at breaching a firewall, and once in, a hacker can find information—like passwords into top-secret systems—so fast that the people in charge of the network can't react fast enough to shut everything down before the damage is done."

"And you wonder why the government is worried?"

"So build better encryption techniques; increase keylength, use digital signature schemes like Lamport signatures, or use quantum cryptography. It shouldn't be too difficult to protect secret information."

"But as it stands, no computerized information is safe, right?"

"Not if there's a way in through the Internet, no."

"But the time and cost for making information safe again—"

"Okay, then, let's just stop where we are. No more computer advances. It won't be safe for corporate America!"

"It won't be safe for anyone, including businesses, individuals, and government. Everyone's privacy is kaput, not to mention their bank accounts. You can't just dismiss the concerns."

"Just killing the technology was incredibly short-sighted."

"I happen to agree with you, but since that has happened, what do you intend to do about it? The government has put the problem you raised right back in your lap. How will you deal with it?"

"As I said, there are potential fixes, and we made them clear to the government. It fell on deaf ears."

"You told the government how to protect its information?"

"I'm no fool. I knew the government would be concerned about the vulnerability of its computer systems, so I gave them some promising ideas for protecting their data from my computer."

"And what about the private sector?"

"Let the marketplace handle it. I can't resolve the problem for everyone."

"I'm sure that didn't impress the legislators. Tell me the truth. Did Qubit sell the missing computers?"

"I don't know. If so, I haven't seen any of the money."

"There you go, then. Give me a demonstration of your computer in action. Find evidence that Rick or Amy got a sudden windfall." He looked at her as if intrigued by the idea, but worried at the same time. "C'mon, Kyle. You don't have anything to hide, do you?"

"No." But he still hesitated.

"Worried about compromising Amy?" Kyle looked at her in fear. "If you trust her, you should have nothing to worry about, right?" He searched for and found Amy's bank accounts. There was nothing amiss. "Kyle, you need to go deeper for this to mean anything."

He sighed and went to work as Erin looked over his shoulder taking notes. He used his computer to hack into anything he could link to Amy by any personal information on her. The speed with which the Qubit computer traced the information and broke the passwords occasioned fright in Erin. *No wonder they shut this down*, she mused. Finding nothing, he did the same for Rick as Erin looked on—and, again, he found nothing.

"I guess they really were stolen," Kyle concluded.

"What about you?" Erin asked.

"I didn't steal the damn things. I'm flat broke. I've really had more than enough of you. I've done everything you asked. Now disappear forever as promised." She sat there looking at him with a pretty pout. "I've told you everything." She continued to pout. "Considering my opening position was fuck off and die, you should be really happy." Pout. He sighed and showed her his only account, a checking account at the Bank of America showing a balance of $1312.58. "That's all I'm worth," he said. "I have a headache. I'm going home." He logged off and told Erin to leave his office as he got his coat and left.

After Amy went to lunch, Erin turned on his computer and logged into the University of Toronto computer using Kyle's password, which she had been careful to take note of earlier. She went through the same steps as Kyle had used for Amy and Rick to track down information on Kyle. After a brief search, she found something interesting enough to check with Rick when he arrived at the office after six PM.

That evening in his office, Rick was being of little assistance. Anxious to get the information she needed to complete her task, she elected to use her feminine wiles to break down his resistance. She sat on his lap and put her arms around him. He kissed her hard and ran his hands over her back. They petted for several minutes. He lifted her sweater up over her head, dropped it on the floor, and buried his face in her cleavage.

She stopped him at this point and said, "Before we go any further, I need some information."

"Is that why you're here now?"

"That's one reason. The other is I find you irresistible. So tell me what I want to know and you can do whatever you want with me." He nodded with a smile. "Those three missing computers really concern me because of the potential for reverse engineering, the loss of fifteen million dollars, and especially the question of possible illegality. I can't get DTC involved in an illegal operation. If the company sold them, I'm afraid I have to recommend against the takeover; if it was an individual, we should be okay."

"They were stolen."

"That's not true, and you know it. Only three people had access to those computers. The door automatically locks and the lock wasn't jimmied. It's so obvious someone here at Qubit sold them." He tried to remove her bra, but she leaned away and said, "Just tell me who sold them and who to, and I'm all yours all night."

"All right I'll tell you, but you didn't hear it from me. It was Kyle. When Amy and I were in Washington, just before the government seized our computers, he phoned to tell us he sold two computers to Canadian customers and took one to his apartment—or so he says. But when we got back, six computers were gone. At first we thought the other three must have been stolen, but—as you know—there was no sign of a break-in, and the alarm didn't go off. Kyle blamed it on me and Amy, which really pissed us off, as you can imagine, but when Amy and I talked about it, we figured he was putting the blame on us to remove any suspicion from himself.

"He blames me alone for the predicament we're in and wants to deal me out, so he takes the computers and admits to selling two to keep the company barely afloat. Then he sells the other three or four on the side before we go down the tubes. That leaves him a multi-millionaire, which he'll use to woo Amy, and me with nothing."

"Who did he sell them to?"

"That I don't know."

"Did you go to the police?"

"No. We'd all be in the soup if the government finds out about any of this."

She kissed him passionately; he dived back into her cleavage. Neither heard Amy and Kyle open the door and enter the office.

Amy stopped short and screamed, purple-faced, "What the hell are you doing?" The entangled lovers detangled and hopped up.

"Calm down, Amy," urged Rick. Erin put her sweater back on.

"What were you doing with her, you son of a bitch?" Amy shrieked.

Kyle, standing at the door, said, "Why are you so upset, Amy?"

Ignoring Kyle, she slapped Rick and started crying. "I hate you!"

"Amy?" said Kyle with tears in his eyes.

Her face expressed the hatred and fury coursing through her; she hollered, "You're the biggest loser ever born, Kyle. You're supposed to be this genius, but we played you for a fool. It was all a ploy to get you to merge your company with ours. I've been married to Rick for two years!"

"No!" he cried in disbelief.

"Yes! Did you actually think I'd be interested in an ugly nerd? I despise you!"

Kyle's eyes overflowed, his nose dripped, his mouth fell agape, his shoulders drooped; his very spirit seemed to quit him, his reason for living gone. Erin could only pity him in his despair.

"Crybaby!" Amy yelled at him. She then ran to Erin and flailed at her, yelling "Harlot! Slut! Get out of here. We'll never sell to your fucking company!" until Rick interceded. She turned her wrath on him, hitting and scratching, until he slammed her against the wall and she fell to the floor.

That reanimated Kyle, who ran at Rick, bellowing, "I'll kill you for hurting her!" Erin stepped in to calm him down as he was winding up to smash Rick. He stopped just short of Erin's face, then shoved her aside.

Amy jumped on Kyle and started biting and scratching him as she screamed, "I hate you! I wish you were dead!" Unwilling to hurt her, he hunched over to try to protect himself. Erin tore her away from the bloodied man.

Walking out in a daze, Kyle turned and said to Rick, "You're dead."

Amy ran out crying.

Erin put on her jacket and left. Her assignment here was definitely finished now.

CHAPTER FIVE

Surprise, Surprise

At 6:45 the next morning, the phone rang. A sleepy FBI agent picked it up and heard, "Agent McAdams?"

"Yes."

"Rick Hugel has been found dead."

"What? How?"

"Shot through the back of his head in his office. Since Kyle Summers threatened to kill Hugel last night and since he's currently on a jet to Vancouver, he looks good for it."

"I thought he was under surveillance."

"He must have figured that out and slipped out the back way. He has a connecting flight to Anchorage. We can't arrest him in Canada, so we'll have agents at the airport in Anchorage to pick him up. I want you to fly there to retrieve him."

"I'm on my way."

"This is a high priority case. One of our jets will fly you directly there. It'll be ready at Midway in forty-five minutes.

You should arrive in Anchorage about a half-hour after he does. Our agents will hold him for you."

"Got it."

Agent McAdams drove to Midway International Airport. By the time the agent had negotiated Chicago's rush hour, the small jet was fueled and ready to go. The pilot welcomed Agent McAdams on board and almost immediately commenced taxiing for takeoff.

Over northern Alberta, the pilot called the agent up to the cockpit and said that the suspect's connection to Anchorage was delayed by fifty minutes, and that they would beat him there.

Two FBI agents met Agent McAdams at Anchorage, and the three walked to the arrival gate. As they waited for the passengers to debark from the jet, a menacing-looking man strolled up to them and said, "You have FBI written all over you."

"And who are you?" said a surprised and irritated Agent McAdams.

"Jeff Norris, CIA." He showed his ID. "As you know, we have an intimate interest in this case."

"How did you even know—"

"We're all on the same team. It is imperative we get some information from your suspect ASAP to head off another disaster in the Far East. I need to question him and I want to escort him back to Washington."

"My assignment is to take him back to Chicago, Mr. Norris."

"We'll let our bosses argue that one out. In the meantime, I want access to him until we take off."

"We?"

"Can't you give a fellow American a ride home on your jet?"

"Not without permission, I can't."

"Well, ask for it."

Agent McAdams called the FBI's Chicago field office and passed along the request. After confirming via computer that Jeff Norris was with the CIA, the Special Agent in Charge told his field agent to cooperate with the CIA agent, but Mr. Summers was to be returned to Chicago.

"You can come with us, but we're going to Chicago."

"All right," replied Norris. "I've arranged with U.S. immigration here for a room to question the suspect in."

The agents spotted Kyle walk down the ramp and out into the small terminal. All four agents followed him to the baggage area. As he waited at the carousel, his jaw dropped upon seeing Erin strolling up to him. "What the hell are you doing here?" he asked in utter astonishment.

"Come with me, Kyle," she said, as two men in suits grabbed his elbows.

"Who are you?"

"Special Agent Erin McAdams, FBI." He tried to free himself from the agents. "Don't!" Erin commanded. "Stop trying to resist and come with us. We're taking you back to Chicago."

"What's the charge?"

"You killed Rick and—"

"You're full of shit!"

Curious passengers gawked as they backed away from the screaming man who was struggling to free himself.

"And you sold your computer to hostile foreign clients."

"What? Are you making this up as you go?"

"Hands behind your back. Now!" He followed her command, and she put handcuffs on him. Erin informed him, "You're under arrest for lending expert advice and assistance to a terrorist organization, and for the murder of Rick Hugel." She read him his rights as he was led to the office set aside for his interrogation. Norris opened the door, yanked the prisoner into the room and tried to close the door before Erin got in, but she put her arm out to stop the door and said, "I'm staying."

"Suit yourself, but let me do my job." He pushed Kyle down on a plastic chair and smashed him across the face with the back of his hand, knocking the chair and its occupant down to the floor.

"Hey," yelled Erin. Norris led her out into the hall and closed the door behind him. She said, "What the hell are you doing?"

"I'm interrogating the bastard who sold those computers and got dozens of our agents killed. More are at high risk as we speak. I need to find out exactly who got the computers, and I'll do what I have to to save their lives."

"Is it really necessary to use force?"

"It is if we want to stop the next mass murder of our agents. We need to know right away who else might be at risk and get them to safety. This is my job. I know how to get any information he has. If you insist on being in the room, either shut up or, better yet, play along. That might help us get to the meat sooner if you're so worried about that piece of garbage." She nodded. "Never mind this good cop-bad cop shit. He has to believe we both mean business. Understood?" She reluctantly agreed.

They went back into the room, and he yanked Kyle up to his feet. "You cost the lives of forty-seven U.S. federal agents so far, you fucking scumbag!"

"What the hell are you talking about?"

Norris punched Kyle hard in the stomach. Kyle bent over trying to breathe. "You have no idea of the damage you've done to your country, do you? Two of those three computers you sold ended up in the hands of enemies of the United States."

Kyle's face showed a mixture of shock and horror. "It wasn't me."

Norris socked him in the cheek, again knocking him down. Erin turned her head away. "The Chinese have one, so does a drug cartel in Colombia. The other was apparently bought by Israel."

"I did not sell those computers!" said Kyle from the floor.

"Then how did you get three million dollars in your bank account?" Norris asked as he kicked the prone man in the chest. "Keep lying, and the hurt will get worse—and I hear from McAdams here that you're a real mama's boy."

"He's the biggest wimp I ever met," Erin said.

Norris laughed as he hauled Kyle to his feet again. "So tell me, Summers, exactly who did you sell the computers to?"

"I sold two computers to Canadians; that's it. I didn't sell any others. If there's three million dollars in my account, I've been framed."

"You want the next shot at him, McAdams?"

Erin looked at Norris in shock, but recovered quickly and said, "No. I'm enjoying being a spectator too much." She hoped Norris was right that Kyle would give in sooner if he knew he had no allies here. Kyle glared at her, and she smiled back. Norris sniggered and kicked Kyle in the crotch. He grunted and fell to his knees.

Norris continued, "A computer in China was used to break what we thought was an unbreakable passcode into top-secret CIA files. It had to be your computer. Those files have the identities of all our agents in the Asian theater. *All* of them!" he reiterated as he punched Kyle again. "A few days later, our agents in China start turning up dead. The next day nine Drug Enforcement Agency undercover agents were executed in Colombia. Those with families got to watch their wives and children die first. That's a lot of blood on your hands, Summers."

"I'm sorry if my computers led to this, but I did not sell them. It's a setup. It had to be Rick Hugel."

Norris thumped Kyle on the head. Kyle reeled, but stayed upright on his knees.

"Come on, Kyle," said Erin, getting more and more uncomfortable. "Just tell us who got the computers so we can stop another disaster, and we can stop this interrogation."

"This is a fucking inquisition, and you won't get away with it!" Norris pulled him up by the collar, pushed him against the wall and cuffed him across the cheek again. "You fucking pussy!" screamed the livid man. "You beat the shit out of a man who can't defend himself, you goddamn sadist. Give me the chance to defend myself, and I'll drop your bloody carcass on the floor!"

Norris burst out laughing. "You?" said the six-foot-four man. "What are you, five-ten, a hundred and sixty? What do you say, McAdams? Can big bad Summers beat me up?"

"Sissy boy couldn't take a little girl."

"Give me the key," said Norris to Erin. She hesitated. "C'mon, let's bring this to a head, then he'll tell us everything, I guarantee it." She gave him the key, and he took off the handcuffs. "Okay, Summers, drop me," he taunted, as he formed fists with his big hands and leveled his left one at Kyle's face.

Kyle parried it and launched a savage lunge punch, and followed it up with a reverse punch, which sent Norris sprawling. He kicked Norris in the face and knocked him out.

Erin, astounded at the proceedings, reacted too late. While she fumbled to get her gun out, Kyle dashed to her and got her by the throat. He shoved her to the wall with his left forearm against her neck, pushing enough to make her eyes bulge and face turn red. With his right hand, he fished her gun out of its shoulder holster. He moved his bloody, sweaty, furious face within inches of hers.

Speaking through his gritted teeth, he growled, "You goddamn bitch! Now you'll feel what it's like to be at the mercy of a madman who would love to see you suffer!"

"I can't breathe!" she squeaked, in obvious panic. He relaxed his arm, but held her in place. She took a big gulp of air. "You can't get away. There are two more agents down the hall."

"As you may have figured out by now, I have a black belt in karate, and I have your gun, which I'll use if I have to to get away from this torture chamber."

"Kyle, I'm really sorry about this."

"Not as sorry as you're gonna be." He let her go, but pointed the gun at her head.

Her face betrayed her anxiety. This man was as enraged as any she'd ever dealt with, and as the only suspect in a murder case, he was willing and able to kill in her judgment. She explained, "He said it would go better for you if I played along. I didn't want any of this. I was just supposed to take you back, then he showed up and—"

"Not interested in your lies. You stood by and cheered and laughed as he was beating me mercilessly." He went over and kicked Norris in the ribs. While he was looking at Norris, Erin reached back for a gun in a holster at the small of her back, but froze when he turned back to her.

"Kyle, please. I told you the truth." He pointed the gun at her again. Seeing arrant hatred in his eyes, she gasped in fear and said in a shaky voice, "Are you really gonna kill me?" She managed a pleading smile as her chin trembled.

"If I was the murderer you think I am, do you think you'd be alive now? I'd have already choked you to death. Then I'd have finished off Norris and shot the two bastards out there who stood by listening while this prick whaled on a helpless man." He lowered the gun, and she breathed a sigh of relief. He continued, "God dammit, this is America. This shit isn't supposed to happen here to innocent civilians. We've become a dystopia that can justify anything in the name of national security."

"Is that how you justify selling those computers?"

"It wasn't me!"

"And you didn't kill Rick either, I suppose?"

"Of course not."

"Since you're holding a gun on an FBI agent, you'll forgive me for not believing you."

"You mean the same agent that just took part in a torture session?"

"I'm sorry."

"Yeah, I'll bet."

"If you didn't kill Rick, why did you run?"

"Last night I went back to Qubit to kick the shit out of Rick. When I got to his office, I saw him lying in a pool of blood with a hole in his head. After I shit my pants, I got the hell out of there. My first thought was that Amy did it, because she was so pissed at her cheating husband."

"She didn't do it. At the time of the murder, she was at the police station, swearing that you stole and sold the computers."

His face fell. "How could she do that to me?" he said with tears in his eyes. Erin slowly removed the gun from the holster. Kyle continued, "I can't believe she would ... While I was driving home last night, I remembered you heard me threaten to kill Rick. I thought, ah, shit, I'll be a suspect."

"And you didn't think running might make you the prime suspect?"

"I thought I had a bigger problem to worry about. When I pulled up to my place last night, I saw two men sitting in a sedan across the street. Did you know Rick was intentionally run off the road into a concrete abutment about four months ago? Only the seat belt and air bag saved him. The police never got to the bottom of it, but I think it was one of our competitors. Our computer would've eventually doomed most of the companies building the old digital technology, from huge multi-national conglomerates down to their small time suppliers. You wondered why I didn't take credit for the breakthrough?"

"Amy gave you your orders."

"That wasn't enough for something so big. I was scared. If it keeps me safe, he can have the credit for now, I thought. So anyway, when I saw those guys in the car, I got paranoid. Maybe the same people came back to kill him, and maybe I was next."

"They were FBI agents."

"I might have considered that possibility if I hadn't just found Rick dead. I was convinced it was the people that killed Rick." He chuckled bitterly. "I felt guilty about suspecting Amy and planned to call her from here to beg her to join me, but she hates me so much she's trying to frame me." He shook his head. Erin got set to make her move. He wiped his eyes and said, "Anyway, last night I packed a bag and ran out the back, hailed a cab, and flew to where I thought I could disappear."

"Give yourself up and I promise I'll investigate it."

"You'll forgive me if that doesn't comfort me. You got everything wrong about me; they fed you disinformation, and you ate it up without thinking. Then you participated in torturing me. You're lucky I'm not a murderer, you bitch. And this fucker!"

He turned to kick Norris again—but as he did, Erin pulled out her Air Taser Gun, pulled the trigger, and took down Kyle immediately. When he collapsed, he banged his head on the floor and lost consciousness. She picked up her pistol, opened the door, and called the agents in. She told them what happened as she put the handcuffs on Kyle.

The two local agents carried Kyle to the jet while Erin roused Norris. He revived quickly and seemed to ignore the pain he must have been feeling. He was all for resuming the interrogation, which Erin adamantly refused. As he walked to the jet with Erin, she told him, "If you lay one finger on my prisoner, I'll take you down with my Taser Gun. Got it?" He laughed as he looked down eight inches to her defiant eyes and nodded.

*

Kyle came to his senses as the aircraft lifted off. His head and body ached from the beating and the uncontrolled fall to the floor. He found himself in shackles in the cabin of the small jet. He was seated behind Norris and across from Erin.

Norris turned and said, "You're in deeper shit than just about anyone on Earth right now, asshole."

"Tough guy again with his opponent in chains, eh? Set me free, and this time I'll qualify you as a eunuch."

Norris laughed and turned his head forward.

Erin offered Kyle a drink and a sandwich. He told her where she could insert them. She made a call to Allen. At the end of a lengthy conversation, she and Allen traded a joke, and she laughed and hung up. Kyle glared at her.

"What?" she challenged.

"You're taking me back so the government can kill me and you just sit there laughing as if it's nothing to you."

"I don't feel guilty for doing my job, Mr. Summers. Console yourself with the thought that it was your own fault."

He turned away from her. A few minutes later he turned back and asked, "Do you know Special Agent Ebbling?"

"Should I?"

"Ebbling came into Qubit and stole a hundred and sixty million dollars worth of computers, but do you think I can find a cop to arrest anyone in a three-letter agency in government that's no doubt using them this very minute?" Erin shrugged. "You're so intent on upholding the law, but shrug at a theft of a hundred and sixty million dollars. Amazing. Your FBI thieves were so uncertain about the legality and morality of what they were doing, they issued a gag order so we couldn't even bring our case to the public. But not even that was enough. They sent out someone else even worse than Ebbling to set me up on a charge of terrorism."

"You think a good defense is a ridiculous charge against me?"

"I know you set me up, you cunt!" She shook her head and tittered, which enraged Kyle further. "This is the government's way of making sure my invention never gets to market, right?"

She offered no response. He snarled and turned to look out the window as Erin typed up her notes on the latest developments.

Norris went to make coffee in the back. A few minutes later, he came forward with two cups of coffee, gave one to Erin, and brought one to the pilot. She took a sip and said to Norris, "Your coffee stinks." Norris went back for another cup. He walked up to Kyle, tipped the cup and poured some hot coffee onto Kyle's lap. He screamed, and Erin warned, "Norris! Cut it out!"

Norris returned, "Just a little payback." Poised to spill more coffee, he asked Kyle, "What's the matter? You hate my coffee, too?"

"I take it with milk and sugar, you sick fuck."

Norris chuckled again as he poured more coffee onto the poor man's lap. Kyle shrieked again. Erin took her cup and threw it at Norris; the coffee scalded his arm that came up to block the missile. He leered at her, then smiled coldly and went to sit in the co-pilot's seat.

"Do you need ice or painkillers?" she asked Kyle.

With a fiery expression and teary eyes, he yelled, "Scalded, electrocuted, and battered, courtesy of the FBI and CIA. What you sons of bitches get away with in the name of national security is beyond belief. You're no better than the KGB or SS."

"Don't lump me in with Norris. I'm sorry about what he did to you."

"As far as I'm concerned, you're more of a threat to our freedom and democracy than the communists and terrorists combined."

"You helped the communists and terrorists take advantage of our freedom. It's because of people like you that we have to restrict our freedom. We're struggling to find a happy medium, that's all."

"We're currently at a sad extreme. You're a cog in a totalitarian regime, Special Agent, and you're too programmed or too stupid to realize it."

"And you're a cog in the Chinese regime, which is totalitarian, and in the Colombian drug cartel, which is pure evil. Rail against me all you want. You're a sleazy traitor and a terrorist, and you will pay for it."

"By what possible stretch of the imagination am I a terrorist?"

"Under U.S. Code Title 18, international terrorism includes any act of mass destruction, assassination, or kidnapping against our government that transcends national boundaries. Therefore, a scumbag who sells a computer to a hostile government that uses it to assassinate our operatives is a terrorist."

"So if my computers were used for a terrorist act, I am a terrorist?"

"Since you sold them, yes."

"I didn't sell them, but even if I did, I would never have suspected they would be used for what they were apparently used for. Doesn't the government have to prove intention to commit a crime?"

"Not in this case. You're held responsible even if you unknowingly helped with a terrorist act."

"Unbelievable. So, I guess if a suicide bomber comes up to me on the street with coat closed and asks me which way to the subway and I tell him, I'm a terrorist?"

"Don't like Title 18? We've got you under other laws, too. Ever heard of the Export Administration Act?"

"It prohibits the export of certain computers to certain countries, presumably so our enemies can't use our technology against us for nuclear weapons and missile design and such. It applies to digital supercomputers."

"Don't play ignorant. You know damn well your computer is much more powerful than any digital one."

"Which is precisely why I did not sell my computer to the Chinese or the Colombians. Hugel and his goddamn wife did it, and when I prove that, *you* will pay for it, Agent McAdams."

"Is that a threat, Mr. Summers?"

"You bet it is."

"Threatening an FBI agent is a crime."

"So is selling computers, so is talking to the media about the outrages the government has perpetrated against me, and so is picking our noses if the FBI decides it is. I can't take the law seriously anymore. So charge me, Special Agent, pile it on. You can only kill me once." She continued typing, and he continued talking. "What did Rick tell you as you were riding him?"

"Don't be so crass. I only kissed him."

"He was bobbing for your apples when I saw him."

"So what? I got the information I needed."

"He said I did it, didn't he? And you believed him." She nodded. "Maybe if I was the handsome one, you'd have chosen me for your erotic interrogation, and he'd be suspect number one. Jesus, you're stupid." She went back to her typing. "Slut!"

*

That did it. She'd put up with enough of his insults over the past week. "What's the matter, Summers? Jealous? You get as much action as a Benedictine monk, don't you, nerd boy?" His downcast eyes confirming her assertion, she smiled and pressed the case. "You're not! You're still a virgin, aren't you?"

"No."

"A twenty-five-year-old virgin." She laughed.

"I haven't been a virgin for, uh, a long time."

"I don't believe you. You'd be pathetic enough to save yourself for Amy."

"No, last year when she put me off for the hundredth time I went out and ... uh—"

"You bought a whore! You paid to lose your virginity at twenty-four." She laughed again.

"A paper bag was all someone needed to subdue your virtue, I'm sure."

"Whereas you had to pay someone to take yours off your hands," she teased.

"Watch out if I get off, McAdams. I will make you pay with so much usury, you'll never recover." Erin smirked at him and kept her cool façade, but she had no doubt that this man was skilled enough and angry enough to ruin anyone he set his sights on. She started to think about how to defend herself against a world-leading computer engineer and despaired about how to do it short of keeping the little cash she had under her mattress. "No smart ass reply to that?" taunted Kyle.

"You'll either be executed for murder or jailed for terrorism, so I'm not worried," she said.

"Which makes you and our government guilty of premeditated murder, you callous shrew. You let that asshole up there abuse your prisoner. You let yourself get taken prisoner by a rank amateur. Some secret agent."

"I have made some mistakes, yes, but in the end, there you are in chains."

So agitated that his head quavered rapidly and spit flew out of his mouth as he spoke, he screamed, "You got the wrong guy, you goddamn moron!" He struggled manically against the chains, all the while screaming at the top of his lungs.

"Shut the hell up back there," said Norris.

Kyle continued to thrash about. When the arm rest came loose, Erin began to worry. Kyle hollered, "If I get free, I'll make you fucking pay, goddamn harpy!"

"Settle down," she ordered as she took out her Taser Gun and pointed it at him. "Now!" He stopped, but maintained his irate expression. She went on, "I'm not arguing this with you. The courts will decide your guilt. Now shut up; I'm tired."

"Tired of screwing up?" She paid no heed. "You better hope I never get to a computer before our friendly fascist government murders me with your help. I will destroy you!" She closed her eyes, feigning nonchalance, but stayed awake for a few minutes worrying about this threat. Finally, exhaustion got the better of her and she fell asleep.

In a slumber over the Canadian Rockies, Erin was dreaming that Kyle was screaming at her and about to kill her. She opened her eyes. Things were blurry and voices had an echo about them.

Kyle was yelling, "What the hell are you doing?"

She looked over to Norris, who had a parachute on. He was opening the emergency exit window. She blinked hard, thinking she was still dreaming. Looking forward, she saw the pilot slumped over in his seat. She turned back as Norris laughed his cold laugh and jumped out. Her jaw dropped.

"Ah, Jesus Christ," groaned Kyle. Continuing to look at the open window with astonished eyes, she heard Kyle laughing nervously and saying, "The end. In chains in a doomed jet."

The loud blast of cold air brought Erin to her feet. She teetered for a moment and had to put her hand on the back of her seat to stay on her feet; she felt dizzy and had a headache. To the cockpit she went only to confirm the pilot was unconscious. Her attempts to revive him were unavailing. She looked out and saw mountain peaks looming on all sides just below them. A buzzer blared. She looked at a flashing light next to the fuel gauge: almost empty!

Dashing back into the cabin she said, "Where did Norris go?"

She looked back at the open emergency exit, then at Kyle, who informed her, "Down."

They both had to yell to be heard over the roar of wind through the open emergency exit. The air was thin and cold.

"Why the hell would he do that?"

"Well, if you're consistent, you'll just blame it on me. Get me my coat, will you? It's freezing."

"This doesn't make any sense."

"Welcome to my world. Did you check his ID?"

"Of course I did. He's CIA, supposedly … God, Kyle, we're out of fuel! What are we supposed to do?" she said, eyes conveying her terror.

"Die."

Desperately trying to reject that notion, she said, "How far do you think we can glide if I take the jet up as high as I can before we run out of fuel?"

"To just below the top of the highest peak in our path."

"How can you possibly joke in this situation?" she yelled at him as she shivered.

"Will it help if I cry or scream? I'm scared as hell, but since my options appear to be dying quickly in a plane crash or returning home to languish in a jail cell until they electrocute me, I choose door number one."

"Well, I choose to live! I'll unchain you if you help me land." She didn't wait for his response as she put the key in the lock and opened it. She hurried to the back to get their coats, tossed him his, and put on hers as she went to the cockpit and sat in the co-pilot's seat.

To her horror, she saw that less than a mile directly in front of them was a sheer cliff. She pulled back on the wheel just as the left engine started to sputter. The jet slowly gained altitude, but was closing quickly on the peak.

"I don't know if we can get above that peak!" she screamed to Kyle as she applied full power. He sat and shut his eyes in silent panic. "God *please*!" she entreated, as she pulled back the wheel to its full extent and banked a little left toward the summit's low point. As the jet passed ten feet above the mountain, Erin exclaimed, "We made it!"

Having cleared the highest peak in the area, Erin was relieved for the moment, but she knew their chances remained bleak. She looked around for a clearing to land in, but saw nothing promising. Directly ahead, and for as far as she could see from her altitude, there was nothing but snow-covered mountains. To the left more mountains; to the right were tree-covered rolling hills along a valley. She turned in that direction to fly along the valley, but could see nothing but steep hills and trees.

"Get up here and help me," she shouted.

"What for? I know nothing about planes. I don't wanna see the end coming."

"I have thirty-one hours as a student pilot."

"A student pilot flying a jet without fuel in the mountains. We're saved!"

"I might be able to land this if we can spot a place. Help me, *please*."

"As I told you, I'd rather die than get back to the States. You're on your own, Special Agent."

"At least check for more parachutes." The left engine coughed and ceased.

"Oh, right. This was well-planned. They'll be no other chutes, the aircraft locator will be gone, we'll be miles from nowhere with nowhere to land, the radio will be out—"

"Shut up. Shut up. Shut up!" She picked up the headset and put it on. "Mayday, mayday, mayday," she shouted. She heard nothing. Looking for the radio controls, she saw it was shorted out. "Shit!" she said. "Bring me my purse," she ordered. He brought it to her. She rummaged through it for a few seconds, then emptied it onto the floor. "Where the hell is my phone?" she asked.

"Norris took it." Erin's face fell. "And there are no parachutes," Kyle said. "Shitty knowing you."

"I'm not giving up. Things are going badly for you, so you just give up."

"Going badly? You have a gift for understatement. It's going so badly, getting splattered in a fiery crash is the best thing that could happen to me right now. I just want this over with."

*

He didn't say so, but the night before, once he'd known he'd lost Amy forever and knew he'd be a prime suspect in Rick's murder, he'd strongly considered suicide. A plane crash might be the best way out.

"You're a coward," said Erin.

"You're escorting me to the electric chair, and you sneer at me because I'm scared? That little shock you gave me hurt like hell. I can't imagine how excruciating the electric chair is. So tell me, pitiless tramp, what would I gain by surviving this? A few months of looking forward to a horrible death? The way you feel right now, that's how I've felt since you put the gun on me. To me, you're the evil agent who bailed on us."

"Oh, what's the matter with the pilot? Please wake up!"

"Some kind of drug that won't be detectable in the autopsy, probably. Norris put it in the coffee, no doubt. I assume that's why you slept through the racket he made when he took your phone, then opened the window and jumped. Too bad for you you only took a sip or two before you tossed it at the bastard. Now you'll see your death coming."

"You're really pissing me off. I've done nothing to deserve this."

"You set me up."

"Do you actually think if I was in on any conspiracy against you that I'd be killing myself, too?"

"Oh, yeah. I can never think straight when I'm about to die. I guess you're just acceptable collateral damage to the CIA in its campaign to end the threat of the quantum computer."

"There!" she said, pointing to her left as the second engine sputtered to a halt, and the jet barely cleared a ridge. A narrow valley opened to the east with a lake about four miles long, but only half a mile wide.

Flying in a southerly direction, Erin had to descend rapidly and bank sharply left to avoid the mountains on the south side of the small valley. It would be a risky maneuver, but it was their only chance. "Where are the flaps? Where are the damn flaps?" She found and lowered them, then pushed the nose down and turned hard. There was no time to find and lower the wheels. "Oh, God, help me!" she pleaded.

Kyle went back to the cabin, sat, and put on his seatbelt. The end now imminent, he began to worry about how much this might hurt. He squeezed his eyes shut as his heart pounded violently. With the plane still in a steep turn as Erin struggled to keep it away from a promontory on the southern shore, it suddenly stalled and plummeted. She managed to level the wings just before the belly of the plane slammed onto the frozen surface of the lake. She was thrust forward against the shoulder belt so hard her left shoulder separated. She cried out in pain. With the ice offering little friction, the plane skimmed rapidly over the surface toward the northern shore.

"Slow down, slow down!" she said as the trees and rocks closed in.

By the time the plane skipped onto land, it had slowed considerably—but not enough. The left wing clipped a tree, and threw the aircraft around. Erin screamed and put her right arm in front of her face to brace for impact. The fuselage glanced off another tree and came to an abrupt halt upon hitting a large boulder. The impact knocked out Erin when part of the instrument panel fell on her head. She also suffered a nasty gash on her left arm that bled freely.

Kyle got away with a cut lip and a minor case of whiplash. After sitting a moment to collect himself, he got out of his seat and checked on Erin. He determined she was alive, but possibly in bad shape. Her left leg was pinned in the wreckage. The left side of the cockpit sustained most of the impact, and the pilot was entangled in the wreckage. Kyle checked the bloody body for a pulse, but found none.

"Lucky bastard," he said. The plane was cracked open to let in the elements. A slow, miserable death after all, he concluded, shaking his head at his bad luck in surviving a plane crash in the wilderness.

Kyle stood there, contemplating his predicament and deciding whether to let Erin bleed to death. Her death would certainly be in his interest, and letting her bleed to death might be the most humane thing he could do in their quandary.

Before he could make up his mind, however, she opened her eyes with a muted moan. He saw her trying to figure out what was happening. She lifted her head and gasped as pain started to register; she began to cry. She looked at the pilot and groaned. She turned and saw Kyle.

To his shock the first words out of her mouth were, "You're all right?"

Those three words, said while she was weeping, saved her life—for the time being, at least. While she continued to sob in pain and fear, he looked for and found a first aid kit. In it was a bottle of surgical glue, disinfectant, gauze, bandages, and other items of no use in this circumstance. He helped her off with her coat, which caused Erin considerable pain with her separated shoulder, and took the cap off the disinfectant.

"This might sting." He poured it on her gash, and she shrieked and swooned, which was a blessing because her insensibility enabled him to clean out the laceration on her arm and the cut on the top of her head, apply the glue, and close the wounds as best he could. Bandages completed the task.

He then tried pulling her from the wreckage, but could not free her left foot from the crushed instrument panel. As he pulled on her leg, she woke up with another yelp. "I'm trying to get you out of here, but your foot is stuck." This took a moment to sink in. "Can you move it? Is it broken?"

"I don't think so." When she tried pushing her arms against the seat for leverage, her shoulder reminded her it was injured. A scream of agony wafted from the wrecked plane. "Help me, please, Kyle."

"I'm trying."

"Try harder. I don't want to die like this." More tears trickled down her rosy cheeks, rosy not only from crying but from the cold. She began shivering. He helped her on with her coat, but she continued to shiver. From the cabin, he fetched two blankets, and covered her and the dead pilot. He got down on his knees to try to find a way to free her foot, but it was no use.

"Is there any pain killer in the first aid kit?" she asked.

"No, but there's a laxative. Didn't they realize we'd shit ourselves on the way down?" She had no smile to offer.

"I had a packet of Midol in my purse. Can you see it on the floor?"

"Oh, that's why you're so grumpy," he jested, but still no smile from Erin. "I guess it's not very pleasant to hear someone laugh or joke when you're screwed. *Is* it?" He pulled the pills from under the seat, and brought them and a bottle of water to her. She took three pills. Kyle swallowed two as well. He put on his gloves.

"Are you leaving me?" she said. He could see the fear in her eyes and hear it in her voice.

"I'm gonna see what our situation is, and maybe try to find something to use as a lever."

She nodded and closed her eyes. He tried to force open the door, but it wouldn't budge, so he climbed out the emergency exit. Surveying their awful desolation—nothing but snow, trees, and rocks in every direction—he cursed and walked along the shore. "Why the hell couldn't she have crashed in a mountain in Hawaii?" he said out loud. He found a solid tree branch that had been another victim of the crash, and took it back to employ it as a lever.

"What's it like out there?" asked Erin.

"Oh, it's a spectacular sylvan prospect breathtaking in its beauty and unspoiled by man, except some thoughtless jackass littered it with a broken plane. Where'd you learn how to land? The John Denver Flight School?"

The stick was too thick to fit into any opening. He cursed and went out to find a smaller one. Returning with three of different sizes, he tried all three, all of which snapped. Three more curses.

"You have to go for help, Kyle."

"How to put this so as not to alarm you? We're doomed! I don't think there's help within a million miles of this place."

"You have to try or we die for sure."

"And let's say I do manage to find help and bring it back here. Either I get arrested and murdered by my government, or murdered by whatever other group that might be after me. I have no incentive to find help."

"There are two lives in the balance here. I just saved yours by crash-landing. You can return the favor."

It's lucky she didn't say that to him when she was bleeding to death. "So, let me get this straight. You saved my life in order to take me back to Chicago to kill me? That's your idea of a favor?" She had no answer for that. "You saved your life only by crash-landing, so don't dare ask me for any favors. As far as I'm concerned, it would've been better if we were plastered on a mountainside."

"Are you really willing to let me die like this? Do you hate me that much?"

"I do, yes." She resumed her weeping. He said, "It's academic anyway. I'm pretty sure there's nothing I can do even to save myself. But I guess I can try." She smiled through her tears, but he dashed her hopes. "I never said I'd help you. If I do, I'm dead, so it comes down to me or you. Sorry, you lose."

"Please don't leave me to die. *Please*!"

"You were taking me to my death, and you think it's terrible that I leave you to yours?"

"I was doing my job."

"If you did your job, you wouldn't be escorting the wrong man to his extinction."

"Everything points to you. You know that because you ran and because you obviously think the death penalty is a foregone conclusion, which I have to say convinces me you are guilty."

"The U.S. government just tortured me and tried to kill me, for Christ's sake. What conclusion would you draw in my shoes?"

"One rogue agent is not the U. S. government."

"Let's say that's true, and I get back to face trial. Then it's flat broke Kyle Summers against the United States of America, which is foaming at the mouth because it is absolutely convinced I'm a terrorist who got forty-seven of its agents killed. Guess who loses?"

"I take no pleasure in taking you back to face the death penalty. I admire you." He lifted his eyes to the sky. "I do! What you've accomplished is so extraordinary. You're brilliant and funny and kinda cute—"

"I bet you say that to all the only guy around to save your life," he said with a phony smile. Supplanting it with an angry expression, he went on, "Maybe if I compliment the sissy boy, he'll spare me; then I can turn around and have him killed. I can even watch him fry and laugh when his eyeballs pop out and his hair burns off."

"That's not fair."

"Don't talk to me about fair, you fucking succubus. I hate you more than anyone I ever met!" She closed her teary eyes. "You may want to take off your jacket. Dying of cold may be the least painful option you have."

"Kyle?" she said with a pleading look.

"Goodbye, Special Agent. I hope there's a heaven for well-meaning dupes of the benighted totalitarian regime."

She lowered her head sadly in resignation and continued to cry. He grabbed a few bottles of water and four sandwiches, along with Erin's gun. He brought some water and food to Erin. Then he left the aircraft and walked along the frozen tarn toward the west. In the silence of the remote mountains, he heard her weeping for almost a quarter mile through the break in the fuselage.

CHAPTER SIX

Trapped

"Oh, what a mess, what a goddamn mess," he carped aloud as he marched on. "I'm really gonna die out here, aren't I?" he asked the trees. At least he was dressed suitably, having prepared for an Alaskan sojourn. Every step he took reminded him of the hot coffee spilled on his lap. He stopped and put some snow down his pants, but decided instantly that was a bad idea; he hopped around and scooped the snow out, then continued on with his burning, frozen balls. In the foot-deep snow, he toiled forward along the lake for forty minutes before coming to its western extremity.

Sitting on a fallen tree to rest, he ate and drank and cogitated. He told himself, *Just forget her, she'll never be found. She's probably already dead.* His conscience in revolt, he tried to stifle it. "You actually expect me to save you so you can kill me? Fuck you!" he bellowed to the mountains.

"Fuck you!" they replied. Even the echoes reproached him.

He stood up to continue his aimless journey, but turned around in place, wondering which way to go. He raised both arms as if to say, "Oh, what does it matter?" and sat back down.

Even if I manage somehow to get out of this, I'm still screwed. God dammit, this is unbelievable. Maybe I should just lie down and die here, he told himself. He lay down on the snow for a few minutes, but then sat up with another imprecation. Lying down and waiting to die was tedious.

He got up and proceeded northwest along the valley. Mile after mile, he trudged, seeing a good deal of wildlife, but nothing threatening. He knew there must be bears and big cats in the area and kept a wary eye out. He'd have been more worried about becoming a meal if he didn't have Erin's gun.

In the early evening, he stopped and squinted. He thought he saw a plume of smoke rising in the distance and altered course for it. When he got closer, he confirmed it was smoke and started jogging toward the source. A few minutes later, he burst through the bushes and startled a young man sitting next to a campfire.

"Jesus Christ!" the man yelled. "You scared the shit out of me."

"I need help," Kyle said. "I was in a plane crash." As soon as he said it, he wondered whether he should have. Now he'd have to answer a lot of unwelcome questions from a lot of people.

"Really?" Kyle nodded. "You look pretty banged up," said the man as he gazed at Kyle's bruised and swollen face. "I have a first aid kit."

"I'm okay. It's just minor bumps and bruises. Can you help me get to civilization?" he said, as he sat by the fire to warm up.

"Sure, but I'm not supposed to contact anyone unless it's an emergency."

"Did I mention I was in a plane crash?"

"Yeah. Listen, I'm a new fish and wildlife officer, and this is my wilderness test." Kyle looked at him as if to say, *I don't give a damn about any test!* The man said, "You said you were okay. It's getting late. Just stay with me until tomorrow morning, and we'll be picked up."

Kyle had wrestled with his conscience during his entire walk to safety, but now that he'd found it, he needed to make the consequential decision. Saving her would doom him. Common sense dictated he let her die, but letting her die would be the worst thing he'd ever done. If she died cold, alone, and in pain in the mountains, he would hear her begging for help and crying as he left for the rest of his life. And chances were he'd be caught again anyway. Since he'd opened his big mouth about the crash he'd have to tell any rescuers where the plane went down. What if they found out he left her to die? Would that be murder? Even if it wasn't they'd blame the crash on him anyway and charge him with two more murders.

He said, "I left a woman behind. She's alive, but she's pinned in the wreckage. Her shoulder might be separated or dislocated, and she might have a concussion. She needs help right away. The pilot is dead." Maybe he could somehow slip away, he reassured himself.

"I have a satellite phone to use in case of emergency." He went to his knapsack and pulled out the phone. He came back and handed it to Kyle.

"Is there 911 out here? Where the hell is here anyway?"

"You're in central B.C., about one hundred-twenty kilometers northeast of Williams Lake." Kyle's expression must have communicated that that information didn't help, because the man added, "We're maybe four hundred kilometers northeast of Vancouver." Kyle nodded. "There's no 911 out here, but I can dial my office. They'll send out help." Kyle gave him back the phone, and the man called for help.

The two sat near the fire and conversed about the crash—Kyle left out the most interesting parts to avoid suspicion—until the helicopter arrived thirty-three minutes later. He thanked the young man and got on board.

On the way to the scene of the crash the paramedic attended to Kyle's minor injuries.

*

Back at the crash site, Erin was still trying to make her peace with fate. She had cried for hours out of pain and fright, but now she just sat there, shivering and waiting to die. She hoped that would happen overnight.

While waiting, she went over and over in her head why Norris would try to kill the three of them. She wouldn't put it past the CIA to kill Kyle for retribution, but why before they'd got any useful information from him? And why would they kill an FBI agent and pilot?

Maybe Norris wasn't really CIA. No, her boss had verified he was. Maybe Norris was acting on his own when he downed the jet. Maybe he was hired by the Chinese to keep Kyle silent. Or the Colombians. Or the Israelis. Or some middle man. Maybe a hit man hired by a major computer firm trying to ensure the technology wouldn't hit the market for a long time yet. There was no way to tell.

All these unanswered questions raised two more: Was it possible Kyle was framed? And whom could she trust? The FBI permitted Norris to get on the jet. Maybe that was simply inter-agency courtesy.

When she first heard the thumping of the approaching helicopter, she thought she was imagining it, but as it got louder, she allowed herself to hope. When she saw snow kicking up in front of the plane, her tears began again, this time out of happiness and relief. A minute later a man with the "jaws of life" entered the broken aircraft and her weeping intensified. "Thank you for coming," she managed to squeak out between her sobs. Kyle came in behind the man and nodded at her. "Thank you," she said.

*

The medic checked her vital signs, got the information he needed, administered strong painkillers, and said, "We have to get you out of here; it's getting dark now." Erin, by this time in and out of consciousness, could tell her rescuers nothing about the fugitive. They extracted her from the wreckage and, having determined that her injuries were not serious enough to warrant a longer trip to Williams Lake in the darkness, flew to the nearest first aid station—all two rooms and one nurse practitioner of it—where her shoulder was mended, her gashes properly disinfected and closed, her blood topped off, and her mild concussion treated. Her foot was swollen and bruised, but otherwise okay.

Kyle was distressed at the isolation of the outpost he found himself in. The town of Likely, B.C., was home to a few hundred souls, fourteen moose and little else.

While Erin slept in the clinic, Kyle was safe, but as soon as she woke up, he had little doubt she would do her duty, and he would find himself again in fetters headed for jail. Any escape from here would take time, and be easy to detect. The nearest civilization, Williams Lake, was about ninety kilometers southwest by serpentine road. There was no bus, but one man operated a taxi service. He'd left two hours earlier to take someone to Quesnel.

"That figures," he said to the lady in the town's country inn. He'd have to hitchhike, which might look suspicious to the RCMP officer who had just pulled into town, here to investigate the crash. And it was too late to consider it that evening. For the moment, he was stuck.

The policeman asked him a few questions about the crash—Kyle told him he didn't really know what happened except the engines stopped and they landed on a frozen lake— and told him he'd do a complete debriefing in the morning. Kyle went to the dining room, sat down to dinner, and ruminated. He decided to leave town in the middle of the night, maybe try a carjacking with Erin's gun.

*

Erin awoke in confusion. As the nurse practitioner administered a sedative, she assured Erin she would be fine. Erin, fading fast, said, "Where is Kyle? The man who was with me?"

"I think he went to the inn. It's right across the street."

"Don't let him get away," she said, as sleep took hold. "Don't let him get to a comp ..." The nurse pulled up the blankets and went back to her crossword puzzle.

*

"Where can I find a computer?" Kyle asked the proprietor when he finished his meal. She pointed to a desk in the entryway. He asked if he could use it, and she said yes. He was a little distressed to see the ancient Gateway PC with its 256k modem link to the world, but it would have to do. In the likely event he was recaptured, he reasoned, at least he would have got his revenge.

He connected to the Qubit computer in Toronto, which he had set up for remote access, intending to use his unparalleled talent to program some nasty surprises for the people who betrayed him. He re-checked Amy's bank accounts and learned she had only $8,800. Rick's account still had about $11,000.

Then he looked for the three million dollars that the FBI connected with him. Sure enough, there it was in a Bank of America account with his name on it. He sat staring at the screen with gaping mouth.

Fuck me! No wonder the FBI is convinced of my guilt, he told himself. *And I showed their agent exactly how to find this,* he mused shaking his head. Had he any inkling Amy and Rick would set him up, he'd have checked his finances long ago. "I'm a damn fool," he muttered.

There was a special note saying that the account had been frozen, not that that could stop him. What to do? Obviously the FBI already knew about it. Would tampering with it now make things worse? A thought occurred to him: he looked up the name of the Assistant Special Agent in Charge of the Counterterrorism squad in the FBI's Chicago field office—and, using Qubit's awesome computing power, located his financial information and transferred $100,000 into his account. This would demonstrate how easy it was to set somebody up using the quantum computer.

Then he transferred the rest of the money indirectly into the accounts of five different charities. Each charity would discover a windfall, but have no idea who had been their benefactor. He sent an anonymous note to each charity telling them it was a gift, that the donor did not wish to be identified, and that he would prefer they did not make a public fuss about it.

He then traced back the original payment and learned it came from a fifteen million dollar account. He worked to track down the missing twelve million dollars. After almost an hour, he had followed the trail to two numbered accounts in the Cayman Islands: one for Amy and one for Rick, he surmised. The trail he followed to the money was so well-camouflaged— he had only managed to stay with it from personal knowledge about Amy and Rick—that it would be impossible to connect the accounts with them without hard evidence. Neither account had been touched since the deposits were made a little over two weeks before. He left these accounts intact to preserve evidence of their crime, but set it up so any access to the accounts would be detected and recorded.

Now to Erin. Even though he now knew she had strong evidence of his guilt, she was the most obvious part of a system that was out to kill him, and she had cheered for his torturer. He found her financial accounts. Savings and checking accounts, IRAs, CDs, and equities amounted to about twenty-five thousand dollars. Leaving one dollar in each account, just to gall her, he transferred the rest to the Canadian Cancer Society.

Erin's $163,456 mortgage at 4.5% interest on her condominium became $363,456 at 6.5%, raising her monthly payments from about six-fifty to about two thousand dollars. Her student loan, which she'd all but paid off now showed a balance of $57,356 owing with the notation "In default." Her two credit cards, on which she owed nothing, were now at the maximum and also in default for non-payment since October. The IRS was alerted to suspicious account information and would be calling on her to pay arrears and penalties amounting to almost $100,000. He briefly considered linking her to child porn sites, posting fake nude pictures of her on the web, and a few other nefarious schemes, but dismissed them thinking she'd be in enough of a bind financially without traducing her reputation to boot.

*

While Kyle was putting the finishing touches on Erin's financial future, Norris crossed the street, walked in the front door of the clinic, and, undetected by the slumbering nurse practitioner, proceeded to Erin's room. Seeing Erin sound asleep, he closed the door, went to the empty bed next to hers, grabbed the pillow, and strolled over to Erin. He paused for a moment to admire the pretty woman. Before doing anything else, he snapped his fingers beside her ear to make sure she was as out of it as she appeared. She didn't stir.

Wanting to admire more of her, he put the pillow down beside her on the bed, lowered the blankets, and opened her hospital gown to expose her breasts. He fondled her breasts, then licked them. Forcing himself to desist before he was discovered, he closed her gown and pulled up the blankets. He gently put the pillow over her face and pushed down hard.

CHAPTER SEVEN

Captive Again

As Norris quietly smothered Erin, the door suddenly burst open, and the policeman who had driven in from Williams Lake that evening commanded, "Get away from her!" as he pointed his revolver at Norris. Alerted to the intruder by Kyle who had seen Norris walk into the clinic from his vantage point across the street, the RCMP officer responded right away. Norris, a former soldier, had reacted by drawing his gun out of his shoulder holster, but had no time to point it. "Drop it!" warned the officer.

"I'm CIA," replied Norris calmly. "I'll take out my badge with my left hand."

"Don't believe him," shouted Kyle as he peered into the room from the hall. "He's the bastard who caused the jet crash and bailed out on us." Kyle got out Erin's gun and held it behind his back, just in case.

"This man is a wanted felon," said Norris. "He betrayed his country by selling top-secret technology to the Chinese—"

"You were in the act of murdering this woman when I got here," shouted the cop. "Drop your gun!" Norris spun quickly to shoot Officer Chianut, but the forty-four-year-old wasn't as fast as he was half a lifetime ago when he proudly served his country as a Navy Seal. The cop shot him dead just before Norris got his shot off, which lodged in the wall. He walked over to the body, picked up the gun and checked his pulse. "He's dead," said Officer Chianut to Kyle. He looked at Erin and saw she was breathing. "Doris!" he yelled out into the hall. The nurse practitioner carefully jutted her head around the corner and gasped at the site of the bloody body. "He's dead, Doris. I had to shoot him. Check this woman, will you?"

Kyle put Erin's gun back in his waistband and turned to walk out, but the officer shouted, "Stay where you are. I don't want any more trouble."

"That guy was lying about me."

"And I know you were lying to me before when you told me you didn't know what happened to the jet, so you can be my guest until I figure out what the hell is going on here."

Telling himself, *I can't get captured again. They'll take me back to kill me!* Kyle pulled out the gun and pointed it at the policeman, who was caught off guard. Kyle was so nervous he was shaking all over.

"Stay cool," suggested Officer Chianut.

"Just drop the guns!" Kyle shouted. The officer held onto them. Evidently he could see how conflicted Kyle was. "I mean it!" Kyle roared. Officer Chianut put both guns on the floor. "Kick them over to me." The officer did so. Kyle kicked them into the hall. "Now give me your car keys."

"This is a dead end for you. There's only one road out of here."

"It's a literal dead end for me if I stay. I've been framed for murder, and she's bringing me back to face the death penalty." He looked at the nurse practitioner, who looked frightened out of her wits. "Don't worry, I won't hurt you," he said to her.

"If you've been framed, you can prove it in court. If a man wanted for murder runs from here with my car and gun, the RCMP will hunt you down, and you could get killed. The smart thing to do is to give yourself up."

"Smart? They'll electrocute me for Christ's sake. It's my goddamn government that framed me. There's no chance for a fair trial."

"You can't really believe the American government is framing you—"

"Shut up! If I were smart, I'd have let her die, but I'm this goody two shoes idiot who saved the woman delivering me to my death. If I don't get bad really fast, I'm dead. Keys!" Officer Chianut tossed the keys. "I'm really sorry about this. I've never done anything remotely bad in my life until now. This is what a paranoid government drives its law-abiding citizens to do. I'm in this unbelievable mess that seems to lead to my end no matter what I do. This way, I at least have a chance. Do you have handcuffs?"

"A good man could never shoot anyone, could he?" said the officer, as he took a step toward Kyle to test his resolve.

"Don't!" Kyle warned. "I don't want to hurt you, but I will to save my life."

"If you shoot me, your life *will* be over. A cop killer will never see the light of day again. And I'm sure you don't want to murder Doris."

Doris started crying.

"I promise I won't hurt you," he said to calm her. Turning to the officer, he pleaded, "Just handcuff yourself to the pipe there, and no one will get hurt. I'm absolutely desperate. My government intends to kill me because they think I'm a terrorist and a murderer. I have to get away."

Officer Chianut took another step. Kyle shot at the floor. Doris screamed. "Think hard about this," the officer advised. "Even if you are innocent of the murder you're wanted for, you'll certainly be guilty of murder here. Put your gun down, and give yourself up before you ruin your life."

Tears streamed down the agonized man's cheeks. There was no good way out of this, he knew. He dropped his head and his gun and fell to his knees. Officer Chianut quickly recovered the weapons, lifted Kyle to his feet, and handcuffed him. "I'm sorry," Kyle said.

Officer Chianut brought Kyle to the clinic's other room and handcuffed him to a pipe. He asked Kyle for his version of the story that led to this point, which he provided. He then called his detachment and informed them of the situation. A quick check with the FBI confirmed Kyle was wanted for terrorism and murder. The officer was instructed to stay in town for the night to guard the prisoner. Help would be sent right away.

*

When she awoke the next day, Erin found herself alone. She felt sure that Kyle would be long gone, but had to check. She called out for help. The nurse practitioner came in and said, "It's good to see you're alive."

"It's good to be alive. Was there any doubt I would live?"

"There was when a man tried to murder you last night."

"What? Who ..." Through her brain rushed the thought that Kyle had tried to kill her to avoid prosecution. *But why would he do that after he told them where to find me?* She asked herself.

Before she could reason it through, the nurse explained, "A man named Norris tried to smother you, but Johnny shot him."

"Johnny?" said Erin, trying to accommodate to this latest shocking development.

"He's an RCMP officer."

Officer Johnny Chianut walked in. He was a tall, husky, First Nations man of thirty-seven. "Did I hear my name?" he asked. "Awake, eh? You're one lucky lady," he informed her.

"I hear I owe you my life."

"Well, me and your fugitive friend."

"Kyle? I don't understand."

Officer Chianut explained the incredible event to the astonished woman, ending the account by informing Erin that he was holding Kyle in the room next door. She nodded and thanked the officer for his actions. He then asked her to explain what was going on, which she did as best she could. The officer told her Kyle had had a Glock M23 pistol, and she said it was hers. He told her he'd hold it for her until she was to leave.

Erin got in touch with her office and learned that American and Canadian authorities were already discussing Kyle's legal status. It was in question, because Canadian authorities, in the absence of exceptional circumstances, must obtain a guarantee against the death penalty before extraditing Canadian citizens to face capital murder charges. American lawyers were going to argue that he was only in Canada because of the plane crash and that constituted exceptional circumstances, but this would likely require a court case to resolve.

Kyle was to be taken to Williams Lake and held by the RCMP to await the decision. Erin was told to return home as soon as she was well enough to travel. She asked her boss to check out Norris, and he informed her that the CIA denied any connection to a Jeff Norris. The FBI was looking into it, but their initial theory was that the Chinese used the quantum computer to insert Norris's name into CIA computer files.

Officer Chianut offered Erin a ride in the car that would be taking Kyle to Williams Lake, where she could catch a flight to Vancouver for a connection to Chicago. She accepted with her thanks.

About an hour before they were scheduled to depart for Williams Lake, Erin walked into Kyle's room. He was lying in the bed with his back to the door. She said softly, "Hey." He curled up and wiped his face with the sheet. "I heard what you did and I came to thank you."

"Fine. Now leave."

"You saved my—"

"Get out!" he shouted in a tremulous voice, with a big sniff.

He was crying, she realized. She found herself disconcerted. Her stomach sank at the duty she had no choice but to carry out. *He must be so scared,* she told herself. *God I hate this.* She wanted to comfort him, but commiseration from the person taking him back to face the death penalty would be ironic enough to qualify as cruel. She said, "Okay. I'll come back in a half hour. We really need to talk."

*

His ineluctable predicament hadn't been topmost in his tormented mind when Erin had entered the room unexpectedly. He had transported his mind back to halcyon days only five months ago. He had just finished the first successful test of the quantum computer prototype. Amy had screamed for joy, and hugged and kissed him. His computer was at long last a reality; the woman he loved was now his forever; fame and fortune were imminent. All his hopes and dreams crystallized in one perfect moment.

Contrast that to the present moment, handcuffed to a pipe in Likely, British Columbia. The woman he loved—the only person he loved in the world—had betrayed him, his computer had been banned, and his very life was at great risk. The hurt, disappointment, rage, and fear commingled in a powerful wave of emotion that engulfed him and emerged in convulsive sobs. He'd buried his face in his pillow to stifle the sounds. Twenty long minutes he spent in this misery.

By the time Erin walked in, the wave had crashed and was receding. He was moaning softly, grieving over the loss of his love. Death seemed almost welcome.

When Erin returned a half-hour later, he was sitting up on his bed composed. She opened with, "Again, I want to thank you for saving me. Twice." He said nothing and refused to make eye contact. She said, "I would've thought you'd be long gone by now."

"The only way out of this shithole is a single taxi, and surprise! It was spoken for, so I was stuck."

"Well, thank God for that or I'd be dead. It's lucky you saw him."

"The only hotel in this metropolis is across the street. I happened to be looking out the window, and I saw him go into this clinic."

"Why did you do it? Why did you come to my rescue?"

"I'm the target. I'm guessing he had to kill you only because you could identify him. After he got you, I was next. My best chance was to catch him off guard, so I called the cop."

"Look at me, Kyle," she said. He turned his eyes to hers. "Thank you for my life," she said with a warm smile.

"You stand there with a sweet smile at the man who saved your life, the man you intend to bring back to face the electric chair. Has there ever been a more paradoxical moment? My *life* is at stake. Do you give that any thought at all?"

"Of course I do. What I have to do really upsets me, but I'm sure you'll get a fair trial."

"Bullshit! Even if I get back to face a trial, I'm sure the frame is unbeatable."

"You've given up on our country the same way you gave up on me in the airplane. It's not as bleak as you think. You will get back, and you will get a fair trial."

"Uh-huh. The RCMP asshole called the FBI, thereby alerting the bastards that their assassin failed, so another is on the way by now."

"You can't really believe the FBI sent Norris," she said.

"FBI, CIA, whatever."

"You watch too many movies."

"Someone tried to kill me and didn't care that you and the pilot would go with me. He had CIA identification. Figure it out, Special Agent."

"I heard about an hour ago his real name was Jeff Foster. He was in the U.S. Navy until three years ago when he joined Blackwater. A year later he was kicked out, if you can imagine, for excessive brutality to prisoners. After that, he dropped out of sight, probably became an independent mercenary. The FBI figures the Chinese used your computer to put Norris in the CIA computer."

"Of course. It's my fault. Why would the Chinese want me dead? They didn't like the computer?"

"If you identified who bought it, it could put them or their fancy computer at risk."

"How? Does the CIA plan to invade China to get it back? It was the CIA wanting revenge on the man they figured sold the computer."

"Come on."

"He tried to kill me before he got any information out of me, so he didn't need any. It was revenge, pure and simple, CIA style. Police, judge, jury, and executioner, without the nuisance of a trial."

"I don't believe that."

"You don't believe it because you can't; the truth undermines everything you stand for. But you have to at least admit something is fishy. Maybe it was a setup."

"Maybe."

"Will you put in a word to stop this extradition business?"

"I'm sorry, Kyle, but I can't."

"Wait a minute while I re-ingest my supreme hatred for you."

"You're still the prime suspect in Rick's murder. And Rick told me you sold the computers to the Chinese and Colombians while he and Amy were in Washington."

"He's the one who did it, you stunned bitch! I'm just the scapegoat. Why are you so ready to believe him?"

"The three million—"

"Part of the setup. Rick and Amy sold those computers because I was gonna deal him out. After we got the government's edict, I blamed him. His only roles for Qubit were finding investors and marketing our computers, and he failed spectacularly. So I told him I planned to set up Qubit in Canada without him.

"You can imagine the look of shock and horror on his face. Amy's face showed the same emotions, which confused me at the time, but makes sense now. So they sold the computers, and set me up for the fall. That leaves them married multi-millionaires—more so if DTC bought us out—and pesky me as someone's bitch in jail or maybe dead. Perfect plan."

"Sounds plausible. I'll investigate it when we get back, I promise."

"You obviously don't work for DTC. They never were interested in buying Qubit, were they?"

"As far as I know, no. They let us pose as employees of theirs for the case."

"Of course they did. Have the government finish us off. Another perfect plan."

"You're the most cynical person I've ever met."

"Can you blame me? Look at what they've done to me. The greed, the duplicity, the lies; it's incredible. Who the hell are you really, anyway?"

"Erin McAdams. I work for the FBI's Cyber Crime squad in Chicago."

"In Chicago?"

"Uh-huh."

"So you do know something about computers."

"Yes. I have a Master's in computer science, as I told you."

"You actually told the truth about something?"

"Obviously an undercover agent can't be forthcoming about who she is. Just as obviously, the FBI couldn't send in a computer novice on this case." She changed the subject. "Tell me, who is Lan Mao?"

"How do you know about him?"

"I'm an FBI agent, Kyle. We know you met him two weeks ago."

"So you used your training and experience to divine that this man with a Chinese name must be the Chinese man who took delivery of the computer. Well, it's true. You got me." Erin looked surprised and disappointed until he said, "Lan Mao is a Chinese-Canadian physicist who works for the University of Toronto. I worked with him to set up a Qubit computer in Toronto for quantum simulation and optimization research projects.

"I sold another computer to a research team at Queen's University headed by Dr. Natalya Fuhrman. That sounds Jewish, maybe Israeli, so you got me again. The ten million dollars I got from those two sales was used to pay over eight million to our creditors and thousands more to our laid-off employees. The rest is still in the company bank account. I took nothing for myself."

"And the three million dollars in your account?" she said as she jotted down notes.

"If there were such an account, it had to be Rick or Amy who put it there for the setup, but there is no such account."

"Yes, there is … Oh, my God! Did you get to a computer?" He smiled. "What did you do? What did you do to *me*?" His smile broadened. "Oh, shit!"

She ran out.

About fifteen minutes later, as Kyle snoozed, he heard someone yell, "You bastard!"

He thought he heard something fast approaching. He propped himself up on his elbow and opened his eyes. It seemed to happen in slow motion. His eyes tried to fix on what it was. They began to converge as the item closed in; he furrowed his brow wondering what it could be. Just as he concluded *shoe*! it bounced off his forehead, then he ducked. "Ouch! What the hell?"

"All my money is gone. My bank account, my CD, my IRA, all gone, you son of a bitch."

"Now don't exaggerate. There's a dollar in each account."

"You think this is funny?"

"Absolutely. I merely kept my promise, Agent McAdams. And anyway, that's only the tip of the iceberg."

Her eyes bulged. "What else did you do?"

"If I recall correctly, I think you now owe somewhere close to half a million."

Erin went pale. After a moment to process the news, she said, "You're kidding, right?"

"Nope."

"Jesus Christ, Kyle! What am I supposed to ... How do I even ... Undo it!"

"Nope."

"Why would you do ... Never mind. I know why you did it, but you can't possibly think you'll get away with it."

"It's a *fait accompli*. Your credit cards are maxed out and in default, your mortgage, which is now something close to four hundred grand—"

"No!"

"You owe a hundred thousand in taxes and the IRS is gonna be pissed."

"What?"

"And your student loan of, I forget, maybe fifty grand is also in default."

Erin stood in the doorway and started to hyperventilate. "I'm sensing some discomfort here," said Kyle. The police officer came to see what the commotion was, and advised her to calm down before she fainted. In her weakened condition, she got light-headed and slumped to the floor on one knee. While Officer Chianut assisted her, Kyle lay down again.

Erin soon recovered and hollered at Kyle, "I'm going to get you a computer, and you are going to undo everything you did to me!"

"Nope."

"You will or I'll rip out your hair and pry out your eyes! Now give me my boot!"

"Nope."

"*Ahh!*" she screamed.

"Disenchanted?" Kyle asked with a smirk.

Erin bolted at the prisoner and began pummeling him with her right arm—her left arm being in a sling—as she said, "You rotten piece of shit! You bastard! Ah, shit, my shoulder hurts. I'll get you for this."

Kyle covered himself as best he could with one arm handcuffed to the pipe, while Officer Chianut pulled her away and back to the doorway. "Officer, this man has robbed me of every cent I had and fabricated debts I don't owe. He's cost me half a million dollars. I want him charged unless he undoes it all."

"No problem."

"So, Mr. Summers, if you get off at home, you're still a criminal in Canada, which should preclude your plan of setting up a company here," noted Erin.

"Officer, this woman has arrested me on bogus charges of murder and terrorism, which is about a million times worse than what I did to her. I want her charged, too." The officer laughed. "Well, then," Kyle continued, "since she is the representative of a government that stole a hundred and sixty million bucks from me and untold billions more in foregone income, I want her arrested and put in jail until she rots." The officer smirked. "You all stick together, I see. So charge away. The U.S. can deliver my cadaver to Canada for incarceration after they murder me. As I go down the drain, at least I have the consolation of knowing she's screwed."

"Bastard!" yelled Erin. "I'm gonna find a computer and bring it here, and you will reverse everything you did."

"Only if you drop all charges against me and rescind the edict against the sale of my computer."

"You know I don't have that power."

"Then I can't help you."

"*Oh!*" She looked around for something persuasive to apply to his noggin.

*

"Come with me," suggested the officer. Erin followed him down the short hall and into the entry way. "Is this going to be a problem if you two go in the same car to Williams Lake?"

"I'll need the time with him to convince him to undo what he's done to me."

"When we return your gun to you, are you going to use that to convince him?"

"I take my job very seriously, Officer Chianut. I would never abuse it."

"Summers told me you participated in a torture session."

At this Erin lowered her eyes. "It's true. Norris—Foster—claimed he had to get critical information from Kyle to stop the imminent murder of more of our agents overseas. He showed me CIA identification—and I had no reason to doubt it, and my boss told me to cooperate with him, so I watched as he beat Kyle, and I'm ashamed to say I acted as if I was cheering Norris on. He said it would be quicker if I played along. I made an error in judgment, and it will never happen again."

"So Summers got revenge by bankrupting you."

"Yes, and not only for the beating he took. He's very insistent he's innocent, and sees me as the system that's out to kill him."

"Do you believe him?"

"The evidence against him seems airtight, but these attempts on his life—our lives—have made me start to wonder. I've told him he'll get a fair trial, but he thinks the government is out to get him."

"The FBI can work that out as he's sitting in jail in Williams Lake. Are you going to press charges against him?"

"Not at the moment. I hope to get him to undo this, but I'd like the option of pressing charges if he refuses."

"No problem."

"When do we leave?"

"A few minutes. Oksana will be driving you two to Williams Lake."

"Oh. I assumed you'd be taking us."

"I've got to answer a million questions about the shooting. Then I guess I'll do what I was sent here to do: help investigate the crash. Oh, here's Oksana now."

An obese, silver-haired woman sauntered in with a cup of coffee. To Erin, Officer Litvin looked like an elderly kindergarten teacher, except for the revolver by her hip. Mindful of Kyle's contention that the people who sent Foster, assuming someone did send him, would send a replacement, she worried that this woman would be little good if a hit man beset them. Officer Chianut introduced the ladies; they shook hands. Since it was too awkward to voice her misgivings about the woman, Erin asked for her gun back. Officer Chianut unlocked a cabinet and gave it to her. He then went down the hall to get Kyle.

Kyle appeared with the officer a minute later. "I won't change my mind," he said to Erin, anticipating her question.

Angry at him, she looked away. His effects, which amounted to nothing more than winter clothing after his suitcase was left behind in Alaska, were returned to him. Handcuffed, he was escorted to the police car by Officer Litvin and put in the backseat. At Erin's request, she took off Kyle's handcuffs once he was secured in the backseat.

As Erin got into the front passenger seat and four RCMP officers talked outside the car, Kyle said, "Grandma Moses is taking me back? What if someone attacks us? She gonna bake some cookies to vanquish them?" Erin kept her head forward and said nothing. He laughed derisively. "This is beyond belief. I saved your life twice, yet you're still intent on getting me killed, and *you're* mad at *me*? If there was a Nobel Prize for sad irony, you'd be a shoo-in."

She turned and said, "We've been over this and over this. I'm an FBI agent. My assignment is to take you back to face trial. It was never personal. It is not and cannot be my job to judge your innocence or guilt. We have courts for that. If I presumed to judge you and act on it I'd be no better than Norris. You threatened to kill Rick, and he turned up dead hours later. Rick accused you of selling the three computers, and you had three million dollars in a bank account. You fled the country. Even you have to admit that the evidence screams guilty on both counts, so if I get to judge, then I would have to shoot you. But then you saved my life. So do I let a murderer go free because I owe him? What if you kill someone else? That would be my responsibility."

"I didn't murder him!"

"And you'll get a trial to make that case with the burden of proof on the government. Stop blaming me for this."

"I've put my neck on the line twice to save you. Do you really think a man who does that could be a murderer, too?"

"I don't know! In a fit of passion against the man who took away your reason for living, maybe. Would you sell those computers to potential enemies of our country? In a fit of passion against the country that took away your life's work and your fortune, maybe. It's hardly outside the realm of possibility. But my opinion does not matter. I was just doing my job and I've almost been killed twice, and now I'm ruined, and that is your fault, Mr. Summers. I'm entitled to be angry with you."

"I did it in a fit of passion against the person set to take me back to the electric chair. The least I can do is bequeath you a life of abject poverty."

She turned her head away from him and fumed. Officer Litvin got in, started the car and their harrowing journey began.

CHAPTER EIGHT

Harried Journey

While Erin and the policewoman engaged in some small talk for the first twenty-four minutes in the car, Kyle looked out the side window at the countryside whisking by and fretted about what he was facing back in Chicago. When he noticed the car slowing down, he looked forward. Up ahead was a car on the side of the road with its hood up, and a man waving to the police car for help. Officer Litvin pulled in behind the car. "Do you think you should stop?" asked Erin.

"We're in the middle of nowhere and it's cold," said the officer. "The prisoner isn't going anywhere."

"Someone has already tried to kill us. This could be a trap," warned Erin.

The woman frowned at her and replied, "It's just a man stranded in the cold." She turned off the engine.

"Leave it on, if you don't mind," requested Kyle. "I'm freezing back here." The officer started the car again and got out to offer assistance to the stranded traveler. "I don't like this," Kyle told Erin.

"Me neither." She slid over to the driver's side and took out her gun, placing it on the seat between her legs. She also slipped her arm out of the sling, just in case. "We're probably just paranoid. Maybe we've both seen too many movies—" As she said this, the officer slumped to the road. "Shit!" Erin shrieked. "He shot her!"

*

Erin immediately put the car in reverse as the gunman turned his pistol on the police car. Bullets rocketed through the windshield as Erin floored the gas pedal. The tires squealed and smoked as they worked to find a grip on the icy shoulder.

At first the shooter was aiming for Kyle, who was in the back seat on the passenger side, giving Erin the few seconds she needed to get the car going. Kyle immediately ducked as the bullets went through the wire mesh screen and proceeded out the back window, shattering it. The gunman gave chase on foot, now aiming for Erin. She ducked and yanked the wheel to the left to turn the car. She overshot the turn, going about 250°.

Putting the car in drive, she noticed the man reloading. She picked up her gun and fired several rounds through the passenger side window just as the man was raising his gun for a second volley. The man fell to the ground, a bullet having struck his thigh. He lifted the gun again, and Erin once more jammed the gas pedal to the floor and the police car took off as the man resumed firing at the car. He hit a back tire, but Erin kept going.

"Are you alive back there?" she said excitedly as her adrenalin continued to surge.

"What?" he said from the floor. His ears were ringing from the blast of the gun in the car.

"You can get up now."

"No, I think I like it down here better. It's not so windy or bullety." He sat up and looked back to see the shooter limping back to his car. "You hit his leg, it looks like. Good shot and good driving, Special Agent. Maybe you're not so bad at this after all."

"Actually, I was aiming at his chest, but I'm glad I hit something. We need to stop to change the tire."

"That bastard might be following."

"The bullet wound will slow him down; he'll have to stop the bleeding. The flat tire is slowing us down. We're sitting ducks driving at this speed." She turned into a driveway that led to a farmhouse and pulled in behind some bushes.

She got out of the police car, opened the back door for Kyle, and opened the trunk. Kyle got out the jack and struggled to figure out how it worked. "Oh, for God's sake, give it to me," said Erin. "You can engineer the world's most advanced computer, but you can't work a jack," she said, as she put it on the ground under a notch just in front of the left rear tire. She gestured for Kyle to take over. "Hurry," she said.

He pumped it until the flat tire rose from the ground. Then he took the wrench and attempted to loosen the lug nuts, but the tire kept turning.

"Lower the jack so the wheel can't turn, genius," she suggested. He smiled and followed her directions.

"There he goes," observed Erin as the assassin drove past. "He'll probably turn around once he hits a straightaway and doesn't see us, so get going!" Once he got the flat tire off, he found the spare wouldn't go on. "It has more volume than the flat one," she pointed out with a wry smile. He thanked her for her running commentary as he quickly jacked the car up more. The tire on, he lowered the jack and tightened the nuts.

"You are hopeless, Kyle," she said as she walked back to close the trunk. Turning back to Kyle, she saw he was walking away. "Where the hell do you think you're going?" she said.

"I don't like this party. I'm leaving."

"No, you're not," she said as she took out her gun.

"Yes, I am. Because while I was being badgered by you when I was changing the tire, I was thinking that even if we manage to get away from the hit men stalking us, I still get killed if you get me back home." He turned and walked away.

"Kyle! Stop right now!" she ordered. "Please don't make me shoot you. Stop, or I swear I'll shoot you!" He kept an even pace away from her. She aimed carefully and squeezed the trigger. The bullet hit the top of his shoulder and knocked him to the ground. "Kyle!" she said and ran to his side.

"You shot me!"

"I'm sorry. I meant to nick your shoulder." She helped him off with his jacket.

"Well, your goddamn nick is more like a deep gouge that hurts like hell." It was closer to a nick, but it was bleeding freely.

"I'm sorry, but I had to stop you. I had to show you I mean business." She looked at his shoulder and said, "It's just a flesh wound."

"Gimme the gun and I'll flesh wound you." He grabbed at it.

She moved it away and said, "No! Can't you see how serious I am about this? Now sit still so I can stop the bleeding." He grabbed again and got hold of the gun. She pushed her fingers into his wound.

"Ahh!" He screamed in agony and let go of the gun.

"I'm sorry, but I have to put a stop to this. How many FBI agents do you suppose would stand for this kind of behavior? Chances are with anyone else, you'd be dead now. You're trying to take advantage of me. Now get up and come back to the car—" She stopped when a bullet ricocheted off the roof of the car, barely missing Kyle.

"What was that?" he asked.

"Get down!" she yelled. Evidently insensible of the imminent danger, he remained on his feet. She kicked him in the crotch, which bent him over and caused the shooter to miss his target again.

"Jesus Christ! Just kill me and have done with it."

"Stand up again, and I won't need to. A sniper is shooting at us, Einstein. You'd be dead now if I hadn't made you bend over."

More bullets shattered the driver's side window in the car. The two scrambled to the open driver's door and got in. With more bullets hitting the car, Erin started the engine, put it in drive, and floored it. She turned south, away from the direction of the shots. Erin said, "The shooting seems to have stopped.

He's probably in a car following us. At least this car has a powerful engine; we should be able to stay in front of him … Oh, shit!" remarked Erin.

A convoy of three logging trucks carrying full loads was just ahead on the winding road. They were lumbering down the road at about forty miles per hour. When they reached the backmost truck, she glanced in her mirror and saw a car fast approaching. "Shit!" she repeated, as she pulled out to pass the first truck on a hill.

She turned on the siren and lights, but in this narrow pass there was no shoulder for the truck to pull over on; it did slow so she could pass more readily. "Oh, God!" she said, praying that nothing would come over the hill in the other direction. She got by the first truck and, unwilling to go blindly over the top of the hill, pulled back in.

No sooner did they crest the eminence than a tight curve to the west commenced. After about twenty seconds, she said, "Does this bend never end?" Behind, the pursuer was passing the truck. Still unable to see more than two hundred feet ahead, Erin pulled out into the oncoming lane. Again, the truck driver slowed to let the police car pass as fast as possible, but as she got near the cab of the truck she spotted a mobile home coming right at them 200 feet ahead and closing fast. She floored the gas pedal, and almost went off the road as the curve ended. She regained control and pulled in ahead of the truck, just missing the mobile home, which had slammed on its brakes.

"Jesus, that was close," noted Kyle, as he dug his claws into his seat.

She caught the final truck just as the road turned sharply south again. Seemingly fearless, the hit man passed the second truck and came up just behind the police cruiser. He began shooting at them. Kyle ducked and Erin cursed as she pulled out to pass on a blind curve, the pursuit car right on her rear bumper and firing through their back window. The tires squealed around the curve as Erin struggled to find the balance between the speed needed to stay in front of her pursuer and the speed needed to stay on the road. The truck driver stopped, presumably to stay away from the danger. Erin pulled back into her lane, with the hit man a few inches behind.

*

The shooting having stopped, Kyle sat up again. Now on a short straightaway, Erin accelerated and opened up a small gap between the cars, but as the road jogged west again, the hit man caught up and rammed the back of the police cruiser. The driver's side tires went off the road, throwing the car out of control. Erin braked hard as she struggled to regain control, but it was no use. As the car tipped over onto the driver's side, Erin screamed. Curtain air bags saved her from serious injury, as did the front air bags when the car slid into a tree, halting it.

Kyle emerged with a few more bumps and bruises. He looked over and saw Erin was unconscious, but he had no time to check on her, for the hit man was lurking. He looked for her gun, but could not spot it, so he clambered through the shattered side window and ran out into the forest. He glanced to see the hit man in the process of reloading.

Kyle figured he had an advantage because the assassin had a bullet in his leg, but the woods ended unexpectedly. Kyle found himself in a clear cut: a hundred acres of newly planted trees stretched out before him. He stopped and shook his head in disbelief that anyone could have such rotten luck. He cursed the Lord and ran back into the forest, but stopped short as several rounds hit the ground directly in front of him. He stood behind a tree with nowhere to run for safety.

"Come out and I promise I'll make it quick," yelled the assassin as he limped toward his prey. Kyle looked around for a solution, but the situation was hopeless. Dashing from tree to tree would at least give him time to think of something, he thought, so he tried that, but stopped when a bullet hit a branch an inch away from his head. While the gunman closed in, Kyle braced for the inevitable. He decided to try one last desperate gambit. He put up his hands and stepped out in the open.

"Can you tell me why you're doing this?" he asked.

"I think you know," said the killer.

"I didn't sell those computers! It was Rick Hugel!" he asserted.

"He already got what was coming to him," said the man as he readied his pistol.

"You killed him?"

"Apparently you did," he answered with a snicker. "Hilarious that they'd pin that on you, not that it'll matter to you in ten seconds or so. Get on your knees," ordered the hit man as he limped up to him.

Trembling, Kyle slowly got down to his knees and said, "But he did it, not me."

"You can get your revenge in hell," he said as he took aim.

Kyle turned away from him and closed his eyes. He heard the shot and wet his pants. The gunman collapsed to the ground. Kyle turned around and saw Erin walking toward the dead man with a smoking gun in her hands. Tears welled up in her eyes.

"Did you know him?" said Kyle, as he sat on the ground and took a few deep breaths to slow his racing heart.

"Of course not. I'm not in the habit of associating with hit men. I just never killed anyone before. It's an absolutely horrible feeling," she said, as she looked at the lifeless body with a hand over her mouth.

Erin and Kyle said nothing for a few minutes as each worked to overcome the emotional trauma. Finally, Kyle said, "Thank you for …" She nodded. He went on, "You're bleeding. Are you all right?"

"I have a headache, but I think I'm okay." She glanced at his lap and saw it was wet, but said nothing.

"It's just snow that got on me," he explained. She nodded. "I was about to be killed and I was scared shitless—no, not that, too. Never mind." She gave him a half-hearted smile. He continued, "Did you hear him admit he killed Rick?"

"I heard him laughing that they pinned it on you, which might suggest you didn't do it. I hope ballistics will confirm it. I'd be so relieved if I'm not taking you back to face the death penalty."

"What a load off my mind that you're relieved, and I feel so blessed that they can't kill me twice."

"I think the maximum penalty under Section 805 is fifteen years, so you don't have to worry about the electric chair."

"Only fifteen years of continual beatings and rape. Oh, thank you! Thank you!" She lifted her eyes. "Maybe they won't extradite me for that trumped up terrorist bullshit."

"On the contrary, without the murder charge there should be no problem with extradition."

Kyle crawled over to get the man's gun, but Erin warned, "Don't even think about it!" as she pointed the gun at him. He backed away. "That may be the gun used to kill Rick. You put your fingerprints on it, and you might get the chair after all. Let the RCMP find the body and the gun."

Kyle checked the man's pockets. He found a cell phone and a wallet. "Keep the wallet and toss the phone. Turn it off and wipe your fingerprints off it first," she said.

"You don't think we should call for help?"

"That'll tell them this guy failed, and we're still alive. He might have a backup close by. There was a gas station we passed a few minutes before we were rammed. We'll call the RCMP from there. Come on, we have to get out of here."

They walked back to the road. At the scene of the accident were a man who was driving by and had seen the police car on its side and one of the truckers. Erin explained she was the driver of the police car, and that she intended to take her prisoner back in the other car. She told them she'd shot a man and recommended they leave the area as more dangerous men might be nearby. They left at once.

Then she and Kyle got in the dead man's car—she made Kyle drive—and turned back toward Likely.

*

141

As she thought of taking a man's life and everything else that had happened, Erin became overwhelmed and began to cry again. She glanced at Kyle and said, "First I'm in a plane crash, then a man tries to kill me, then the biggest ass in the world robs me of every cent I own and puts me a half a million dollars in debt—then I get shot at, then I'm driving like a mad woman trying to get away from a crazed killer, then I'm in a major car accident, then I shoot a man—"

"Two men."

"Shut up! God, you're childish."

"Childish? Oh, boo-hoo, you're carrying me back to the electric chair. Mommy, Erin shot me."

"All you do is whine."

"While you sit there feeling sorry for yourself, think of what's been done to me over the last three weeks."

"I feel bad for you."

"Yes, I'm sure you felt pity for the better part of a second over my misfortune as you helped them take me down. They cost me more than you can possibly imagine. Maybe tens of billions of dollars in the long run. That's probably more than all the robberies in the whole history of mankind. And you close your eyes to it."

"If the law is unfair, work to get it changed. In the meantime, I'll do my job."

"Nazi."

"Vagabond."

Looking through the wallet, Erin said, "Kentucky license. His name was Richard Demeter—almost certainly an alias."

Kyle pulled into the gas station. Erin picked up her gun from the seat between her legs and told Kyle to get out of the car and come in with her. Inside the station, Erin called Officer Chianut and told him his colleague had been shot and most probably killed. She explained what happened and told him where to find the bodies. He promised to send help right away.

She rejoined Kyle as he was picking out some chocolate bars. "We have to stay put here. The RCMP should be here in twenty minutes or so."

He gave her a mock "Whoopee!"

As Kyle paid, Erin looked out to the car and saw a man checking it out. The man headed toward the store. "Kyle, we have unwelcome company. Out the back. Now!" she commanded. "Get out of sight!" she yelled to the station attendant as she and Kyle sprinted to the rear exit.

The man followed them, killing the proprietor—his decision to ignore Erin's advice proved improvident—on the way through. Erin went behind a dumpster, but Kyle ran for a garage about seventy-five feet away. The man got to the back door, spotted Kyle, and took aim with his pistol. Erin, who had drawn her gun as she was running, shot at the hit man. The bullet bounced off the steel door a few inches from his head. He ducked behind the door frame and returned fire at Erin.

A much better shot than Erin, he pinned her down. Every few seconds she'd pop up and squeeze off a round and got down before the return fire could hit her. Knowing she was overmatched she took to peering under the dumpster, which was on wheels, to try to head off a charge by the man. If he got to the other side of the dumpster, she would probably be killed. She saw him girding to make the sprint, and popped out to take a shot at him. Again, she missed her target, but he reconsidered the frontal assault.

There was an interval of silence. She looked under the dumpster, but could not spot his feet. "Where the hell is he?" she said out loud. Her heart pounding, she struggled to keep her cool. She looked over to the garage, but doubted she had a chance to make it. She tried to move the dumpster, but it would not budge.

She popped up, and a bullet nicked the top of her right ear. The man had elected to go out the front of the store and around the side of the building to get close enough to take her from the side by surprise. Erin screeched and ran to the far end of the dumpster. She jutted her head out the other side and shot twice, sending the man back behind the wall.

Where was he now? Looking at the back exit, she saw the potential for ambush and tried to decide whether to move back to her original position, to the back exit of the store or to the garage. If she guessed wrong what her nemesis would do, she'd be dead.

While Erin crouched and wondered how she would survive this latest assault, she heard a roar from behind her. Startled, she spun and just about shot at Kyle as he approached on a snowmobile. Realizing who it was at the last second, she held her fire. He was waving to her to jump on as he passed by. She ran to the snowmobile and hopped on behind Kyle. He applied full throttle, and sped off into the open field behind the store as the hit man ran out the back exit firing at them. One bullet hit the mirror on the left side, but the rest missed, and the two sped away.

Erin looked back to see the hit man run to his car.

"Thank you," she said, as she held on tight. If he responded, she didn't hear it. After a few minutes at full speed, he slowed down, turned into the woods, and stopped. "Not too bright getting stuck behind that dumpster," he said.

"If I didn't, one or both of us would be dead now. He was aiming at your back when I took the first shot at him."

"Oh, well, thanks then."

"How did you get this?"

"Add another charge to the list, Special Agent. I stole it."

"This was an emergency."

"So you do act as judge sometimes."

"I have some discretion, but it doesn't extend to murder or terrorism."

"I hate to tell you this, Agent McAdams, but if I am a terrorist and you just aided me, that makes you a terrorist, too. You better arrest yourself now."

"I'm out of my jurisdiction; I can't arrest me."

"Which means you can't legally prevent me from escaping, right?" She didn't answer. "Stumped, Special Agent?" No answer. "Where to?"

"I have no idea. Just stay away from the main road."

He headed deeper into the woods, taking a northeasterly direction. They found an old logging road, and followed it into a shallow valley. Forty-five minutes later, with the sun setting, Erin said, "It's getting dark out. We have to find shelter."

A few minutes later, through a clearing in the trees, they saw a frozen lake. Erin looked out across the lake, tapped Kyle on the shoulder, and said, "That's a cabin over there, isn't it?" He looked and nodded. "We should stay there tonight." He stopped the snowmobile and looked across the lake. "What are you waiting for?" she asked.

"I'm trying to decide whether to take the chance of crossing the lake. May is just around the corner, which probably means the ice isn't very thick. We should try to find a way around."

"We can't take the chance of trying to go around the lake with nighttime coming fast; it's miles long, but only half a mile or so wide." She got off the snowmobile and walked down the slope and out onto the ice. She jumped up and down a few times and proclaimed it "perfectly safe." She added, "We've been leaving a trail in the snow a blind man can follow. The snow's mostly blown off the ice, so we might be able to shake anyone tailing us. Let's go down the road a little way, go out onto the ice, and double back to that cottage. Let's go!"

He followed the road along the shore for about a mile, then, holding his breath, he took the machine onto the ice. She could feel him tense up and said, "Relax, chicken." The ice held. He turned and headed diagonally across the lake toward the cottage.

By the time they realized the ice was perilously thin where the current was strongest near the opposite shore, it was too late to stop. They looked down and realized the ice was no longer opaque. About eighty yards from shore, Kyle gunned the engine. The snowmobile sped across the next fifty-five yards before it broke through the ice, bringing its passengers down with it.

Erin ended up next to the snowmobile, which had settled upside-down on the lake bottom. She scrambled onto it and stood, which brought her head above the water. Her head ached from the terrible cold. She shuddered as she looked for

Kyle and called his name. Turning around in every direction, she finally saw his fist come up against the ice about ten feet to her left. He was going away from the hole! She took a deep breath, dived under the ice and swam to him.

Reaching him, she dragged him back to the hole as he was beginning to black out. She struggled to put his feet on the snowmobile. As his feet found purchase, Erin felt him go limp. She quickly stood on the snowmobile and lifted his head above the surface. "Kyle!" she said. "Kyle!" She put her mouth over his, pinched his nose, and pushed her breath into him. He coughed water into her mouth, and he revived.

"Are you all right?" she said with teeth and chin bobbling.

He nodded slowly as if in a daze.

"We'll die here in no time," she said. "We have to get to shore and into that cottage."

His senses returning and registering mostly temperature, Kyle stood there shivering. He said, "You should've left me under the ice. I have nothing to live for; it would all be over now if you just let me be."

"You're welcome," Erin replied. She turned her head to the right and saw they could reach the ice in that direction. "Push me onto the ice, then I'll pull you up," she suggested. He pushed her onto the ice surface. Remaining horizontal, she turned and took his hand and pulled him up. The ice began to crack under their weight. "Hurry!" she said, "Push yourself to shore." They used their arms and legs to propel their prone bodies toward the shore. Breathing hard against the agonizing cold, the pair stood and ran to the cabin. Finding the door locked, they broke the bedroom window to gain entry.

Benumbed by the frigid air on their bedraggled bodies, they shuffled into the main room. There was no electricity or heat.

"We have to find dry clothes and start a fire," said Erin, as she dropped her sopping gloves and jacket on the floor. She squatted down and tried to take off her boots, but she was shivering so hard, she couldn't do it. "Sh-sh-sh-shit!" she said as she sat on the floor, and managed to undo her laces and remove her boots and socks. Then she stood and lifted her sweater over her head, then unbuttoned and unzipped her pants, pushed them down her legs, and stepped out of them. Through her wet, white bra Kyle could see her hard nipples.

As he stood there, shivering, with gaping eyes and mouth, she covered her breasts with crossed arms and mocked him by imitating his face. He shifted his gaze to her crotch. Her pubic hair showed through her soaked white panties. She yelled, "Stop staring, pervert, and light a fire!"

"Stop issuing orders. I'm not your slave," he protested as he disrobed down to his underpants.

"I know, Amy owns you. But unless you want to die of exposure, start a goddamn fire!"

There was wood next to the fireplace. Kyle, by this time shaking violently, put some kindling in the fireplace. He looked around the hearth for matches, but found none. To the kitchen he went in quest of paper and matches, while Erin went to the bedroom in search of dry clothes. Her search proved fruitless, but she took a blanket off the bed and put it around herself; she took off her wet bra and panties. She then removed the sheet and walked out to see how the fire was coming.

From the volley of curses emanating from the kitchen, she gathered it wasn't going well. She joined the search.

"I found some paper lining the cupboards, but no matches."

"I got this for you," she said holding out the sheet.

"I can see right through it," he returned as he took it and put it around him. He took off his drenched underpants.

"There's nothing else in this entire cabin."

"Why do you get the thick blanket and I get this useless sheet? It's your fault that we got wet."

"I thought it was safe."

"Perfect epitaph."

"We'll trade off. Wait'll I warm up a little."

"Which should be just about the time I die of exposure."

They resumed the search for matches. "Here's some," she said, as she looked in a drawer. She opened the matchbook and said, "There's only two left." They took their booty to the fireplace. Erin tore up the paper and put it under the kindling. She lit a match, but it went out as soon as she touched it to the paper. "Dammit!" she said. "There's a breeze coming through the chimney."

"Don't worry," Kyle replied. "Just know that if the next one goes out that blanket is mine."

She looked at him as if to say, *Try it, bub*! and took a piece of paper out of the fireplace. She lit it and used it to light the remaining paper in the fireplace. The paper went up quickly, but the kindling was proving more uninvolved. "We need more paper, quick!" she said. Kyle ran to the kitchen and got the last two sheets lining the cupboards.

By the time he returned, the fire was reduced to some red ashes. He gave her the paper. Erin put the tip of one sheet against the embers and blew gently on it. After almost half a minute, it finally caught. She picked up the smallest piece of kindling and put it on the burning paper. As the fire died out again, she put the last piece of paper on the fire. "Find more paper!" she said.

"There is no more," he responded.

She looked at him and ripped off part of the ancient sheet that was doing little good preserving his warmth, and put it on the fire. It burned almost as well as the paper, but the wood remained impervious.

"Dammit! This must be fireproof wood," she griped. "We'll need more of that."

He tore off several more strips amounting to most of the sheet, leaving him with a loin cloth. By the final strip, the kindling was sparking to life, but worried it might still go either way, Erin reached back and, without a word, ripped the rest of the sheet off of him, leaving him naked. She threw it on the fire and smiled as the fire engulfed the logs. Turning back to smile at Kyle, she had to suppress a guffaw as she glanced at his penis, which had retreated into itself seeking warmth, and was smaller than his nose.

"Don't you dare laugh," he said as he blushed and covered himself with his hands. "This is what happens to a man when he's freezing."

"I know," she said as a laugh escaped. "I'm sorry. It just looks, so, um, cute and harmless and blue now."

"Don't call my dick cute, for Christ's sake. A man wants to think he's got a monster down there, not a Smurf. How would you like if I said your pussy is, I don't know, a gaping maw?"

"Not very much, but I know it's not true, so I'd just write you off as a jerk."

After warming up for a few minutes, she got up and went to the kitchen. She brought back two kitchen chairs and put them to either side of the fireplace. Then she went to the window, and ripped the cord off the blind. She came back and tied one end to each chair. While she tied the cord, she gazed at the man before her kneeling in front of the fire.

Reflecting on the last few days, on the incredible machine he had invented and the genius that must have taken, on what he had done for her despite what it might cost him, on his sangfroid and strength of character in facing their current crisis, on his trenchant sense of humor and the fun she had prodding him to display it, on how appealing he could be when he cared to be … reflecting on all that, she realized how much she was beginning to enjoy his company. Rejecting a compelling notion to go to him, throw her arms around him and kiss him, she averted her head and went to pick up their clothes.

She came back, tossed him half, and said, "Wring them out, and hang them on the clothesline. We have to dry these before it gets light outside. The assassin will be able to track us here in daylight."

Once all the clothes were hanging to dry on the line and the chair backs, Erin went to the bedroom and dragged out the mattress. "It's too cold to sleep away from the fire," she explained. She put the mattress just outside the ring of clothes drying by the fire. "We'll need to sleep together, but I'm warning you, Mr. Summers, you'd better keep your hands off of me." He smiled. "And that goes for cuddly little Smurf, too," she teased, with her own saucy smile.

His smile withered away. "Pulsing Anaconda Smurf wants nothing to do with you," he answered to her laughter.

She lay down, unwrapped the blanket, and spread it over herself. "We lie with you facing away from me. I can't sleep on my left side because of my sore shoulder and arm, so you have to sleep on your left side."

"I'm not sleeping on the shoulder you shot."

"C'mon, milksop. It's just a scra—"

"Don't say it!"

"Goodnight," she said. He grunted. Exhausted, he fell asleep right away. Twenty-five sleepless minutes later, she asked, "Are you asleep?"

"Not anymore."

"I'm still shivering. I'm too cold to sleep."

"You're in no danger of feeling comfortable here."

"Move closer to me, but behave yourself. Talk about something. Your complaining always makes me snooze. Tell me, Kyle, leaving aside who sold the computers to the Chinese and Colombians, do you feel guilty that your technology was used to find and kill our agents?"

"Of course I do. At the same time, it's really unfair to be held responsible. I mean, it's not a new issue. Do we hold munitions companies responsible for the millions of lives their products take? And, unlike their bullets and bombs, my computer could be used to help mankind, maybe help stop terrorist plots, cure cancer, or something great like that.

"Our country cannot bury its head in the sand and pretend this technology does not exist. We can't go back to the way it was, no matter how much people may want to. The new reality is a lot riskier, but we better get used to it before we lose what made us great in the first place."

"I know. You don't have to convince me. The problem is, the new reality was sprung on us too abruptly, and we were caught unawares. It's not as straightforward as a quick hop from the old world into the new. A lot of people get hurt in an upheaval of this magnitude, so we have to do what we can to minimize the damage while we figure out how to get there."

"Yeah, well, our enemies aren't waiting while we muddle our way through."

"What the Chinese and Colombians did with your technology proved the government's case that your technology is dangerous in the wrong hands. How do we protect against that?"

"Better encryption technology, as I told you before. Since the Chinese have the computer, we have no choice but to go that route now."

"Is that it in a nutshell? Your admission? Is that why you did it? To make it necessary for the government to approve the sale of your computer?"

"I did not do it! Rick and Amy did it."

"All the evidence points to you."

"I know, I know. It's a setup."

"Prove it at your trial."

"How?"

"I don't know. Your our own naïveté—your blind devotion to a witch—got you into this. How to get out of it, I don't know."

"I'll get away. Tonight, tomorrow, the next day, I'll get away from you."

"Maybe, but then you'll be the subject of a manhunt. Both the law and the outlaws will be gunning for you. You're not exactly a field agent. You won't last a day. Stop fighting the inevitable; stay with me. It's for your own good."

"From my perspective, here's what you just said: 'Kyle, why don't you dip your nuts in boiling oil, and shove a hot poker up your ass? It's for your own good.' You're taking me back to jail. How can you do that to me?"

"I just told you. I don't want you dead. And I believe in what I'm doing."

"Then you're the same as they are. Damn Luddites. They're the ones risking this country's future, not me."

"Dress it up any way you want. It will never justify selling forbidden technology to the Chinese."

"I did not do that! Shut up, I wanna go to sleep." He moved away from her, but she was cold and closed the distance again. She cuddled up against him, bunching part of the blanket between them. He rose to the occasion. She turned her face to him and said, "I hope you're not expecting something."

"Nope," he said resolutely.

"Part of you is."

"That part has bad taste."

"I'll take your word for it."

The two closed their eyes and started to get drowsy. A few minutes later, Kyle, half asleep, rolled over and put his arm around Erin. With part of the blanket still between them, she smiled and drifted off to sleep. Another few minutes later, he kissed her cheek. That woke her up. She turned to him to whisper, "Don't do that," but he kissed her on the lips.

She knew this could go no further. He was a suspected terrorist and her prisoner—but she found herself pleased at this attention, at least until he said, "I love you, Amy."

She yelped, "Amy! You bastard!" Half awake, he seemed only dimly aware of his crime. She continued, "Amy, Amy, Amy! Grow up, will you?" she yelled as she put her feet against him and shoved him out of the bed. "She's treated you like garbage ever since you met her. She is in no way worthy of the love you've devoted to her. Get it through your thick head: you're nothing to her but a free lunch ticket. And she set you up, so you say, to take the fall for the contraband computers. If that's true, she's the one who ruined you, not me. Can't you see that? How can a real man let a woman treat him like that?"

"Look at me. I have nothing to offer a woman. I thought I had to put up with whatever she dished out, otherwise she'd leave me."

"That's nonsense."

"You just said it yourself, I'm not a real man. No woman ever showed any interest in me before Amy or since I met her. I never believed any woman could ever love me. I still don't. She never told me she loved me; I wouldn't have believed it if she had.

"When she promised to marry me I thought it was just because she was betting I'd be rich some day, but that was okay since I didn't believe I could possibly be worthy of her otherwise. That was why I was so desperate to invent my computer. It was all I had to offer her. Meanwhile, whatever she asked, I did—anything not to lose her until I could provide for her the life she deserved."

"How can someone who's accomplished what you have think so poorly of himself? I think you're a great man, and more important than that, I think you're a good man. But you lost your way because you followed your fantasy right down to hell. She does not love you; she must loathe you to have done what she's done to you."

"She set me up to go to jail, and you're doing her bidding. You're no better."

"I've put my life on the line for you more than once, Mr. Summers. What did she ever do for you? You're hopelessly naïve when it comes to women. She knew that and took advantage of you."

"She fooled me to steal my computer. You fooled me to quash my computer. Not much difference."

"There's a world of difference. I did it for my country, not for any personal benefit. If you sold those computers and jeopardized our country's security, if you're partly responsible for the death of forty-seven agents and counting, then, yes, I'm taking you to jail and I will not feel guilty about it."

"I sold two computers in Canada, period, so fuck you!" he said, as he crawled under the wet clothes and lay down next to the fire.

"Come back here. It's too cold to sleep alone." He lay motionless and silent, so Erin curled up and eventually went to sleep.

At one point, Erin woke up and saw Kyle sitting up next to the fire and staring at it. Obviously, he'd been stoking it. By his posture, breathing, and sniffling, she could tell he was crying again.

As an FBI agent, she wasn't accustomed to feeling any pity for the people she arrested, but as she lay there gazing at Kyle, she too began to cry. He'd lost everything: the government had outlawed his invention and blotted out an incredibly bright future; the woman he loved so deeply had used him in the worst way imaginable; she and Rick had framed him for the crime of terrorism—by this time, with all this man had done for her and with his adamant denials, Erin was becoming convinced that this man could not be a terrorist; he was being hunted by killers; she was escorting him back to prison.

Any one of those reasons was enough to make a grown man cry; combined they were enough to make him want to—*Oh!* she realized. *He really does have a death wish! He said he has nothing to live for. That's why he's put his life on the line for me again and again. A death wish makes a man willing to take great risks. That poor man. He invents an amazing machine that should have made him rich and famous, but look what it got him. It's so unfair.*

She desperately wanted to go to him and comfort him, but she couldn't. As distasteful as she found it at that moment, this was her job and it would be unprofessional to sympathize with her prisoner. It might give him false hope that she would let him go. Besides, being a man, he'd probably be embarrassed if he knew she saw him weeping, she told herself. She turned over and went back to sleep, eventually.

Erin dreamed that Kyle was being hooked up to the electric chair. She was pounding on the glass in the observation room screaming, "No! This is a mistake! Stop this travesty!" when: Crash!

She awoke, terrified, when a man smashed open the front door with his shoulder, and ran into the cabin. She sat up, her heart thumping wildly.

"Where is he?" the man, the one from the store the day before, demanded to know with a pistol pointed at her.

"I don't know," she answered, still in shock. "He must have snuck out while I was sleeping." She looked at the table where she'd left her gun, but saw it was missing.

The assassin cautiously went to the bathroom door, fired five times through it, and pushed the door open. He saw no one. He then checked the bedroom. Empty. She stood with the blanket wrapped around her.

"Hold it there," he advised, as he turned his gun to her. "Nothing against you, but I can't leave any witnesses," he said.

Panicking, she started shaking and breathing fast. In sheer terror, she tried desperately to think of a way to save her life. "Who do you work for?" she asked. "Just tell me if you're a federal agent."

"What's the difference? You'll be dead in a few seconds."

"No! *Please!*" she begged. "You must know I'm an FBI agent. If you kill me—"

"They'll blame Summers."

"I was just doing my job taking a fugitive to justice."

"And I'm just doing mine," he said.

Erin tried a last ditch gambit. She let the blanket fall open and gave him the best *Don't you want me?* pout she could muster under the circumstances.

He smiled and said, "I know your game, but it won't work. Too bad I have to kill such a fine-looking creature," he said, as he pointed the gun at her chest. She screamed as a loud bang reverberated around the room. The hit man fell to the floor, hurt but alive. He dropped his gun.

Erin turned and saw Kyle looking in shock at the man he'd just shot. The hit man, who was struck in the upper chest, scrambled to get his gun. Kyle ran in and said, "Stay still!" The man remained motionless. When Kyle bent over to retrieve the gun, the man tried to kick him in the face. Kyle blocked it with his arm, but lost his gun in the process.

The stricken gunman reached over for his gun, got hold of it and, as he brought it to bear on his victim, he stopped short when a bullet struck him in the head. Erin dropped her gun and collapsed to the floor. After a few moments, trying to come to terms with killing another man, she crawled over to Kyle, pulled him down to his knees, threw her arms around him and exclaimed, "Thank you!"

"I screwed up. If you hadn't rescued me, we'd both be dead."

"You tried to get away again, didn't you?" He nodded. "But you came back to save me again?"

"Just like last time: I was next, and it was my chance to catch him by surprise."

She looked him in the eyes and kissed him on the lips. "Thank you, Kyle," she whispered as she held him close.

"Get dressed," he said. "We need to get away from here right away." She stood, picked up both guns, grabbed her clothes, and went into the bedroom to get dressed. When she came out of the bedroom, Kyle was checking the dead man's pockets. "Nothing but cash and a cell phone again. Alberta driver's license. William Veibl."

"This whole thing is out of control. I have to take the chance and use this phone to call the police." When Erin tried to dial Officer Chianut, she got no signal. Cell phone coverage was spotty in the mountainous region.

They decided to leave the cabin and resume their trek. They walked northwest along the lake until they left it behind and turned north. Since they were on foot, and making their way through a thick forest, their progress was slow. Every so often, Erin would try the phone but with no luck.

Kyle said, "Just to check, you're turning off the phone between tries, right?" She shook her head with a quizzical look on her face. "Are you aware that cell phones periodically send signals to nearby cellular towers?"

"Of course, but obviously there are none since I can't get a call out."

"If we happen to move into the line of sight of a tower and the phone happens to transmit the ping then, which it can do if it's on, it says loud and clear to anyone watching 'Here I am.'"

"I'm trying to call every few minutes, but I guess it's better to be safe than sorry," she said as she switched off the phone.

*

The person responsible for monitoring the hit man's phone had just transmitted their location to their last operative in the area.

CHAPTER NINE

The Alpine Excursion Comes to a Bloody End

While they walked, Erin made small talk and Kyle mumbled answers here and there as he tried to fashion a plan of escape. *"What I should do, what I would do if I had any balls, is punch her in the face, take her gun and run. But where would that get me? Lost in the wilderness with the police and hit men shooting at me. She's right; I wouldn't last the day ...*

"Yeah, I'm hungry, too ..."

Christ, there must be some way out of this mess. If I could somehow convince her I'm innocent, but how the hell to do that? At least she believes I didn't kill Rick now. Maybe that will help get her on my side ...

"Yeah, it's a nice morning, positively sultry ..."

If I could get her on my side, convince her I could never do what I'm accused of, maybe she'd help me. No, she'd never go for it. Too dedicated to her job, to what she thinks her country stands for. If saving her life hasn't stopped the little trooper from doing her duty, nothing will ...

"It's beautiful country all right ..." *Who gives a shit about the scenery when I'm being marched to prison? Jesus woman! She's smiling a lot at me this morning. Probably her way of keeping me in line until she can dump me off in jail. Or it could be that she's really grateful that I shot that prick. She actually kissed me. Amy never kissed me like that ...*

"Yes, the fawn is cute, and delicious, I bet ..."

Got her laughing. Good, keep doing that. Maybe if I try being nice to her and joking with her she'll see me as a human being and not a prisoner. That might be a start, anyway. Nothing else has worked ...

"What am I thinking about? Oh, how sweet that little fawn was. What the hell do you think I'm thinking about? ..." *Okay, I'm off to a bad start being nice. Get with it ...* "Sorry. I was actually thinking about you."

"Nothing bad, I hope."

"I was wondering what made you decide to join the FBI."

"It's not something I set out to do, that's for sure," answered Erin. "I was kind of a wild child, a real tomboy. I loved sports and was better at them than most boys I knew. I liked the company of boys better than girls because to me they had so much more fun—this was before anyone thought of sex. I just liked the roughhousing, you know? Anyway, the point is, I like action. Sitting at a desk all day typing into a computer would kill me. No offense."

"Some taken. Yet you took a degree in computer science?"

"That was strictly laziness. I never liked it, but I found it incredibly easy, so I majored in it. But when I graduated, I thought, *Ah shit, I don't want to do this for a living*, so I went to graduate school, which put off work for a while. When I began looking for a job, an FBI recruiter came to Dartmouth looking for computer science graduates.

"My impression of the FBI was like most people's, I guess: straight-laced police types. Yet I'd seen enough movies and TV shows that I thought the job could be exciting. I went to talk to him, but warned him at the outset that I wasn't interested in sitting at a computer screen all day. He said the FBI liked computer scientists not only for their programming skills but for their logical minds—a logical mind lends itself to investigation. So I signed on."

"Was it what you expected?"

"At first, they had me in the office all the time, which I didn't like—but after a year, I started working in the field. Now I love my job. It's challenging, it's often exciting, it's occasionally dangerous, which gets my juices going, and I get to meet lots of criminals and get the satisfaction of making them pay for their crimes."

"What was your most dangerous case?"

"This one by far. As I told you, I'd never shot anyone before—and I've never been a target."

"Lucky me to be part of that. Your most interesting case?"

"You're kidding, right? Do you think my typical case involves terrorism, murder, intrigue, the highest technology yet invented, and running for my life?"

"Don't forget the naïve nerd."

"That *is* typical in most of my cases," she noted with a smile.

"I never fooled myself into believing she loved me, but it never occurred to me that it was a setup from the get go."

"How did that happen?" she asked as it began to snow.

"Seven or eight years ago, Hugel tried to get me to join his firm after he read my thesis, but I knew his ideas wouldn't work, so I said no. A couple of years later, I read about this amazing invention for controlling decoherence by Hugel Quantum Corporation. I thought, *Ah, shit, I've been scooped*, so I looked into it further.

"I discovered it was my design. You can imagine how furious I was. I went to see him to impress upon him that stealing my idea was unacceptable. He informed me that copyright law doesn't confer any protection against people using ideas; only a patent does that, and he had the patent. I thought that was bullshit and said I'd sue him. He laughed and called me a sucker—and, not finding that altogether pleasing, I impressed upon his skull with my fist. The prick pressed charges.

"He steals my multi-billion dollar idea, then has the nerve to press charges against me. He told me he'd drop the charges if I joined his firm. He was stuck because all his ideas were dead ends. I told him I'd never work for a thief and dared him to meet me in court. He backed off and dropped the charges. He didn't need his investors knowing the trouble he was in."

"He knew he needed you, so he sent in Amy undercover."

"Apparently. She worked for a venture capital firm called Comptech Venture Partners—at least, that's what she told me. I had a lawyer check out the contract, so she must have worked for them."

"She did, although she never passed that contract on to Comptech," Erin said. "Allen contacted Comptech," she explained. "They told him she'd been fired almost two years ago because they discovered a conflict of interest. She had fallen in love with their client and was lying for him. She had been submitting glowing reports on Hugel, but Comptech later learned those reports were at odds with their other indicators. They sent someone else in, and discovered that Hugel had gotten nowhere and had fired his researchers, and they found out the research money was being diverted to a subcontractor."

"Summers Quantum Computers?"

"You got it. Probably the smartest thing Hugel ever did, but Comptech didn't see it that way. They decided to pull the plug on Hugel's firm and threatened legal action."

"That's why we piled up so much debt; our venture capital was cut off."

"That's right. Hugel threatened to declare bankruptcy. Comptech then threatened to auction off your component to the highest bidder, but they decided against it. Apparently they'd been checking into your progress since all their money was being spent by you, and were very impressed by what they found."

"I remember a bunch of suits infesting my lab, and asking stupid questions."

"They must have liked your answers, because they negotiated and agreed to drop any proceedings against Hugel in return for twenty-five percent of the new company."

"Comptech only owns twenty-five percent?"

"That's my understanding."

"Amy told me it was thirty-nine percent. So Rick and Amy must own thirty-four percent between them."

"You should know this. Did you not sign a contract?"

"Yes. I read to the part that said I owned forty-one percent and trusted Amy on the rest."

"You can be really naïve, can't you? They tricked you into a partnership and took a much greater percentage for themselves than you knew."

He nodded and chuckled bitterly. "I handed those buggers thirty-four percent of my firm, and what did I get in return? A botched plan to unveil the computer that gave our competitors the notice they needed to shut us down, and a charge of terrorism after they sold three computers in a last desperate attempt to get rich off me. Jesus, I'm stupid!" He shook his head. "You knew all along, didn't you? You knew Amy was playing me for a fool."

"We knew she'd been fired from Comptech, and we knew she was in love with Rick, but we had no idea she was married to him. When we got there and found out you two were engaged, we were thrown for a loop."

"Guess I can't blame you. Why would she ever drop Adonis for Cyclops?"

"You may not realize it, but when you put yourself down like that, it sends all the wrong signals. You're telling people you're not worth getting to know. You're also communicating that you hold women in low regard, because you think them incapable of seeing you for who you really are."

"Can you blame me? Every woman I ever trusted has betrayed me."

"Your mother and Amy?"

"You know about my mother?"

"Yes. I'm far from perfect, but I'm good at my job. That's two women who betrayed you, Kyle. There are three billion more out there. Don't paint us all with the same brush."

"You betrayed me, too."

"I refuse to have this argument again." The flurries got heavier.

"Fine, Special Agent. Just tell me, after what you've learned about me in the past two days, how do you see me now?"

"Bear!"

"Bare? What does that mean? What's the matter?" he said as Erin took flight.

"Bear, idiot!" she screamed, as she pointed back while running. Kyle looked around and saw a bear walking up to him.

"Jesus!" he prayed, as he took off behind Erin. The bear trotted leisurely behind them. "He's chasing us!" he screamed. She scrambled up a tree, groaning because of the pain in her shoulder. He followed, hollering in pain and making little vertical progress. She looked down and tried to help. All she could reach was his hair, so she pulled it up. The pain on his head and in his shoulder and the bear swiping at his dangling feet with his paw spurred an ear-splitting skirl that seemed to spook the bear. It turned and walked away.

"Your girly scream scared it away. My hero," she teased. He smirked. They sat on their branches silent for a time, watching the bear. It disappeared into the bush. "Why did you stand there like an idiot after I screamed 'bear'?"

"Here and there lies Kyle Summers, the victim of a dastardly homonym." She furrowed her brow in confusion. "You know," he continued, "until I met you, I would wake up

every day and think, *Ah, shit, here comes another lousy day,* because there's been an uninterrupted string of them for twenty-five years—but I could always comfort myself with the thought that at least I wasn't gonna get eaten by a fucking bear. Thank you for shading the only ray of sunshine in my life."

"Don't give it a second thought," she replied with a titter. "I guess the bear wasn't really hungry. Lucky for you or the only way they would've had to identify you would be from dental records after it shit your teeth out." He sniggered. "Hey, maybe if you climb higher, you can get a signal."

"No, but next time I'm looking for a great way to crack my skull open, I'll give that some consideration."

"But my shoulder ... Oh, never mind." Erin climbed another thirty feet, showing no fear and great dexterity despite her injured shoulder. She pulled out her phone and dialed Officer Chianut.

"It's ringing," she called down to Kyle. "Hello Officer Chianut. It's Erin McAdams. We're in trouble ..."

After bringing him up to date on the fireworks since they last spoke, she hung up and climbed down as the snowfall intensified. She told Kyle, "Officer Chianut figured out where we were last night. He said he'd meet us there, but he's now at the scene of Officer Litvin's murder, which is at least forty-five minutes away. He recommended we hurry back to the cabin because there's an intense snow squall on our doorstep." Kyle nodded. "I'm not sure he was all that pleased to hear from me again," she added, as she hopped down to the ground.

Get her on your side, he reminded himself. *Joke with her.* Jumping down, he replied, "Maybe the heap of corpses we're leaving in our wake is annoying him."

She chortled and said, "He said he was glad we got away from the bear because he wouldn't wanna have to tell my parents I was eaten by a bear. That would be hard."

"I'd say nothing. They'd figure it out when they went to claim your intestines and gnawed-off foot."

"You're terrible," she said, chuckling. "You'd have to say something to prepare my parents for that."

"They'd sense something was awry when they were told you'd be coming home on Flight 816 *and* Flight 457."

She laughed again as they hurried back the way they came, until their old footsteps disappeared under new snow. "I can't tell which way to go," Erin said as the wind picked up. "I can't even see with the snow blowing in my eyes. We have to find shelter."

"Maybe we can build an igloo."

"Do you know how to? You're from Saskatchewan."

"Of course. First we find a bunch of snow. Check. Then we find an Eskimo." She punched his shoulder. "Ow!" he cried.

"Oh, I forgot about your shoulder. Sorry." He punched her sore shoulder, and she shrieked. "I made a mistake, but you did it on purpose, jerk!" She punched his sore shoulder again. He yelped and reared back to punch her shoulder again, but she beat him to the punch, hitting him directly on his wound, and he fell to his knees in pain. "Now I suggest you accept my apology and stop this."

He got to his feet and said, "Apology accepted." As she smiled in victory, he walloped her shoulder again, and she screamed in pain.

She jumped on him and buried her teeth in his wound, and his yowl spooked every bird in the forest. "Now cut it out!" she ordered as she walked away. He followed, rubbing his shoulder. A moment later, she said, "Maybe we can build a lean-to. Do you know how to do that? And don't say sticks and a Boy Scout or I'll kill you."

"You're a violent person, McAdams. I know we need fallen branches, and they're all under the fallen snow."

They walked another few minutes until Kyle pointed to a fallen tree next to a large Engelmann spruce tree. "There's our shelter," he said. "The tree is dense enough to provide cover, and the log will block most of the wind. All we need to do is pile up some snow on this side to block the rest of the wind."

She nodded, and they got to work, pushing some snow into a mound with their arms. Then they crawled under the tree and crouched close together.

Get her on your side, he repeated to himself. "That's six," he said to her.

"What's six?" she asked.

"The number of times I've saved your life."

"Where do you get six?"

"One just now when I built our snow fort."

"I was cold, I wasn't dying."

"We'd have died of exposure if I left it up to you. Once when I shot the guy in the cabin."

"You admitted you messed up. I had to finish him."

"You wouldn't have had the chance without me. Once when I rescued you with the snowmobile."

"I'd have got him—and, anyway, you only got that chance because I shot at him as he was about to kill you."

"Once when I stopped Norris from smothering you."

"The RCMP officer shot him."

"Only because I called him. And there was taking the rescuers back to the plane and there was stopping you from bleeding to death on the plane."

"You can't count saving me on the plane twice."

"Why not?"

"Because, well, say I was never rescued—then it wouldn't have mattered that you stopped my bleeding. It would be like a surgeon telling the waiting family, 'I have good news, and I have bad news. The good news is I saved his life. The bad news is he died a little after that.' Only the final outcome can be counted."

"The final outcome for me is you're taking me back to die or rot in jail. Your sense of gratitude needs work. "

"If you're innocent, you have nothing to worry about."

"As I said before, the United States government against a poor man: foregone conclusion."

"The burden of proof is still on them. I have faith that justice will prevail."

"You would."

"And, anyway, I don't owe you. I saved your life seven times."

"Oh, I can't wait to hear this."

"Once when I crash-landed the plane."

"You did that to save your life."

"Once when I got us away from the hit man who killed the RCMP officer."

"You did that to save your life."

"Once when I kicked you in the balls so you bent over and the sniper missed you."

"That just made up for shooting me and kicking me in the balls."

"Once when I shot him just before he was going to shoot you."

"You can't count the same guy three times if I can't count the plane twice."

"Once when I shot at the man in the store who would've killed you."

"He probably would've missed anyway."

"Once when I saved you from drowning."

"I was only drowning because of you! In that case, I saved you from choking to death when I stopped choking you to death."

She chuckled. "Once when I shot the killer in the cabin. Oh, and once when I pulled you up the tree away from the bear."

"Oh, come on. My girly scream scared it away, remember? Anyway, I'd rather be oozing through the intestines of a bear than lying here listening to the most aggravating person on Earth."

She smirked.

The two lay under the tree for a few minutes, saying nothing. Then Erin, looking out at the snow, remarked, "We've been through a lot together in the past couple of days." He concurred. Turning to him, she pleaded, "Kyle, please fix what you did to me. *Please!* It's not fair to bankrupt me for doing my job."

Oh, that's why she's smiling at me and joining me in friendly banter: she wants something from me. I'm not making any headway with her at all. Why do I keep fooling myself that a woman would ever take me seriously? He said, "Don't get me going on what's fair again. I'll tell you what: help me escape and I'll fix your finances."

"You must think very little of me if you think I'd do that."

"Okay, then, on the infinitesimal chance I'm found not guilty, I'll undo what I did to you. Our fates are linked, Special Agent. If they screw me, you get it, too."

"But—"

"No! Drop it."

She turned her head away in anger. A while later, she turned back and asked, "What did you do with the three million dollars?" He shrugged. "Did you move it to another account?" No response. "I've seen some of your tricks, and I'll use them to find the money."

"Believe me, Special Agent, if I wanted to cover my tracks, no one would find them. And I changed the password, so you can't log into the U of T computer again."

"We have thirty-one of your computers."

"Is that your admission? The government is using the machines it stole from us?"

"I don't know the answer to that question, but it's a good guess."

"Bastards. How can you close your eyes to that? One hundred sixty million dollars—actually, one hundred sixty-five million since, as you just implied, they clipped the one in my apartment, too. One hundred sixty-five million dollars stolen by the government of the United States. Stolen to drive us out of business. How can they get away with that?"

"Your computers were used in a terrorist act. Sixty-one Americans were murdered because of your computers. That gives the government the right to shut you down."

"You really are brainwashed. It's all linked. The government's unconstitutional edict to forbid the sale of quantum computers led to all this. It made me desperate enough to sell two computers to Canadians to avoid bankruptcy, and it made Rick and Amy desperate enough to sell to the Chinese and Colombians."

"Which led to the murder of sixty-one—"

"I didn't commit murder. Not even Rick or Amy committed those murders. The computers did not commit those murders. They weren't even a proximate cause. Chinese agents and Colombian drug lords did it. Are you after them? They used guns and bullets. Are you after Smith and Wesson? Cars or trucks transported them to the murder scene. Are you after Ford? How the hell does the act of selling a computer equate to murder? To terrorism?"

"I already told you how international terrorism is defined by our government, and I don't get to disagree with it, so I'll do my job. Where is that three million dollars?"

"Gone and there's no proof it was ever in my account."

"Mr. Summers, you may be able to erase the money, but you can't erase my memory and the memories of the other agents who saw the money in your account. We know the money was there; we documented the evidence, we talked to the Bank of America, and they substantiated it and supposedly froze it. So erasing your account achieved nothing. Where is that money?"

"Never had it, never touched it, but feel free to use the tricks I taught you. You might be surprised what you find."

"What did—you didn't put it in my name?"

"No, but that would've been comical. Oh, I should maybe mention that when I was trying to find what became of the proceeds from the three computers, I just happened across a payment of a hundred thousand dollars in the bank account of the Agent in Charge of the Counterterrorism squad."

"You didn't!"

"I figured he was the one who deputed you to capture the terrorist nerd."

"Do you think this is a big joke or something?"

"Just think of what a funny sitcom it would be: the government absolutely demolishing an innocent man, then arresting him for murder and terrorism, then sending assassins after him, then tossing him in jail. Has to be the most hilarious set of events since those wacky Saudis flew into the World Trade Center," noted Kyle as the snow let up.

"You must know that every time you tamper with evidence, you hurt your own cause."

"Evidence? Come off it. Be consistent, Special Agent. A large deposit into my bank account was enough to condemn me, so it should be enough to condemn your boss. If not, you're tacitly admitting that it's a trivial matter to fabricate this bogus evidence, which thereby exonerates me."

"The difference is I know you've done this to the special agent in charge. I don't know if you were set up."

"Which you'll testify to."

"I have no choice."

"Then I have no choice but to leave your finances in tatters."

Angry at him, Erin crawled out from under the tree. The brief storm had spent all but a few flurries. Suddenly, Erin screamed, and a rifle shot resounded through the forest. She fell to the ground. Her hand was bleeding, and she was crying in pain. Realizing she'd been shot through the hand, Kyle reached out and dragged her behind the fallen tree.

"I'll let the FBI agent live if you come out alone, Summers," yelled the gunman from the distance. "You have one minute to decide."

Kyle looked at her in terror for a moment, then managed a nervous smile. He quickly took off his jacket and his shirt. He tied his shirt around her hand tightly, which elicited a shriek of pain from Erin, and he put his jacket back on. He said, "Try to sneak away when he's focused on me. I don't imagine an assassin is good for his word."

She took a deep breath and cried, "No, Kyle! Don't go out there. He'll kill you for sure."

"Jesus, Erin, I'm screwed whatever I do, remember? No sense you dying for this."

"I don't want you to die! You can't just give up. Take a gun. We'll fight him."

"Time's up," said the gunman as he fired five more shots. The bullets hit the log. The gunman walked leisurely to the east so he could get a clear shot.

Kyle saw him about a hundred yards away, but there was nowhere to run for better cover. "I'm useless with a gun, your shooting hand is out of commission, and he has a rifle of some sort. Your only chance is for me to give myself up."

She looked at him with pleading eyes. He took a pistol and waited for the gunman to move again. When he did, Kyle fired several shots. The man scurried behind a large tree trunk, but no shot came close to him. Then he raked the log with dozens of bullets. Kyle and Erin cowered and covered their heads.

"I'm out of ammunition," said Kyle. "I'll give myself up. You stay down."

"Don't do this!" said Erin. "I still have the other gun."

"Which you can't shoot."

"You take it. You can't just give up!"

"Even if he were thirty feet away, I'd miss him; he's a hundred yards out with a rifle. This will give you a chance. Just keep your head down. You haven't seen him, so he might just leave after he does his job. I'll take out the empty gun and drop it so he can see. If he decides to come after you, he might figure you're unarmed; shoot him when he gets close."

"I know you have a death wish, but please don't throw your life away. You're too special."

"Stay down!" he commanded, as he stood with his hands above his head.

"No!" she bellowed.

While he walked fretfully toward the hit man with his hands up, Kyle dropped the pistol and yelled, "The FBI agent hasn't seen your face. She's wounded and unarmed, so she isn't a threat to you. Don't kill her!" he pleaded. With the man taking aim at Kyle, Erin squeezed off a shot with her left hand. The bullet missed its target by twenty feet. She fired twice more and missed. Then she ran out and stood in front of Kyle.

"Erin!" screeched Kyle in exasperation. He tried to shield her.

"This man is my prisoner, and I'm taking him back to face justice," she hollered. "If he's guilty he'll pay for his crimes. You don't need to kill him!"

*

As the gunman aimed for Kyle's head, someone behind him roared, "Drop your weapon!" The gunman slowly lowered his rifle, but didn't drop it. "Drop it or we drop you!" yelled Officer Chianut. The man let the gun fall to the ground.

"Hands above your head, and hold perfectly still," came the next order as another RCMP constable approached. He put on handcuffs, frisked him for weapons and stood guard. Officer Chianut radioed for the helicopter to come to his location and went to help the stricken FBI agent. She had collapsed and was sitting in shock on the ground. Kyle was kneeling next to her trying to comfort her.

"The bullet went through her hand," Kyle said as the good officer knelt to help. Kyle added, "Thank you. We owe you our lives."

"You're welcome," he answered as he took out his handcuffs and put them on Kyle.

Fourteen minutes later, the helicopter arrived. A medic saw to Erin's immediate needs, and carried her to the chopper. Kyle and Officer Chianut got in. The other RCMP constable put the gunman on board then went back to the snowmobile they had left a couple of hundred yards back to run toward the gunfire they'd heard. The helicopter flew to Williams Lake.

CHAPTER TEN

Bargains in Williams Lake

At Williams Lake, Erin was brought to the hospital, and Kyle was brought to the police station and put in a cell to await extradition. While recuperating in the hospital, Erin wrote up the incredible events of the two days in the wilderness—typing with her left hand—and emailed her report to the Chicago field office.

She speculated that one of the guns used by the hit men might be the murder weapon used to kill Rick Hugel. She turned out to be correct, but it was not Veibl's or Demeter's—it was Jeff Foster's gun. The murder charge against Kyle was withdrawn, clearing the way to extradition.

Kyle was brought before a judge the next morning, with Erin in attendance. The judge ordered his detention. With the Americans pushing hard for a quick turnaround, the Justice Minister commenced the extradition process against Kyle Summers by setting a date for the hearing three months hence.

Before leaving for home, Erin went to visit Kyle. She came with a portable computer and video camera. She set up her equipment, and had him brought to the interrogation room. When he entered, she patted on a chair next to her. He sat. The camera was behind them, focused on the screen.

"Show me," she said. "Show me you're innocent. Prove you were set up."

"How?"

"Get access to your computer in Toronto."

"That's impossible," he asserted.

"I saw you do it in Chicago, Kyle. I did it myself after you left that day. That's how I found the three million dollars, and I know that's how you erased your three million dollar account and played havoc with my finances."

"I have no idea what you're talking about."

"C'mon, Kyle. It's so obvious who did those things we don't even need your confession, but Officer Chianut and I will testify that you admitted it. I'm giving you the chance to demonstrate your innocence. Take advantage of it. Use your computer to find the money Amy or Rick got from the sale."

"Turn off the camera."

"But we need it on record."

"Turn it off or go to hell." She reached back, and turned the camera off. He continued, "How stupid do you think I am? You want me to admit on camera that I removed the three million dollars from my account?"

"I'm not trying to hurt you; I'm trying to help. Surely you must trust me after what we went through together."

"I'm in jail, Special Agent, and you put me here. I trust you to do your job like any other automaton employed by the FBI."

"My job is to find the bad guy. You've maintained all along you've been set up. I'm asking you to prove it. Can you?"

"Before I messed up your finances, I spent an hour tracing where the three million dollars came from in my account. I found out it was part of a fifteen million dollar deposit, the price of three Qubit computers. I followed a well-camouflaged trail to two numbered accounts in the Cayman Islands, six million dollars each."

"Rick and Amy?"

"Who else? But I found nothing to link them to the accounts."

"Still, the money in those accounts is important evidence. Let me record you tracing the money to those two accounts."

"The prosecutor will simply say I split the proceeds into three accounts, or say it was a team effort. The evidence is useless against anyone but me, because the only person in the world the money is linked to is me. I found it only because Rick's ruses on the computer were so predictable."

"I can assure you this: the prosecutor will add a tampering with evidence charge against you. You're already linked to the money. Whether it's three million or fifteen million doesn't really matter. There was a lot of money deposited into your account right when those illegal sales took place, and we can prove it beyond the shadow of a doubt. Take me up on this, Kyle. It can't hurt, and it could help you a great deal."

He considered a moment, then said, "I need to pass this by the court-appointed lawyer just out of law school who seems convinced my case is hopeless."

"Fine. I'll wait to hear from him." Erin left, and Kyle was taken back to his cell.

That afternoon, she got a call from the lawyer who told her that Kyle had agreed to demonstrate what he did with the three million dollars in his account on the condition that no additional charges would be laid for tampering with evidence. She told him she didn't have the authority to make that decision and would have to get back to him after checking with her office.

The federal prosecutor, John Feinstein, decided to negotiate with Kyle and his lawyer via teleconference. Beginning the discussion, the televised prosecutor said, "Mr. Summers, I understand from Special Agent McAdams that you've been busy tampering with evidence, and you want me to forget about that in return for showing us what you did with the evidence. Do I have that right?"

"You not only have that right, you have that correct," replied Kyle.

"Jesus, I'm dealing with an English teacher. You better start taking this seriously, Mr. Summers."

"I've been tortured, I've been in a plane crash, I've been shot, I've been in a car crash, I almost drowned, I almost fed a bear, and I'm now in jail for the crime of inventing a computer. That should tell you two things, Mr. Feinstein: I take this more seriously than you can possibly imagine, and you can't intimidate me, so meet my demand or piss off."

"You make a poor negotiator, Mr. Summers."

"That's it!" barked Kyle. "No deal," he said, as he got up to return to his cell.

"Kyle!" said Erin as she clutched his elbow. "Think hard about this. This is your chance to make your case. Just calm down and talk with him." Her look implored him to resume his seat. He did.

"Make your case," suggested Mr. Feinstein.

"My case? My case is I invented a computer, and the government is trying to kill me for it."

"Kyle, *please!*" supplicated Erin.

"All I did was invent a goddamn computer!"

"Agent McAdams," said Mr. Feinstein, "you found the three million dollars in an account in Mr. Summers's name?"

"Yes."

"Mr. Summers, you removed that money from your account, *correct?*"

Kyle conferred with his lawyer for a moment and responded, "Right."

"But you had no such right."

"So if my neighbor steals fifteen million dollars from a bank and stashes three million in my garage and phones the police to tell them where to find it to throw them off their scent, I have no right to get it out of there?"

"You have no right to tamper with evidence."

"I know damn well the cops will fall for it. They'll charge me for the robbery with all the evidence right there. I have no alibi. So my choice is to get rid of the evidence or to go to jail for certain. Any reasonable person would dump the evidence and try to find out who stole the fifteen million in the first place. I've done that, but you're ignoring the evidence in your zeal to prosecute the wrong man."

"Your problem is we caught you with the three million dollars before you removed it, and we have only your say so that the twelve million was traced to Mr. Hugel and Ms Janssen."

"My client will show you what he did with the three million dollars if he has his deal," piped up the lawyer.

The prosecutor said, "Very well. I will not charge your client with tampering with evidence if he shows us how he moved the money and where every cent is now." With the camera showing the computer screen, Kyle walked the observers through the steps he used to unfreeze the three million dollar account and move it to several charities and to the FBI agent's account.

"You tried to frame an FBI agent, Mr. Summers," noted the irritated prosecutor. "Had I known that, I wouldn't have agreed to this deal."

"I did it to show how easy it is to fabricate this evidence, to show how easy it was for someone to put the money into my account with the quantum computer. There was no intent to frame anyone," Kyle protested.

"Special Agent McAdams tells me you claim to have traced the money in your account to a fifteen million dollar payment and that you traced that to two accounts in the Cayman Islands?" Kyle looked askance at Erin. "Show me that evidence."

"And if I do show you, won't that work against me?"

"How? We already have the proceeds from the crime linked to you. The number of millions doesn't matter. Show me the other accounts, and we may be able to link them to Hugel and Janssen."

Kyle again conferred with his lawyer and decided to comply. He showed how he traced the three million dollars in his account to the original fifteen million, then followed the trail to the two accounts of six million dollars in the Cayman Islands.

Satisfied with the information he'd gotten, Mr. Feinstein said, "Rest assured, we'll keep tabs on the two numbered Cayman Islands accounts. Any computer used to gain access to either account will be immediately identified."

"Good. So where does this leave me if that doesn't happen?" said Kyle.

"It leaves you with the original charge of selling your computer to the Canadians, which I understand you've admitted to, and the much more serious charge of lending expert advice and assistance to a terrorist organization," answered the prosecutor.

"But I showed you how I traced the money to Rick and Amy."

"You showed us how you traced it to two numbered accounts, and how easily you could have manufactured that."

He looked at Erin as if to say, *See?* He said to Mr. Feinstein, "And I showed how worthless the three million dollars in my account was as evidence. And, tell me, why would I settle for three million and give them six million each? I own forty-one percent of the company."

"To throw us off the scent?"

"So I left the three million that implicates me right out in the open and buried the twelve million so deep that only—"

"Only you could find it," completed the prosecutor.

"That still doesn't answer why I would leave the three million dollars in my garage with the door wide open for everyone to see."

"Every criminal makes a mistake somewhere along the line. If you confess now, I may be open to another deal. I may consider dropping charges for the sale of the two computers to the Canadians in return for a guilty plea on selling to the Chinese and Colombians."

"I'll never in a million years plead guilty to something I didn't do. And the law against the sale of my computers to Canada is so clearly unconstitutional, it borders on the fantastic."

"I'll tell you what, Mr. Summers. Waive your right to the extradition hearing, and I'll agree to drop the charge on the sale of computers to the Canadians. We have you on that, and I'll be seeking five years in jail for that crime. That's an incredible deal, Mr. Summers."

"Anything to keep this immoral and unconstitutional mess out of public eye, eh? Go to hell."

"Kyle, don't—" said Erin.

"Shut the hell up, Special Agent. I'm through talking to him."

"Mr. Summers! A word, please," said his young defense lawyer. "I strongly advise you to take the deal. Your government is pulling out all the stops to get you extradited, so I think you should take his offer."

"In other words, you admit you can't defend me properly."

"I have two months of experience. How can I fight the U.S. government? I'll gladly step aside if you can afford—"

"I haven't got a cent to my name since the goddamn government froze the assets of my company."

"You'll spend three months in jail here waiting for your hearing—and, if you decide to appeal, maybe a year or two longer. After that, you're facing five years in prison on a charge you've already admitted to. You have to be realistic. Common sense dictates taking his deal."

"I thought you told me that Canada's Extradition Act prohibits extradition for political offences."

"The Americans know that. They'll likely seek extradition on the lesser charge, the one you already admitted to."

"Selling computers is not illegal in Canada. I thought you told me it has to be a crime in Canada for the extradition to succeed."

"They won't argue you were merely selling computers, they'll argue it was forbidden technology. And if they fail on that charge, they'll come forward with the serious one."

"Then you can argue that their real intention is political persecution."

"I can try, but are you willing to bet several years in jail on it?"

"Jesus Christ! Don't they have to prove anything?"

"In an extradition hearing, the judge isn't weighing the evidence to determine guilt or innocence. The Americans simply have to testify that they have strong evidence—your confession to their agent—and that they intend try you on that charge. I honestly don't see how you can win. One more thing: you've been charged with pulling a gun on an RCMP officer here. The Justice Minister has agreed to stay that charge in the event of extradition, but if you win the extradition case, you face jail time here anyway."

Kyle folded his arms on the table in front of him and dropped his head into the crook of his right elbow. After a few moments, he raised his head and said in resignation, "I'll waive my right to the extradition hearing if you drop the charge for selling to the Canadians."

"Good decision, Mr. Summers. I'll send the paperwork," said the prosecutor as he signed off. Kyle's lawyer took his leave as well, after arranging for another meeting to ensure the paperwork was in order and signed.

As Kyle got up to leave, Erin said, "You made a smart decision."

"I made the only decision I could after the government passed an unconstitutional law, then stole my means to defend myself against it. You've done your job, Special Agent. Now get out of my life for good." He knocked on the door and was led back to his cell.

Looking forlorn, she went to a hotel to await her flight to Vancouver the next morning.

Kyle was transported to Chicago by two heavily armed FBI agents two days later.

CHAPTER ELEVEN

Pre-Trial

Special Agent McAdams was given two weeks to recuperate before being assigned her next case. Without telling her boss, Erin went to see the prisoner. The thought that Kyle hated her for doing her job distressed her. She had no idea how she would change his mind, but she had to try.

When the guard brought him into the room he gave her such an irate glare that the guard stayed between the two. Kyle had just learned that the government was charging him separately for the sales of the computers to China and Colombia, which would double the amount of time he was facing, and he was furious with her. She apologized, saying she had no idea they would do that, but he told her he'd never forgive her.

The IRS had also issued Qubit Inc. a demand for payment of over two million dollars for taxes related to the Canadian sale. Qubit's accounts had been seized as proceeds from a criminal act, so it was forced to declare bankruptcy. As the most obvious representative of the government that destroyed his firm, she felt his wrath for that act as well.

"Never come near me again!" he warned as she left, depressed.

*

Kyle petitioned for help from the American Civil Liberties Union and the Electronic Frontier Foundation. Both declined to represent him. He was left to rely on a public defender.

When Helena Csonka first walked into the room, Kyle sighed and fought a natural reaction to frown; he forced a feeble smile. Before she uttered a word, Kyle had inwardly cursed and surrendered to his lousy fate.

Afflicted with polio as a toddler, she walked with a cane. She was barely five feet tall and maybe ninety-five pounds; she wore an ugly yellow pantsuit, and an uglier brown face. She saw his disquietude, and knowing the first impression she made was often uninspiring, the black, disabled woman jested, "Don't worry, I'm three tokens in one, so judges never dare rule against me." That spawned a natural smile from the defendant.

Her father had been an engineering student who fought the communists during the Hungarian revolt, but was forced to flee for his life when the Soviets invaded. Not knowing a word of English and without a cent in his pocket, he ended up in Chicago in 1957. The Hungarian community there helped him get on his feet, but it was a young black woman who took pity on him and helped him through the darkest days. They fell in love and married—despite many warnings against it—and had a baby girl.

"I'm Helena Csonka," she continued, as she sat across a small table from him and laid her cane on the table. They shook hands as Kyle introduced himself. Helena continued, "I'm an Assistant Federal Public Defender. I got a call from Special Agent Erin McAdams, which surprised me, because last year I tried to crucify her in court. She held her own, but I would've thought she'd hate me. But she told me she respected my tenacity and talent, and since I seldom get compliments from the FBI she had me right there before she even asked her favor.

"She suggested off the record that I ought to defend you rather than assign your case to one of my staff, which is a highly irregular occurrence for an FBI agent. Either she thinks very highly of you or very poorly of the case against you—or both.

"Anyway, I looked into the particulars of your case, and I must say I'm outraged at how the government has treated one of its citizens on the most flimsy of circumstantial evidence." That brought another smile to his face and hope back to his heart. He liked her authoritative tone of voice and confident manner. "So, Mr. Summers, I'll be defending you as long as you agree to be utterly straight with me."

"I'll be completely honest."

"Start from the beginning: tell me about the computer, how you invented it and what it can do; tell me how the government reacted, and how you reacted in turn; tell me about why you fled, and what happened while you were a fugitive; tell me what you've admitted to, and what the prosecutor promised in return. Tell me everything that has happened from the time the government passed the unconstitutional law against your firm to the minute we met."

Kyle regaled her with the entire story. "So what are my chances?" he asked once he'd finished.

"Sounds like they have nothing solid linking you to the sale of the computers to China, Colombia, or Israel. It's all circumstantial. But I'll need to verify that. Once you're indicted, I'll get the evidence they have against you including the little film you made."

"Will I get indicted? What about this grand jury business? The prosecutor told me it was set up to guard American citizens from unfair prosecutions, and that it couldn't decide guilt or innocence—only whether to indict. If we win there, he told me, the case won't even come to trial."

"There is no *we* at the grand jury, only you and the prosecutor. Originally it was set up to protect citizens from government excess, but today grand juries are the puppets of federal prosecutors. The only evidence it hears is presented by the prosecution, which tends to be damaging to defendants. You have no right to present evidence, and no right to defense counsel. You're not permitted to hear the testimony of witnesses against you—you can't even testify in your own defense. And everything is held in secret, so there are no protections against abuses.

"There's usually not even a judge present, so the prosecutor wields complete power. He can withhold evidence that works against his case and use evidence that a court would never allow, even hearsay and rumor. He can even compel witnesses to testify against their will, thereby emasculating the Fifth

Amendment. And he can choose a biased jury. With the deck thoroughly stacked, the grand jury votes to indict in virtually every case."

"But that's still not a guilty verdict, and there's a chance I won't be charged, isn't there?"

"A trivial chance weighed against the damage a grand jury decision to indict can inflict on your case. It also stretches out the time you'll languish here, waiting for the inevitable decision. I strongly advise you to waive grand jury proceedings and agree to be prosecuted by a written charge of crime."

Exasperated once again, he said, "I've been giving in time and again against all these incredible injustices. I need to stop retreating and make a stand somewhere."

"Make your stand in court where I can defend you."

He ran his hand through his hair and said, "All right. Dammit, I swear, our justice system is no better than you'd find in an African dictatorship."

"I'm sure you'll change your mind on that after you're found innocent. Your hearing is tomorrow. We'll plead not guilty on both counts and ask for bail, but don't get your hopes up. The prosecution will be asking for you to be held without remand, and since you ran once, they'll almost certainly get it."

"So I'm stuck in jail at least until the trial is over." Helena nodded. "And when will the trial start? I have a right to a speedy trial, or is that, too, an illusion?"

"Within sixty days, although if the defense requires more time, the defendant can waive—"

"No more waiving. I'm in jail for inventing a computer, and it's so goddamn unfair I just want to scream!" He got up, took his chair, and flung it against the wall. Helena sat there unfazed; she'd apparently seen it all. "I'm sorry," he continued, "but this place has lost a lot of its charm." He managed a halfhearted smile, but only briefly. "I've been destroyed by the government, and every second I spend in here, I get more angry. I swear to God if they find me guilty for something I didn't do, I'll earn my fucking sentence when—"

"Command your temper, Mr. Summers. Don't start making threats that can be recorded. Keep your head, and we'll get through this. I know you believe a guilty verdict is a foregone conclusion, but let me assure you, you're wrong. They cannot deny you a fair trial. Believe me when I say their case is weak. We can win it, but you need to stay cool and follow my advice." He nodded. Helena proceeded, "Tell me, is she in love with you?"

"Amy?"

"No, Erin."

"Erin? Of course not."

"She's acting like a woman in love. Did she say anything to you that might indicate her feelings toward you?"

"One minute she seems all concerned about me, and the next she throws me in jail. She saves my life, then shoots me, then saves my life again. She tells me she admires me, then tells me what a loser I am. I hope the hell that isn't love."

"Well, she definitely has strong feelings for you, so she'll pull her punches. We can use that for your advantage."

"Good."

"One more thing: apparently Amy Janssen has disappeared."

"What do you mean? Do they think she was killed?" he asked with concern.

"Do you still love that woman?" Helena asked. Kyle looked down, embarrassed about his feelings for the woman who betrayed him. "You really are a glutton for punishment. The police have evidence she skipped the country. She flew to Mexico and probably went into South America."

"If she ran, that should help my case, shouldn't it?"

"We'll say it suggests her guilt, but the prosecutor will counter that she probably feared for her life after Hugel was shot and all the attempts against you. The prosecution still has her statement against you, but I'm certain I can get that excluded, since we won't get the opportunity to confront her regarding the out-of-court statement. I have to go. See you tomorrow." She left.

*

At the hearing the next day, bail was denied, and the out-of-court statement was excluded.

The prosecution next asked the judge for a media blackout of the trial, but the defense balked. It required another hearing before the judge, which took place early the next week.

"All right. Make your case, Mr. Feinstein," said the judge.

"Your Honor, it is imperative that this trial be held in camera, because it will bring to light the operations of our CIA and DEA agents in the field. Considerable damage has been done to both services already by Qubit Inc."

"That has not been proven," pointed out Helena.

Mr. Feinstein continued, "As we know, the intelligence community requires a high degree of secrecy to be effective. The last thing we need is to shine a spotlight on what our agents are doing in foreign states. Too many uncomfortable facts will be aired in this trial, facts that we do not want shared with potential enemies of this country."

"Ms Csonka."

"Your Honor, that is a smokescreen. The real reason the government wants to hold the trial in secret is because the legislators are terrified that their unconstitutional laws will be spotlighted by the media and because the petty bureaucrats are terrified that their outrageous actions against an American citizen will become known to the public. Those are the uncomfortable facts they're worried about. They don't want their hands tied by the Constitution, and they know that this case may well lead to that if it comes to the attention of the public. Don't let them get away with it, Your Honor."

The judge considered for a moment and ruled: "I'm persuaded that the needs of our intelligence community outweigh the need of the public to hear the details of this case."

"But, Your Honor," protested Helena, "the government needs the pressure of public opinion to force it to abide by the Constitution."

"I've made my ruling, Ms Csonka. You'll get your chance to demonstrate the unconstitutionality of the laws at issue here whether or not the trial is held in public. I'm ordering a media blackout of the proceedings."

After the hearing, the prosecutor offered a deal to the defendant: twenty years in a medium-security prison in return for a guilty plea. Kyle responded, "I didn't sell those computers, so go to hell."

"You're facing two life sentences."

"What? *Life*?" He looked at Helena, and she nodded. He went on, "McAdams told me the most I would get was fifteen years. Then I find out the government is charging me separately for the sales to China and Colombia, so I thought I was facing thirty years."

Mr. Feinstein replied, "The penalty for each crime is fifteen years, except when death is involved in which case the maximum penalty is life in prison, so our offer of twenty years is incredibly generous."

"Twenty years snuggling with my cellmate Longfellow Bangbottom. How can I ever thank you? By the way, Santa Claus, where's my goddamn sled I asked for in third grade? That set of crayons was pathetic, you cheap fuck."

"Helena, this deal is off the table when I walk out."

"Then walk out."

He did and the trial was on.

CHAPTER TWELVE

The Prosecution

The judge invited John Feinstein to make his opening statement.

Mr. Feinstein began: "Good morning, Your Honor, and ladies and gentlemen of the jury. The case we will present to this court will seek to prove that the defendant, Kyle Summers, willfully sold dangerous technology to enemies of the United States, technology our enemies used to slaughter sixty-one Americans. This man invented an impressive machine, the most powerful computer in the world, a computer that can break any secret passcode, including those protecting your bank accounts and those protecting our country's most vital secrets.

"Imagine the damage our enemies could do to us with such a machine. Imagine, for example, if they used the computer to identify our agents within their country—and anywhere else, for that matter. Imagine the damage that would do to our intelligence efforts, and imagine what that would mean for our agents. The American government was so concerned about this possibility, it outlawed the technology until its impact on our security and economy could be established ...

"Unfortunately, the fearful scenario I asked you to imagine became all too real this past April. Twenty-eight CIA agents in China, ten more in other countries who were studying Chinese activities, and nine DEA agents in Colombia were murdered on two bloody days—April sixth and seventh. As if this weren't disastrous enough, fourteen wives and children of the DEA agents were murdered as well, many in front of our agents before they were killed.

"This massacre occurred just days after the defendant's firm, Qubit Inc., defied Congress and began selling its computers. We will show that five computers were sold, one of which found its way to China and another to Colombia. No coincidence there. Heaven knows what else they now know about us that they will use against us whenever they please.

"It's a nightmare scenario, ladies and gentlemen, and we intend to prove that Kyle Summers is responsible for it. As the inventor of the machine, Mr. Summers knew what it was capable of; he knew selling his computer to our enemies invited disaster ...

"The CIA and DEA had to shut down their networks to protect against further incursions, and expend thousands of man-hours and millions of dollars to learn what top-secret information was compromised. Today, many weeks after the cyber attacks, CIA and DEA internal computer networks remain offline, with no links whatever permitted to the Internet, not even email. The DEA has had to pull all their other operatives out of Colombia to protect their lives.

"And it gets much worse: the CIA data files breached included the names of all CIA operatives throughout the Far East. We've had to withdraw *all* of them. We currently have no intelligence-gathering capability on the ground anywhere east of India. You can well imagine how much that hinders the ability of these critical agencies to protect our interests and to fight terrorism ...

"Why do we believe Kyle Summers is the guilty party? Undercover FBI agents went into Qubit and quickly identified him as suspect number one. They found millions of dollars in his personal bank account. Jill, can you pull up Exhibit 17? As the highlighted section shows, this three million dollar account belonged to Kyle Summers. It was opened March 27, 2008, just three days before the intrusion into top-secret CIA and DEA computer files.

"By the way, Mr. Summers used his computer to erase this evidence after we established its existence. We'll play a tape where Mr. Summers shows how he did this. The FBI also heard his business partner accuse him of the crime. And, ladies and gentlemen, Mr. Summers fled to Alaska when he learned he was under suspicion.

"You will be asked to determine if these are the actions of a guilty man.

"Jill, Exhibit 6, please." The exhibit outlined the charges against the defendant.

Exhibit 6

Formal charge: *Federal crime of terrorism.* U.S. Code Title 18, Section 2332b(g)(5) defines the federal crime of terrorism as an offense that is calculated to influence or affect the conduct of government by intimidation or coercion; offenses stipulated include the killing or attempted killing of officers and employees of the United States.

	U.S. Code Title 18	
Section of code:	2339A	2339B
Charge:	Providing material support to terrorists	Providing material support or resources to designated foreign terrorist organizations
As clarified under Section 6603 of the Intelligence Reform and Terrorism Prevention Act of 2004, "material support" includes:	Providing expert advice or assistance and other physical assets to terrorists	Providing expert advice or assistance and other physical assets to terrorist organizations
As amended by Section 805 of the USA Patriot Act:	Covers assistance rendered for the commission of murder of federal officers or employees (18 U.S.C. 1114)	Covers assistance rendered for the commission of murder of federal officers or employees (18 U.S.C. 1114)
Specifically:	Provision of a quantum computer to the Chinese qualifies as a physical asset; setting up the computer qualifies as expert assistance	Provision of a quantum computer to the Autodefensas Unidas de Colombia (AUC) qualifies as a physical asset; setting up the computer qualifies as expert assistance
Consequences of the crime:	38 CIA agents murdered	9 DEA agents murdered along with 4 spouses and 10 children
Maximum penalty:	Life in prison when death is involved	Life in prison when death is involved

"Mr. Summers is formally charged with the federal crime of terrorism, specifically violations of U.S. Code Title 18, Section 2339A—providing material support to terrorists, and Section 2339B—providing material support or resources to designated foreign terrorist organizations. Material support or resources to terrorists includes about two dozen categories, but this case will focus on two: expert advice or assistance and other physical assets.

"We will show that the provision of a quantum computer to the Chinese qualifies as a physical asset, and that setting up the computer qualifies as expert assistance. The defense will doubtless argue that the Chinese are not terrorists, but as the definition at the top of the exhibit shows, the killing or attempted killing of officers and employees of the United States fits under the definition of the federal crime of terrorism. The maximum penalty is life in prison when death is involved. We are seeking the maximum sentence.

"The other charge, violating Section 2339B, carries the same penalty when people die, and again we are seeking the maximum. The organization that carried out the murders has been identified at the Autodefensas Unidas de Colombia, a terrorist paramilitary organization that protects cartel drug routes, drug laboratories, and cartel members and associates. The U.S. State Department includes the AUC on its list of forty-two foreign terrorist organizations. It is critical to point out that the government does *not* have to prove an intention on the part of the accused to commit this crime, only that the accused contributed to a terrorist act.

"During the trial, we will call on twenty-four witnesses, including leading experts, to make a compelling case for conviction. We will call Dr. David Drotch, a leader in the field of quantum computing and a professor at MIT, to introduce you to the key concepts you'll need to know for this case. Then you will hear from Dr. George Sykes, one of the nation's foremost experts on supercomputing technology.

"At this trial, you'll no doubt hear the defense claim that other means could have been used to identify our agents, but Dr. Sykes will demonstrate beyond any doubt that only the Qubit computer could have wreaked this havoc. You will also hear from Tina Daley of the CIA, who will list the names of the agents slaughtered, and tell you what their loss means to this country and to their families. Javier Tavares will list the names of the DEA agents, spouses, and children killed in Colombia, and tell you what damage has been done to our effort to keep illegal drugs out of our country. We will hear from the wives of two of the dead operatives.

"And, finally, you'll hear from Special Agent Erin McAdams of the FBI who led the field investigation, pursued Mr. Summers to Alaska, and returned him to face justice.

"The evidence I just summarized, and much more that you'll hear during the course of the trial, will demonstrate that Mr. Summers's computer caused the disaster, and that he sold the computers to those who perpetrated the murders. At trial's end, I will request you find the defendant guilty as charged on both counts. Thank you."

The judge thanked the prosecutor and invited the defense to open.

Ms Csonka stood, thanked the judge and jury, and began her statement. "I'm pleased to be here on behalf of my client today for two important reasons. First, as we will prove, Mr.

Summers is innocent of the charges against him, so I am here to prevent a grave miscarriage of justice.

"Second, and with apologies to my client, I'm here for an even more important reason: to do what I can to stop our security establishment from running roughshod over the rights that the Constitution is supposed to guarantee each and every one of us. I'm confident that as you hear what the government has done to this young man, your blood will run cold, you'll shudder to think it can happen in your country, and you'll worry that you or your loved ones could be next.

"As we just heard, the government will be relating a litany of woes, even to the extent of subjecting you to the misery of those who lost loved ones to play on your sympathies. We all grieve for them and respect their sacrifice, but we will prove that Mr. Summers is in no way responsible for these calamities. He built a computer, the most impressive one ever built. We are happy to concede this point.

"But the government must meet a higher standard for you to convict Mr. Summers. It has to show that the Chinese and Colombians are in possession of his computers, and that Mr. Summers sold the computers to the perpetrators. I trust you see the irony that this higher standard is itself atrociously low, yet even at that we will show the government's case fails to meet that low standard.

"We will explore this concept in depth: how can the act of selling a computer constitute terrorism? I will make a strong case that the law itself is unconstitutional because it disregards the critical notion of any intent to commit the ultimate crime.

"Why did the government decide to charge my client under two sections of Title 18? It is not just because it is mean-spirited. It has to do with the low standard of proof, as I mentioned at the outset. This gets a bit complicated, so please refer to the prosecution's Exhibit 6 when you need to.

"The government of China is not a terrorist organization, so Section 2239B could not apply, but the Chinese government can perpetrate a terrorist act under our incredibly broad definition of terrorism, so Section 2239A could apply. On the other hand, the AUC is a terrorist organization as defined by our government, so 2239B can apply. But so can 2239A. Certainly the AUC can carry out terrorist activities.

"So why bother bringing in another statute? Because the government has a much easier task in prosecuting my client under Section 2239B. Why is that? Because, as Mr. Feinstein admitted, it doesn't have to prove any intention to commit terrorism to label someone a terrorist. That is truly terrifying, ladies and gentlemen. Did you know that if you sell something to the AUC, you are a terrorist? I mean, what isn't a physical asset? So if you sell a car, an outhouse, a light bulb to the AUC, you are a terrorist. If you didn't know the AUC was a terrorist organization, too bad. As long as you know they have committed violent acts, you are a terrorist; the government doesn't have to prove any intent to further terrorist activity.

"If someone sold the Qubit computers to the Chinese government and to the AUC, that is an irresponsible act to be sure, but to define this as terrorism defies reason. If we let the government get away with this, we better expand our prisons a thousand-fold, because anyone who builds anything that could be of use to terrorists will soon find themselves behind bars. You may think this is hyperbole, but I assure you, by the end of the trial, you'll believe your government capable of any madness when it comes to fighting terrorism.

"In conclusion, I submit that we will prove my client is innocent, and that he has been caught in the post 9-11 mania that seems to have convinced our security establishment that they can get away with anything they please in the name of national security. You'll be privileged to send them a clear message that destroying our Constitution and Bill of Rights is not acceptable! You'll be able to brag to your grandchildren about your service to your country in delivering this message. Thank you."

With the opening statements completed, the prosecution was invited to call its first witness. Mr. Feinstein called Dr. Drotch and established his credentials. Answering a series of questions posed by Mr. Feinstein and with the aid of over a dozen exhibits, Dr. Drotch outlined the basics of how a quantum computer worked.

Helena asked Kyle to whisper to her whenever the expert made a mistake, but he kept the presentation at such a general level that Kyle could pick out no specific miscues. During cross-examination, she asked Dr. Drotch only three questions: "How would you characterize the breakthrough that Mr. Summers made in inventing the computer?"

"I haven't been fortunate enough to use the computer, but from what I understand, it's remarkable."

"Remarkable. MIT must have access to some of the best minds in the world in this field." The man nodded. "Have your world leading experts at MIT come anywhere close to the Qubit computer?"

"Again, I haven't used the Qubit computer, but we remain a long way from producing a working quantum computer."

"What do you think of the government's decision to shut down this remarkable technology?"

Before the witness could answer, the prosecutor had objected that the doctor's opinion in this matter was immaterial to the case. The objection was sustained.

The prosecution went on to call Dr. Sykes. The witness contrasted the capabilities of the leading supercomputers with those of the Qubit quantum computer, and concluded it was like "comparing the first airplane to the space shuttle." Following the lead of the prosecutor he extended the metaphor to conclude, "Breaking into the CIA computer is a challenge akin to sending an astronaut into orbit and you can't do that with the Wright brothers' plane. It is clear that only a quantum computer could do this."

During cross examination, Ms Csonka asked Dr. Sykes if he could state with certainty that the Chinese hadn't developed their own quantum computer, and he conceded he could not. During redirect, he stated it was "highly unlikely the Chinese had developed the technology and virtually impossible that the Colombians did, especially at exactly the same time."

The prosecution's next witness, Mr. Ying, was a computer expert from the FBI who had been using for the past several weeks one of the computers confiscated from Qubit. Using a series of exhibits, he illustrated how the Chinese and Colombians would have used the technology to break into top-secret government files. Mr. Feinstein asked him what specific training he had for operating a quantum computer, and the agent answered, "None. Anyone with basic training in computer programming can operate the computer."

During cross-examination, Ms Csonka focused on the unconstitutionality of Section 806 and the expert advice and assistance clause of Section 805. She began, "Where did you get the Qubit computer, Mr. Ying?"

"It was one of the computers seized from Qubit."

"Seized? And how many computers did the FBI confiscate from my client's company?"

"I believe it was thirty."

"At five million dollars apiece, that's one hundred and fifty million dollars. By the way, company records show the FBI actually took thirty-one computers, including one from Mr. Summers's apartment, and components for two more. But let's not split hairs, it's only an extra fifteen million. Tell me, Mr. Ying, is it government policy to use the assets it has seized from American firms?"

The prosecutor objected, but the court overruled him, and directed the witness to answer.

"I don't know the official policy."

"How many Qubit computers is the government using?"

"I don't know."

"For what reasons is it using the computers?"

"I'm sorry. I don't know."

"Maybe to foil terrorists plots?"

"Objection! Calls for speculation."

"Withdrawn. When the government needs jets, does it steal them from Boeing?" Before Mr. Feinstein could object, Ms Csonka said, "Rhetorical, Your Honor."

"Keep your rhetoric to a minimum, Ms Csonka," suggested the judge.

"Do you know this, Mr. Ying? Was the real reason for seizing the computers to drive this fledgling company out of business because of the threat it represented to established computer conglomerates?"

"Objection, Your Honor!" shouted Mr. Feinstein. "This is beyond the scope of the direct. This case is not about the seizure of Qubit computers, it is about the sale of Qubit computers. The sale caused the seizure, not the other way around."

"Sustained," said the judge. "Keep your focus on this case, Ms Csonka," he warned.

"Your Honor," protested Ms Csonka, "the government precipitated this ungodly mess when it decided to label the computer as illegal. It doomed the firm with its seizure of Qubit assets, and deprived my client of any means with which to defend himself by freezing company bank accounts and driving it out of business. This case is all about arbitrary government decisions, and I need to be able to cite them at this trial."

"Why don't we consider your points on a case by case basis, then? There'll be no blanket prohibition against discussing government decisions regarding the company or the defendant."

Ms Csonka thanked the judge, and proceeded to Section 805. "What assistance would the computer's seller have to render to get the computer up and running?"

"It requires special engineering expertise and equipment to set it up," answered Mr. Ying.

"And did anyone from Qubit show you how to install it?"

"No."

"You figured it out?"

"Well, there is a detailed installation guide included with the computer. My colleagues and I were able to use that to figure it out."

"Do you suppose the Chinese or Colombians would also be able to figure this out?"

"Objection," interrupted Mr. Feinstein. "Calls for speculation."

"Sustained."

"Is it possible that only the FBI could figure out how to set this computer up with the help of the installation manual?"

"As I said, it requires high-level computer engineering expertise."

"You didn't answer my question, Mr. Ying. Has the FBI cornered the market on this expertise?"

"It's possible that others with the expertise can set this up on their own."

"Thank you. Tell me, Mr. Ying, does merely providing an installation manual qualify as expert advice or assistance under Section 805 of the Patriot Act?"

"Objection! Insufficient foundation, Your Honor."

"Sustained."

Ms Csonka spotlighted Section 806 in cross-examining Agent Ebbling, focusing on the nature of the authority for seizing the computers and information pertaining to the technology.

"Agent Ebbling, by what authority did the FBI seize the Qubit computers?"

"Section 806 of the Patriot Act authorizes the government to seize and forfeit all assets of any individual or organization engaged in terrorism against the United States."

"And how did the FBI classify Qubit as a terrorist organization?"

"The CIA and DEA detected intrusions into their top-secret files, and a few days later their agents started disappearing. Their computer people said it had to be the quantum computer, so we went to seize the rest of the computers before any others got to our enemies."

"That doesn't answer my question. How does selling a computer constitute terrorism?"

"I believe I just answered that."

"Agents disappeared, and it had to be the quantum computer. That's enough to make Mr. Summers a terrorist? Am I missing something here?"

"If he didn't sell those computers, our agents would be alive."

"Your Honor."

"The jury will ignore that last statement. After all the evidence is in, you will make your own assessment."

"Thank you, Your Honor." Turning back to Agent Ebbling, Helena went on, "I recall reading in the paper a couple of years back that someone went nuts and deliberately ran down two people at a bus stop. He killed a woman who worked for Health and Human Services. He drove a Buick. If GM hadn't built and sold that car, that poor federal employee might be alive—unless the crazy man used another car. Tell me, Agent Ebbling, should the FBI seize all assets of GM?"

"Objection, Your Honor—"

"Withdrawn. I mean there would actually be more of a justification to seize GM's assets than to seize Qubit's assets, because surely the computer itself wasn't used to perpetrate the killings. What I'm asking is what standard did you use to condemn whoever might have sold technology to these terrorists, for how could they possibly know how a buyer was going to use their technology? How can the government possibly hold manufacturers responsible for the uses to which customers put their products? You must see what a slippery slope this is. Yet you ignored this thorny problem and proceeded on the basis of … On what basis, Agent Ebbling? What proof did you have it was the Qubit computers?"

"The computer people said–"

"Hearsay. Someone said it was Qubit and it became gospel. Is the mere assertion that a Qubit computer was involved in terrorism enough to take all the company's assets?"

"We had probable cause—"

"You ruined maybe the most promising new company this country has seen in a generation based on probable cause? Without any solid evidence, you drove them out of business. Did you give the company a chance to defend itself before seizing its assets?"

"The computer is obviously dangerous."

"I'll take that as a no. Does the FBI intend to keep the one hundred and sixty-five million dollars worth of computers it seized?"

"Forfeiture is standard."

"Have you declared forfeiture yet?"

"Not to my knowledge."

"Why not?"

"That's not my business. I'm just a field agent."

"Could it be because the intention all along was to drive Qubit out of business?"

As the prosecutor started to object, Agent Ebbling yelled, "I hope so! That scuzzbag got forty-seven of our agents slaughtered!"

"So, Agent Ebbling," said Ms Csonka while looking at the jury, "we see the standard of proof that the government requires. Someone points a finger at someone else, and you take them down without a shred of proof, without notice, without a hearing."

"I'm not a lawyer; I simply followed orders."

"And why did you arrest Mr. Summers?" she asked.

"Because he was resisting the orders."

"Resisting the seizure of one hundred and sixty-five million dollars worth of his company's product that left the company with nothing? Resisting the seizure of proprietary information on how to produce the computer? Resisting the seizure of high tech machinery to build the computers? Resisting the government's gag order because the FBI typed up a letter? How completely unreasonable of him," she said to the chuckling of some of the jury.

The judge pounded his gavel, and the prosecutor objected that the counsel was giving her personal opinion, which the judge sustained.

The prosecutor had called the witness to demonstrate to the jury that the defendant was livid enough to strike out at his country, and he succeeded in conveying this, but he was uncomfortable with Ms Csonka's Big Brother insinuations that were resonating with the jury. He was also worried about his star witness, Special Agent Erin McAdams, who, during coaching, had betrayed a marked predilection for the defendant. She needed more coaching, but she was wrapping up a case that had taken her to Florida. He remonstrated with the FBI, but was told her case was at a critical juncture and she could not be withdrawn at present. She would present herself to him as soon as practicable.

The case seemed to be favoring the defense early on, but the tide was about to turn.

*

The next day, the prosecution set about to portray the damage done to the country's security and to the individuals involved in the mass execution. First, high-level officials with the CIA and DEA argued that America's intelligence efforts in China and Colombia had been dealt a serious blow, which rendered the country more exposed at a very dangerous point in its history.

One example of potentially calamitous consequences involved the loss of an agent in China who was keeping close tabs on the sale of missile technology to the Iranians. "Our agent was inside the Chinese defense bureaucracy and was making a strong case against the sale, but now he's dead, and the sale will almost certainly go through. That makes Israel much more vulnerable to attack, and Iran a much more significant threat to our interests." In conclusion, he predicted, "It will take decades to rebuild our assets in those areas of the world."

The defense took issue with the government's failure to protect its top-secret computer files against attack from the new technology. Ms Csonka asked the witness to read a highlighted passage in Exhibit 59, which was a submission from Qubit Inc. to the Congressional panel that had heard the case to stop the sale of quantum computers.

The CIA witness read, "Quantum computers can theoretically render the current measures used to protect top-secret government files ineffective, but there are measures the government can take to protect its information. The following pages advance three methods that should prove effective in protecting sensitive computerized information."

"This document was provided to the U.S. government five months before the CIA files were breached," said Ms Csonka. "Tell us which if any of the suggested measures the CIA used to protect its information."

"None that I know of," conceded the witness.

"Why not? You knew how vulnerable your computers were to this new technology."

"Because the technology was not supposed to be out there."

"The genie was out of the bottle; that made it inevitable. Wasn't the sensible course to take immediate steps to protect your information from intrusion?"

"We were in the early stages of considering the issue."

"Committees, meetings, studies, but no action, and all the while you remained vulnerable." With that Ms Csonka was through with the witness.

As the prosecutor promised, the CIA and DEA representatives read out the names of the forty-seven agents killed and the fourteen family members butchered. The weeping wives of a CIA agent and DEA agent aptly demonstrated the personal dimension of the case. The CIA agent's wife related how her husband was murdered as he was phoning her to tell her he was discovered, and wanted to say his final goodbye. Emotional as it was, that was nothing compared to the account from the DEA agent's wife.

"Mrs. Gutierrez, thank you for being here. I know how difficult this must be for you," opened the prosecutor. "You lost your husband and daughter in this tragedy?"

"Yes," said the somber widow.

Mr. Feinstein turned to the jury to inform them, "Gilberto Gutierrez was working undercover for a Colombian drug lord named Miguel Flores. For four long years, he risked his life working undercover for our country. He had worked his way into the inner circle of the drug cartel and had been passing invaluable intelligence to the DEA. Last year, he was responsible for alerting the DEA about a shipment of nearly a ton of cocaine; the shipment was intercepted in the Gulf of Mexico and six drug smugglers were arrested. Earlier this year, Mr. Gutierrez tipped off the DEA that Flores's right-hand man had entered the United States under an assumed name. He was arrested and is now serving a twenty-five year sentence.

"But there'll be no more coups for Mr. Gutierrez, and the drug cartel can almost rest assured that its shipments and its kingpins will be safe, because Gilberto Gutierrez and many of his DEA colleagues were murdered last April. Mrs. Gutierrez, please tell the jury what happened on the evening of April seventh this year."

"Um," she began as her tears stirred. "We were cleaning up the kitchen after supper, and the phone rang. My husband answered it and he looked terrified. He dropped the phone and ran to the window to look outside. I asked what was wrong. He said, 'Get the children; we have to get out now!' I screamed for the children to come, but only Andres came."

"Your seven-year-old son?"

"Yes. Then my husband screams, 'Too late! They're here. Hide in the closet behind the clothes!' I was too shocked to move, so Gilberto took me and Andres to the closet and shut the door. He ran to get Christina—"

"Your twelve-year-old daughter."

"Yes. By the time he got her, the men had kicked open the front door and come in our house. I couldn't see anything, but I heard them yelling at my husband. I got behind the clothes in the closet and pulled my son back and covered his mouth. Then there was a gun shot, and my daughter screamed. My heart fell to my stomach, and I started to cry and shake.

"Then one of the men starts to search the house for me and my son. They opened the closet, and I held my breath and closed my eyes. I squeezed my son's mouth harder to let him know to be perfectly still. By God's grace, they didn't see us, because that closet had so much clothes and toys in it. They left the door open, and I could see that my husband was ..."

Here Mrs. Gutierrez broke down crying.

"Take your time, Mrs. Gutierrez," the judge said sympathically.

She resumed: "Gilberto was on the floor with blood all over his stomach. They shot him in the stomach. He was alive, but I could see he was in great pain. While one man finished looking for us the other one held my daughter; she was screaming for her father. When he finished searching the house, the other man came back, and he punched Christina in the face.

"My husband pleaded for them not to hurt her, but they tore off her clothes." Mrs. Gutierrez again paused to weep. Several jurists were also in tears listening to her testimony. She took a breath and continued, "Then they rape my beautiful little girl in front of my crying husband; both of them rape her. I was crying so hard I had to bury my face in some clothes so they wouldn't hear me. I didn't know whether to cover my son's mouth or his eyes … He hasn't said a word since that horrible day." Again she stopped as her weeping intensified.

"Your Honor," protested Ms Csonka, "the jury obviously understands the pain this woman has suffered. Is there any need to prolong the testimony? Asking Mrs. Gutierrez to relive this horror any further is cruel."

"No!" the woman responded. "I want to finish. I want the jury to know what this man did to my family!" she yelled while pointing at Kyle.

"Your Honor!" said Ms Csonka.

"Please, Mrs. Gutierrez, try to keep to the facts," said the judge. "The jury will ignore that accusation."

"When they were finished violating my daughter, they shot her in the face. I screamed, but my husband's scream must have drowned it out, because they didn't come. Then they shot Gilberto in the testicles, then his chest, then his face.

"After they left, I stayed in the closet for a long time. I died that day too in the closet." Then she turned her wrath on Kyle, screaming, "Was your blood money worth it? Worth the lives of my daughter and husband?" As Ms Csonka rose to object, Mrs. Gutierrez finished, "Take your blood money to hell with you!" The judge admonished the woman and again directed the jury to ignore her denunciation.

Mr. Feinstein summed up for the jury, "This heartbreaking story illustrates so clearly that this trial is not about an evil government agency ignoring the Constitution to tread over its law-abiding citizens. It is about the government's obligation to do everything it can to protect its citizens from the pervasive evil in today's world. The Constitution and Bill of Rights are still in place. Your government has no intention of undermining those cornerstones of our nation. Only those intent on terrorizing our citizens or helping terrorists to do that need worry about their rights, because they have no right to hide behind the Constitution to carry out their agenda."

At this point Ms Csonka rose to ask the judge, "Is there a question coming at the end of this speech?"

"Save it for closing," said the judge.

The defense had no questions of the witness, wanting her off the stand right away. Two mothers were next in line, but Ms Csonka objected that enough was enough, and the judge agreed. They were sent home without testifying.

Exhibits showing pictures of all sixty-one victims elicited more tears from the jury, particularly when the slide of the sweet, smiling three-year-old daughter of one of the slain DEA agents was shown. The next slide, which showed her with half her head blown away, educed gasps and shrieks. Observing the emotional reactions in the jury, Helena knew that the "parade of victims," as she privately characterized it, had done serious damage to her case.

During cross-examination, she sympathized, but pointed out that the prosecution had not proven conclusively that the

Chinese or Colombians had the computers and that the defendant had sold the computers. Then she asked Javier Tavares of the DEA, "What gun was used to kill the little girl?"

"I'm not sure," he responded. "What difference does it make?"

"So the gun that actually killed her makes no difference, but the computer that may have identified her father as an agent made all the difference?" Mr. Tavares shrugged. "I presume then that there is no court case against the gun manufacturer?"

"No."

"What about the owners and designers of the web hosting service that the AUC used as a platform to break into the DEA computer?"

"You're being ridiculous."

"Yes, I am; every bit as ridiculous as holding a computer designer responsible for this reprehensible crime. Is the person who pulled the trigger on trial?"

"We don't know who pulled the trigger."

"Is the person who ordered the killings on trial?"

"That investigation is underway."

"Sounds like our government needed someone to pin this on, so it chose the only one it could get its hands on."

"Your Honor!" Mr. Feinstein interrupted. "Counsel is arguing her case."

"Sustained. It's the jury's job to draw conclusions," said the judge.

Helena left it at that. She felt she minimized the damage, but knew the prosecution had scored points with the jury.

The final witness for the prosecution was Special Agent Erin McAdams. Away on another case, this was the first time she had been present in the courtroom for this case. The Summers case had had to break for three days until Agent McAdams could testify, since her other case was at a critical juncture. She had just concluded that case by arresting the suspects the evening before.

She was sworn in and introduced herself. Mr. Feinstein began, "How long had you been a field agent when you were assigned this case?"

"One and a half years."

"Why was such an inexperienced agent assigned to such an important case?"

"Well, an in-depth knowledge of computers was vital for this case, and I have a Master's in computer science. Most of our computer experts aren't in the field. Also, I'd learned a lot in my nineteen months in the field."

"I don't mean any disrespect, and I hope this doesn't sound sexist, but is it possible you were assigned this case in part because your superiors thought Dr. Hugel may be more forthcoming with an attractive woman?"

"It's possible."

"And was he forthcoming with you?"

"Once coming at least," commented Kyle audibly. Erin blushed and lowered her eyes.

"Mr. Summers, keep your snide comments to yourself," reproved the judge.

"Well, since Mr. Summers brought it up," said the prosecutor, "we'll hit the nail on the head. Agent McAdams, how did you extract Dr. Hugel's confession that Kyle Summers sold the computers to the Chinese and Colombians?"

"I sat on his lap and began to seduce him. I implied I would have sex with him."

"But you didn't have sex?"

"No, just petting."

"Did you do this to further your investigation?"

"Yes. He gave me much more information than I'd gotten from him prior to that."

"Okay, let's move on. What was the nature of your assignment?"

"There weren't supposed to be any Qubit computers on the market, but when someone broke into the top-secret computer files at the CIA and DEA, it was obvious someone had them."

"Objection, Your Honor," said Ms Csonka. "That has not been established. No one has offered conclusive proof that the Chinese or the Colombians are using the Qubit computer."

"That is a matter of judgment, Ms Csonka. I'll let the jury decide for themselves. Overruled."

"Continue, Special Agent," said Mr. Feinstein.

"My assignment was to determine who sold the computers and who to. We posed as representatives of DTC. Our cover assignment was to do the due diligence prior to making an offer to buy out Qubit Inc."

"Okay, let's go through what you and your partner learned. You were surprised to find out that two computers had, in fact, been sold to Canadian customers, correct?"

"Yes, that's right. The three owners admitted that."

"But more computers were missing?"

"We found out that thirty-six computers were built—and again the owners admitted this—but the FBI had seized only thirty. The two to the Canadians plus one we found boxed up in Mr. Summers's apartment made thirty-three. Three were missing."

"How did the owners account for the missing computers?"

"They said they'd been stolen."

"And did you believe them?"

"No. The CIA had traced the source of the leak to a computer in China; the DEA traced their leak to Colombia; I'm not privy to how the CIA determined the other computer ended up in Israel."

"So three Qubit computers were missing, and our government had evidence that three extremely advanced computers were in use in three foreign nations. Coincidence?"

"Extremely unlikely."

"You next determined that Kyle Summers was the real inventor of the machine?"

"Yes. It became obvious that Dr. Hugel had only a surface knowledge and that Mr. Summers knew far more. In fact, Mr. Summers told me he invented the computer. I wasn't sure whether to believe him, since he was drunk when he made the claim, so I confronted Ms Janssen. She admitted Mr. Summers was the genius behind the machine. And, at about the same time, Allen Levinson, my partner for this assignment, found out that Mr. Summers owned the largest share of the firm."

"Why did Qubit Inc. represent Dr. Hugel as its spokesman and lead the public to believe he was the one who invented the computer?"

"Because he had a PhD and he was well-spoken and very handsome—charismatic."

"And the true inventor, the defendant, has no PhD?"

"No."

"And is not well-spoken?"

"Well, yes, he is, but he can be very brusque."

"Charismatic?"

"Well, not really, no," she said, with a worried glance at Kyle.

"What did you do with the information that Mr. Summers was the brains behind the operation?"

"I turned my focus to Mr. Summers. He'd been very uncooperative to that point. He was so angry that the government had disallowed the firm to market the quantum computer. It was unfortunate that we chose DTC as our cover, because Mr. Summers hated them for leading the lobbying effort to stop the sale of the computer."

"He was against the sale of Qubit to DTC?"

"Adamantly, but his two partners were all for it. Kyle … excuse me, Mr. Summers immediately hated me, so I had a real uphill battle, but I could see he loved Amy Janssen and he listened to everything she told him to do, so I asked her to intervene. Otherwise DTC wouldn't buy her firm, I told her. She insisted Mr. Summers tell me everything about the computer."

"And he did?"

"Eventually. Using a regular Dell computer on his desk, he logged into the Qubit computer he had sold to the University of Toronto, and walked me through how to use it to break passwords."

"If it's that easy to log into the quantum computer remotely, doesn't that support our government's decision to delay the introduction of this computer?"

"Objection!" shouted Ms Csonka. "The witness's opinion on this matter is irrelevant, and she is not qualified to answer the question in any case."

"Sustained."

"Continue with how you identified Mr. Summers as the key suspect, Agent McAdams," said Mr. Feinstein.

"I challenged him to use his computer to find evidence that the three missing computers were sold, you know, were there large deposits in any of their names? He did this for Dr. Hugel and Ms Janssen and found nothing incriminating, but did only a perfunctory job on his own name, so when he left I used what I'd learned from him to look into his affairs, and I found an account in his name in the amount of three million dollars."

"When was it deposited?"

"March 27, 2008. Three days later, the breach of the CIA computer system occurred."

"What did you do with this information on the deposit?"

"I advised my superiors and confronted Dr. Hugel. I told him I knew the three computers were not stolen; they were, in fact, sold by at least one of the owners. He told me Kyle Summers sold the computers."

"Then what happened?" said Mr. Feinstein.

"Well, I was sitting on Dr. Hugel's lap at the time, and Ms Janssen and Mr. Summers walked in on us. Ms Janssen got wild because she was in love with Dr. Hugel—married to him, as she said at the time. I didn't know this when I was seducing him. The revelation devastated Mr. Summers, who was deeply in love with her; she had promised to marry him, in fact. A fight ensued between the men. Mr. Summers ended up threatening to kill Dr. Hugel and then he left."

"And the next morning Dr. Hugel was found murdered?"

"Yes, and Mr. Summers had fled to Alaska."

"So he was the prime suspect for both the murder and the sale of the computers?"

"Yes. I was ordered to fly to Alaska to pick him up and bring him back to Chicago."

"You had quite a time returning Mr. Summers to Chicago." Erin nodded. "There were several attempts on Mr. Summers's life, and, because you were escorting him back, several attempts on your life as well. Can you briefly tell the jury about your incredible experience?"

The jury was transfixed as Erin related the terrifying episodes on the jet, in the clinic, in the car, on the snowmobile, in the cabin, and on foot.

When she finished, Mr. Feinstein said, "Why would Mr. Summers save the life of the person bringing him back to face jail or even capital punishment?"

"It became apparent that he had a death wish. His life was in ruins, and he was facing a long prison sentence or even the death penalty. He said more than once it would be better if he was dead, so he took great risks in saving me."

Kyle leaned over to whisper to Helena, "So much for her loving me."

Helena responded, "I'm sure Feinstein coached her on that answer."

Mr. Feinstein said to Erin, "Sounds like he was certain he would be convicted."

"Yes.

"Why would an innocent man be so convinced he would be found guilty?"

Ms Csonka objected to the speculative quality of the query and it was sustained. The witness was turned over to the defense.

CHAPTER THIRTEEN

Crossing McAdams

"You and Mr. Summers went through a lot together," observed Ms Csonka. Erin nodded. "You gave a very … shall we say 'careful' reply when Mr. Feinstein asked you why Mr. Summers would save the life of the person taking him back to face these charges. Surely there was more to it than a death wish. If that's all it was, he would've simply stood still while people were shooting at him. So, Agent McAdams, why did he save you again and again?"

"Objection, Your Honor," said Mr. Feinstein. "Calls for speculation."

"Ms Csonka?" said the judge.

"Your Honor, I'm trying to establish that Mr. Summers's actions were not those of a guilty man as the prosecution implied with the witness's limited response to the very same question."

"I'll overrule the objection, but stick to the facts, Ms Csonka. The witness will answer the question."

"I'm not sure why he saved my life. I think maybe he's that kind of person."

"I'm sorry—what kind of person?"

"A good person."

That pleased Helena, who was banking on Erin's obvious regard for her client. She continued, "You think highly of him?"

"Yes."

"Yet despite this, and despite everything he did for you, you still did your job and brought him back to face the charge of terrorism?"

"I believe in what I do, and I believe in our justice system. If he's guilty, he has to pay for his crime; if he's innocent, he'll go free. It was not my right to make that determination, no matter what he did for me and no matter what I think of him. Still, it was the hardest thing I've ever had to do."

"Okay, I want to explore with you a few of your presumptions about this case. As I understand it from your testimony, your case against Mr. Summers rests on four pillars: the accusation of Dr. Hugel, the money in Mr. Summers's account, his frame of mind at the time, and his flight. Let's consider the first pillar. Dr. Hugel accused him outright of selling the computers. Tell me, Special Agent McAdams, do you believe a guilty man will lie to frame someone else and thereby remove suspicion from himself?"

"Of course."

"Would a man lie to get sex from a pretty woman?"

"Of course."

"You're sure you didn't focus on Mr. Summers as a suspect because you were physically attracted to another obvious suspect?"

"I had no preconceptions based on the looks of the suspects."

"Do you think if you instead chose Mr. Summers for your special interrogation and he pointed to Dr. Hugel that you would have believed him?"

"I didn't find three million dollars in his account."

"Let's skip to that. You had by then observed Mr. Summers as he broke into the accounts of Ms Janssen and Dr. Hugel. You saw how easy it was with the Qubit computer. Isn't it possible that either one or both of his partners put that money into his account?"

"Well, yes, but at the time I had just witnessed Mr. Summers delving into their accounts and turning up nothing—in effect exonerating them, as far as I was concerned, and when I did the same with his accounts I found the three million dollars."

"But to frame him, isn't that exactly what his partners would do? Put the three million in an easy to find place?"

"Objection, the question is leading," interrupted the prosecutor.

"Sustained. Rephrase, Ms Csonka," ordered the judge.

"Is it possible the three million dollar account was set up by someone other than Mr. Summers?"

"Yes."

"Mr. Summers must be brilliant to have invented his computer."

"Yes."

"Would a brilliant man be stupid enough to leave that account where anyone could find it?"

"Calls for improper opinion, Your Honor. The witness has no basis to answer that question," said Mr. Feinstein.

"Sustained. The jury will answer that question when it renders its verdict."

"So much for two pillars …"

In response to the prosecutor's objection, the judge said, "The jury will ignore defense counsel's personal opinions, and counsel will refrain from making them."

"Let's turn to the third pillar. Mr. Summers's frame of mind. How did you expect him to feel after he toiled for years, gave all his blood, sweat, and tears to invent a machine that would have changed the world and earned him billions of dollars and the hand of the woman he loved, or so he thought? How should he feel when the government issued an edict against the sale of his computer?"

"He's entitled to be angry," replied Erin.

"Angry? Isn't that a huge understatement? They took everything from him with a blatantly unconstitutional law—"

"Objection, Your Honor: assumes facts not in evidence. No court has ruled Section 806 unconstitutional," said Mr. Feinstein.

Ms Csonka said, "Of course not, he has no money to bring his case to court. The government saw to that by bankrupting the firm."

"Ms Csonka," said the judge, "I've been very patient with you thus far. You will allow me to rule on the objection before speaking."

"Sorry, Your Honor."

"I'll sustain the objection. This court cannot consider the constitutionality of that law. The jury will ignore that outburst."

"So, Agent McAdams, are you telling the court that Mr. Summers was the prime suspect in part because he was more upset than his partners were about the government's decision?"

"He seemed most motivated to defy the law."

"Could that be because the computer was his brainchild?"

"Yes."

"He stood to lose much more than his partners?"

"Yes."

"Doesn't it seem unfair to suspect him for that reason?"

"Maybe so, but—"

"You've answered the question, Special Agent. The computer was his brainchild and no one else's?"

"Yes."

"His brainchild, maybe the most impressive machine ever invented, light years beyond anything on the market. An expression of his genius, work that took a decade of his young life. He put everything he had into it. When he talks about it, you can hear the pride in his voice, almost the way a father might talk about his child prodigy. Did you pick up on that?"

"Yes."

"Why, then, would he risk something so precious to him with a reckless deal to sell computers to potential enemies of the United States?"

"Objection, Your Honor," interrupted the prosecutor. "Calls for speculation."

"Sustained. Move on, Ms Csonka," instructed the judge.

"You testified that Mr. Summers was adamantly opposed the sale of the company to DTC."

"Yes."

"As far as Mr. Summers knew, the offer DTC had on the table for Qubit was for one hundred million dollars?"

"That's right."

"He owned forty-one percent of Qubit. That means he was adamantly against parting with his brainchild even with forty-one million dollars on the table. Correct?"

"Yes."

"Did you question why Mr. Summers would settle for twenty percent of the proceeds of the sale when he owned forty-one percent of the firm?"

"Before we could consider those kinds of details, Mr. Hugel had been shot, and Mr. Summers had fled to Alaska."

"Don't you find it strange that he would make a deal that could easily risk the company, not to mention his freedom, for three million dollars?"

"Assuming he found it risky, I suppose."

"I mean, if and when he gets the go-ahead to sell the computer, he stands to make many billions of dollars. Why risk that for a few million? Rhetorical.

"Now, let's consider what his partners were risking with a sale to the Chinese and Colombians. They had no emotional investment in the technology. How could they? Neither had anything to do with inventing any part of the machine. They brought nothing to the partnership for their thirty-four percent share, did they?"

The prosecutor's objection that the question was leading was sustained. Ms Csonka proceeded. "Special Agent, do you know if Amy Janssen and Rick Hugel did anything to get their thirty-four percent of Qubit?"

"We know the reason Mr. Summers agreed to the partnership was that Dr. Hugel owned the patent for an essential piece of the quantum technology, the method for controlling decoherence."

"But didn't Mr. Summers design that method?"

"Yes, he did, in his bachelor's thesis at the University of Chicago."

"Dr. Hugel used Mr. Summers's thesis to build the component?"

"Yes. Mr. Summers assumed copyright law would protect his design, but it doesn't work like that. Dr. Hugel built the component according to Mr. Summers's specifications and patented it. He was the legal owner at the time the partnership was struck and Qubit was incorporated."

"So all Dr. Hugel and Amy Janssen brought was a component that they, shall we say, acquired from Mr. Summers without his approval and without any recompense?"

"That's my understanding."

"You mentioned that Ms Janssen was married to Dr. Hugel, but had also promised herself to Mr. Summers. Was this to dupe Mr. Summers into the partnership?"

"Yes. Even though he needed the component he designed, he was ready to design another one because he hated Dr. Hugel for, uh, acquiring his idea, so Ms Janssen promised to marry him to seal the deal."

"Fast forward two years. Mr. Summers has successfully built the world's first quantum computer, but Qubit is on the verge of bankruptcy because the government has outlawed the technology. Assuming each owner acts purely out of self-interest, what would he or she do? Mr. Summers has every interest in keeping the company alive, because what happens if the firm slips into bankruptcy?"

"From what I understand, it would be auctioned off."

"Precisely. If the company goes bankrupt, anything worth money goes up for auction, and the technology is potentially worth billions. Maybe not now, but some day. We can well imagine the auction would fetch the owners a pretty penny. Bring up Exhibit 68 please ...

"This is the first notice of an auction of the quantum computer technology to take place in two months. This ad was sent via the Internet to hundreds of potential investors by Comptech Venture Partners, twenty-five percent owners of Qubit. This is why that company didn't step in to rescue Qubit. They knew they could realize an immediate golden return on their investment. If Qubit was rescued, their investment remains locked up until the government allows the sale of quantum computers, and that could be many years—or never. But bankruptcy is the last thing Mr. Summers wants.

"With his life's work at risk, he does everything he can to keep the company afloat. What does he do?"

"Sells some computers."

"Sells two computers to the Canadians. And earns just enough to pay the creditors and keep the company afloat. Make sense?"

"Yes."

"Mr. Summers's absolute refusal to sell out to DTC is consistent with this. He is driven to keep the company alive because that keeps his computer in his hands and Amy on the hook. But what about the other owners? What is in their interest? Wouldn't it be the same as Comptech's?"

"Objection. Calls for speculation."

"Nice try, counselor," said the judge. "Sustained. Ask another question."

"When the government issued the edict against the sale of Qubit computers, Mr. Summers blamed Dr. Hugel because his job was to market the computers. His failure to stop the law doomed the small company. Mr. Summers threatened to move Qubit to Canada and deal Dr. Hugel out?"

"I believe so, yes."

"He intended to include Ms Janssen, though?"

"That should be obvious."

"But that couldn't work, could it? She was married to Dr. Hugel. When Mr. Summers found out, she would be out, too."

"Definitely."

"That would leave them with nothing—or with a messy, drawn-out court case to try to get something. So it would be in their interest if the firm went bankrupt. They'd get thirty-four percent of the proceeds from the auction?"

"I assume so," answered Erin.

"But what if Mr. Summers succeeded in rescuing the firm? Hugel and Janssen know he's in Canada delivering the computers. Where does that leave them if the firm doesn't go into bankruptcy? Owners of a firm that can't sell its product— it leaves them with no money and no prospect of any in the foreseeable future. They needed an insurance policy or they would be at great risk of ending up with nothing after four years of playing Mr. Summers to get rich off his genius. They had a lot to gain by selling those three missing computers and risked virtually nothing, as long as they could pin it on Mr. Summers."

"Objection: counsel's personal opinion," charged Mr. Feinstein. "She's drawing conclusions again."

"Sustained. Ask questions, Ms Csonka."

"To pillar four. Mr. Summers's flight from Chicago. You figured, 'He ran, so he must be guilty,' right?"

"Right."

"The defense is willing to concede that running tends to make the suspect look guilty and this might be damning evidence against my client except for two key facts: first, Mr. Summers did not murder Dr. Rick Hugel, correct?"

"Correct. He was killed by a man named Jeff Foster."

"And, second, when Mr. Summers ran, he had no idea he was under suspicion of being a terrorist. Isn't this true, Special Agent?"

"Well, his computers and machinery had been seized by the FBI, so he may have had an idea."

"Maybe if he was guilty of selling the computers to the Chinese and Colombians, he might have been able to make the huge mental leap from *the government took my computers* to *I'm a terrorist*. If he didn't sell the computers, how could a reasonable person have any clue that he would be considered a terrorist? I mean, he had no idea the FBI was snooping around."

"That's right."

"In any case, we now know that he had a good reason for fleeing. Tell us what your investigation uncovered, Special Agent."

"Four months prior to his murder, Dr. Hugel had been run off the road. The police concluded someone did it deliberately, though they have not been able to identify the perpetrator. The police theorized it was a competitor trying to do in the main competition; I know Mr. Summers was convinced of it. Mr. Summers told me that when he found Dr. Hugel murdered, he worried the same perpetrator had returned and worried he might be next. When he spotted two men watching his place that night, he thought it might be the murders after him. They were actually FBI agents."

"But you didn't know about his reason for fleeing when you set off to Alaska after him?"

"No, but our investigation was not yet completed. When he ran just after the murder, he forced our hand. When your prime suspect bolts, you go after him. It would have been irresponsible to do otherwise."

"No reasonable person would dispute your obligation to go after him. But you admitted your investigation wasn't complete at that point. You must have continued the investigation after you returned Mr. Summers to Chicago."

"No. I took two weeks to recover from my injuries, then I was assigned to a new case."

"Why was that?"

"Uh, my judgment concerning Mr. Summers was considered biased by that point."

"Because the prime suspect saved your life again and again."

"Yes."

"Were you upset by this decision?"

"Yes, but I understood it."

"So, tell us, Special Agent McAdams: what did you tell your bosses about this man upon your return to Chicago?"

"Objection, Your Honor. That is immaterial to this case," opined Mr. Feinstein.

"Your Honor," protested Ms Csonka. "Agent McAdams's professional opinion is what landed my client in hot water and still has him steeping in it."

"Overruled. Answer Agent McAdams."

"I told my boss that I found it hard to believe that a man who did what he did for me could be a terrorist, and that it was possible that Mr. Summers had been framed by his partners."

"And their reaction was to take you off the case."

"Yes."

"Did anyone else pursue the leads you had turned up while in Mr. Summers's company?"

"The FBI put a tracer on the Cayman Islands accounts and issued an arrest warrant for Ms Janssen. And there is an investigation into who ordered the assassination attempts and killed the FBI pilot."

"No investigation of my client's obvious motives against the illegal sale of his computers? No investigation of his partners' obvious motives for selling them?"

"No."

"So the FBI concluded it had its man. He ran, so he's guilty; no need for further investigation. But as we've established he did not run to get away from a charge of terrorism because he knew nothing of the FBI investigation, and thus crumbles pillar number four. Thank you, Agent McAdams. I have no further questions, Your Honor."

During re-direct, Mr. Feinstein focused on the number of computers Kyle attempted to sell. "It wasn't just a case of Mr. Summers intending to sell only enough computers to keep the firm afloat, was it, Agent McAdams?"

"No. We know he tried to complete the deals he had with twenty American customers."

"So he actually did try to get as much as he could out of the sinking ship?"

Ms Csonka's objection was overruled, and Erin was told to answer.

"It would appear so," she said.

"So, is it a great stretch to think he tried to complete three more sales overseas?"

The judge sustained Ms Csonka's objection, and the question was left unanswered.

*

When the prosecution rested, Mr. Feinstein felt he had the upper hand, because the parade of victims had had a dramatic affect on the jury, but he worried that the case could go either way since the defense had not yet begun its case. He decided to try to make a deal with the defendant. This time he offered ten years in jail.

He considered Kyle's "Fuck off" a definitive rejection.

CHAPTER FOURTEEN

The Defense

Erin hadn't had the chance to bring herself up to date on the Summers case while she was working in Florida. On Sunday afternoon, she went to her office to read the FBI file in chronological order from the time she left off, learning a few unimportant details and one startling fact: there had been a hit on one of the Cayman Islands accounts two days earlier. Two hundred thousand dollars had been transferred to six different accounts in Brazilian banks under one name: Rita Johnson. A picture of the woman was provided by one of the banks. It was Amy Janssen.

Erin went to her boss the next morning to ask what the FBI was doing with this information. She was told they asked Brazilian officials to arrest Ms Janssen, which they had done the morning before. The United States would be seeking her extradition.

"Will the government be dropping the Kyle Summers case?" she asked. That was the prosecutor's decision, she was told.

Erin went to the prosecutor and said, "Mr. Feinstein, you have irrefutable evidence that Amy Janssen sold those computers. You'll be dropping the case against Kyle Summers now?"

Mr. Feinstein smiled at the inexperienced agent. He said, "That Amy Janssen is guilty does not mean Kyle Summers isn't. They were partners, after all. Yesterday evening, Ms Janssen attested that all three owners were in on the scheme. We'll be offering Janssen a deal to testify that they were partners."

"But what if she's lying?"

"That's for the jury to decide. Why are you so concerned, anyway? I have to say, your stated high regard for Summers did little to help our case. We're supposed to be on the same side."

"I'm on the side of justice—period. You appear to be concerned that you get a conviction whether or not it's just."

"Don't lecture me, Special Agent."

"Have you informed the defense? This qualifies as exculpatory evidence."

"In your professional opinion? It's bright and early Monday morning. This all happened over the weekend. We will carry out our duty to inform the defense."

"When?"

"We are required to report reasonably promptly and we will. As you're aware, there are many national security issues involved in this case, so we are justified in proceeding carefully—"

"Oh, come off it! You're delaying until you can make your deal with Janssen."

"I'm through justifying myself to you. Leave my office, and keep your mouth shut about this if you value your job."

"Save your pathetic threats for the criminals, Feinstein. You don't have the grounds, the right, or the authority to fire me!" she exclaimed as she left.

The prosecutor immediately called Erin's boss, and asked him to forbid her to bring this information to light until the prosecution was ready to release it to the defense. When her boss warned her to keep her mouth shut, she began yelling. He told her she had a very promising future with the Bureau, and suggested she start her planned vacation right away before she put it in jeopardy. She stomped out and went home to stew.

*

The defense opened its case later that morning by calling experts in quantum computing, who testified that the government's decision to stop this technology was a "monumental blunder" and "an outrage that defies reason." A top lobbyist then deconstructed the case his fellow lobbyists used to bring about the delay, and characterized it as the classic strategy used by industry to hinder unwelcome competition. At the prosecution's objection that defense counsel was wasting time with this detour through Section 806 of the Patriot Act, when this case focused on Section 805, the judge cut the testimony short, and told Ms Csonka to get on with this case. The defense called its key witness: Kyle Summers.

Ms Csonka opened: "For the record, Mr. Summers, please tell the jury if you sold the computers to the Chinese and to the AUC."

"No I did not."

"But you did sell two others to clients in Canada?"

"Yes."

"You knew you were breaking the law. Why did you do it?"

"Three reasons. The most pressing one was the imminent bankruptcy of my firm. We were eight million, one hundred-thirteen thousand dollars in debt. Obeying the law meant the failure of my firm, of my computer, and the loss of the woman I loved, and I could not let that happen. The ten million from those two computers gave us a critical reprieve in the battle against the insane law forbidding the sale of my computer.

"Second, I was convinced the law was so unjust and outrageous that it practically invited defiance. I mean, how can the United States government tell me, a citizen of Canada, that I can't sell my computer to Canadians?

And, third, I thought once the computer was on the market that the American government would have no choice but to reverse its bonehead decision."

"Why not extend that logic and sell more computers overseas, say to China and Colombia?"

"I know that supercomputers can't be sold to some countries because they are potential enemies of ours, so I assumed it would apply to my computer. On a business level, it would be idiotic to risk the future of my firm by selling to those nations. On a personal level, I never wanted something I invented to be used against us. I can't say I invented the computer to better mankind—although it has that potential—but its use to hurt or kill people horrifies me."

"What did you think when the government accused you of being a terrorist?"

"I thought it was so ridiculous that I didn't believe it. I thought it was another means of preventing the computer from reaching the market. I still do."

"Let's consider the motives the government alleges were behind the sale to the Chinese and Colombians. First, good old fashioned greed. Fifteen million dollars. That's a lot of money, especially for a company on the verge of bankruptcy. How do you react when the government says you did it for the money?"

"If I just wanted money, I'd have used my computer to steal as many millions as I wanted, and I could've easily done it without any danger of getting caught. Why risk all this by selling to our enemies?"

"So why didn't you use your computer to steal?"

"Because I'm not a thief. I never even considered stealing to keep the company afloat; I just needed to sell two computers for that."

"The other main motive the government cites is revenge against your country for ruining you. What say you to that?"

"Again, why risk involving a middleman? That would make it much more likely I'd be caught. If I just wanted revenge, I could've used my computer to do untold damage to any government computer I wanted without hurting anyone and without leaving any clues."

"But you didn't do that either?"

"No. All I cared about at the time was keeping my invention alive. I needed to sell two computers for that, so that's what I did."

"But you tried to sell more to American customers."

"More computers on the market would have given us more breathing room to fight the law, and made it harder for the government to keep up the charade that their edict was something besides protecting entrenched interests."

"So tell us what the FBI did to you."

"Well, first they raided our factory, and served me with a gag order, so I couldn't complain publicly about what they were about to do to me."

"You mean a National Security Letter?"

"Yes. The FBI simply typed up a memo and said it entitled them to take our documents and computers."

"Objection," stated Mr. Feinstein. "National Security Letters only pertain to financial documents, and that's all the FBI took in connection with the Letter."

The judge stated, "To clarify for the jury: National Security Letters do not permit the seizure of computers. Section 806 of the Patriot Act does permit this if the organization was involved in an act of terrorism."

"Go on, Kyle," said Ms Csonka.

"Okay, anyway, they were welcome to our documents. I just cared about my computers and I inferred at the time that the Letter covered the seizure of our computers as well. Ebbling said I couldn't tell anyone anything. Anyway, I didn't believe they had the right to do that in this country, so I threatened to call the news, so they arrested me. Then they proceeded to steal all of our computers and computer components."

"Objection, Your Honor. The FBI legally seized the computers," said Mr. Feinstein.

"Sustained," held the judge. "Refrain from hyperbole, Mr. Summers."

"Thirty of our computers and parts for two more were permanently borrowed, which apparently is legal now in this country. They were trying to bankrupt us."

"Objection. Mr. Summers is again drawing unwarranted conclusions. The motive for the seizure was to stop more mass murders overseas."

"Sustained. What did I just say, Mr. Summers?"

"Okay, they borrowed our computers, which were our only assets, and that just happened to lead to our bankruptcy when the IRS finished us off. The FBI must know a private company can't survive without anything to sell and a prohibition to build more of its product. We can't go on piling up debt; we're not the government. Our creditors were demanding the money we owed them. So I sold two computers and used the proceeds to pay our bills and our employees."

Ms Csonka said, "Assuming the Chinese and Colombians have your computer, how did they get them?"

"Only the three owners had access to the computers and the storage room had not been broken into. Three computers went missing when I was in Canada, hooking up my computers. It had to be one or both of my partners."

"Do you have any hard evidence for your theory?"

"As we saw on the video the prosecution played, I used my computer and traced the three million dollars in my name back to a fifteen million dollar deposit made on March 27. I then traced that fifteen million to two numbered accounts in the Cayman Islands, six million each."

"Dr. Hugel and Ms Janssen?"

"Objection, Your Honor," said Mr. Feinstein. "Assumes facts not in evidence. The link to the other owners has not been established."

"Sustained—"

"Yes, it has!" screamed Erin from a back bench, no longer able to hold back. "The prosecution knows that Amy Janssen accessed one of those accounts last Friday."

"Order!" hollered the judge. "You're out of order, Agent McAdams."

"Approach, Your Honor?" appealed Ms. Csonka.

"Both of you and Agent McAdams to my chambers at once!" he exclaimed. "It's 11:15. We'll recess until after lunch. Jury members, be back by one PM."

*

In the judge's chambers, the judge again rebuked Erin and said, "What the hell is going on?"

"Your Honor, forgive me, but I couldn't stand the lies anymore. Mr. Feinstein knows full well that Amy Janssen is under arrest in Brazil. She withdrew two hundred thousand dollars from one of the Cayman Islands accounts last Friday."

"Mr. Feinstein?"

Clearly flustered and angry, Mr. Feinstein replied, "The investigation is at a very preliminary stage. We've concluded nothing as yet—"

"You deliberately withheld exculpatory evidence from defense counsel," said Ms Csonka.

Mr. Feinstein protested, "We don't necessarily consider this evidence exculpatory and we had full intentions of informing defense counsel once we ensured that national security would not be jeopardized."

Ms Csonka returned, "This business of justifying any outrage by citing national security is past contemptible."

"Hold on for a minute!" the judge instructed. "Mr. Feinstein, when did you get this information?"

"I was told on the weekend, but I didn't attend to it until Monday, just two days ago. As I've said, we are busy getting our facts straight and checking national security implications. We intended to inform defense counsel once we understand what's going on ourselves."

"Come on! You just lied to the court," said Ms Csonka. "You knew full well there was a link between the Cayman Islands account and Amy Janssen. That is strong grounds to dismiss the charges against my client."

"Get me the evidence right away, Mr. Feinstein. I need to see it for myself."

"We need to assemble it—"

"Get me what you have right away, Mr. Feinstein."

Mr. Feinstein sighed and called his office.

The judge then said, "Now get out of my chambers, all of you, until the file arrives. I have a headache."

Out in the hall, Mr. Feinstein warned Erin that this would mean her job, and she told him to go to hell.

The file arrived forty minutes later, and the judge examined the evidence for another twenty. He called the three back into his chambers and said, "I have determined that the records contain materially exculpatory evidence and that disclosure should not harm this country's interest, at least in the context of a trial under a media blackout."

Ms Csonka, greatly incensed about the prosecution's malfeasance, asserted, "Your Honor, you have the power to dismiss the charges against my client. The prosecution purposefully withheld exculpatory evidence."

"Calm down, Helena. I won't do that, but I will overrule Mr. Feinstein's objection. You may now establish your link. Mr. Feinstein, consider yourself fortunate that I don't cite you for contempt. Same goes for you, Agent McAdams. You will remove yourself from my courtroom. We'll reconvene at one."

"Your Honor," spoke up Mr. Feinstein, "since this information is now to be included in the trial, we should be allowed to read Ms Janssen's statement in court."

The judge handed Ms Csonka the signed statement. It read:

Kyle was furious at the American government. He said if we let them get away with it, we'd all be ruined. He convinced me and Rick that we should sell as many computers as we could. He said if we got our computer out there, the genie would be out of the bottle, and the government couldn't get it back in. He delivered two to Canada, and called all our U.S. customers, who expressed the intention to buy our computer. All three owners, Kyle, Rick, and myself, knew we had been contacted by a Chinese woman and a Colombian man who wanted to pay cash for our computers. We said no at first, but when we got the government's ruling, we said to hell with it. They screwed us, so we'll screw them. We sold to them. We all knew about it.

"You've already ruled on this for her previous statement, Your Honor," pointed out Ms Csonka. "The witness is unavailable, so we can't confront her regarding her hearsay testimony. The government has already abridged my client's First, Fourth, and Fifth Amendment rights. Let's not add the Sixth to that."

"The statement is out, Mr. Feinstein," ruled the judge.

"What if we produce the witness in court, Your Honor?" he asked.

"So we get to the bottom of the prosecution's tactic," averred Ms Csonka. "Delay informing me about her access to the numbered account until they can work out a desperate deal to get her to testify against my client in court. What are you offering her, Feinstein?"

"As long as she agrees to extradition, the same offer we recently made to your client: ten years in prison. She was smart enough to take it first."

"She was smart enough to invent a new lie to minimize her penalty," said Ms Csonka. "Ms Janssen signed a deposition in April that Mr. Summers alone sold the computers. Now that that has been shown to be a lie, she's changed her story to suit her new predicament."

"She's said all along Mr. Summers was in on it. The only thing that's changed is she admits she and Hugel were a part of it," responded Mr. Feinstein.

"And when can you get her here?" asked the judge.

"Your Honor! You can't be seriously considering this," said Ms Csonka. "Mr. Feinstein has provided a rich incentive to lie and her lies would be incredibly prejudicial against my client. Besides, the prosecution has rested its case."

"I've ruled that Ms Janssen's link to the Cayman Islands account is in, so both the defense and the prosecution can have a stab at her if she can testify in court. When can you get her here?"

"Well, the wheels of justice are slower in Brazil than here. It might take weeks."

"Which is why he tried to delay, then tried to get her statement admitted," said Ms Csonka.

"I was on the fence on this one, since Ms Janssen obviously has a talent for lying. Since you can't produce the witness in a reasonable timeframe, I'm not delaying the proceedings. Her statement is out. Now get out; I'm hungry."

*

After the break, Ms Csonka resumed with the defendant. Looking at the jury, she said, "You'll be pleased to know, Kyle, that there has, in fact, been a link established between Amy Janssen and one of the numbered accounts. Though we cannot presume her guilt without a trial, it is alleged she transferred two hundred thousand dollars to six bank accounts in Brazil, where she apparently resides. The prosecution has known about this for days, but failed to inform us. It is clear why, ladies and gentlemen: they knew it would strike a fatal blow to their case against my client."

"Objection. Defense counsel's personal opinion; she cannot know what I knew," said Mr. Feinstein.

"You dug this hole, Mr. Feinstein. Overruled."

Ms Csonka said, "Now, the prosecution has built its case around the three million dollars found in Mr. Summers's name. And we have heard Mr. Summers's contention that one or both of his partners put this money in his account. Recall that we questioned why Mr. Summers, as forty-one percent owner of Qubit, would settle for three million dollars while each of his partners got six million. Mr. Feinstein objected on the grounds that we had no proof those two six million dollar accounts were linked to his partners. This morning's revelation that Ms Janssen allegedly accessed one of those accounts lends new credence to my client's contention.

"No sane person would settle for twenty percent of the proceeds if he owns forty-one percent of the company. So how did the three million dollars get into an account with my client's name on it? Your Honor, with your indulgence, I would like my client to demonstrate to the jury how simple it is to fabricate this evidence."

"And how would he do this?" inquired the judge.

"By hooking in remotely to the computer in Toronto."

"Objection!" said the prosecutor. "The defense wants to turn this into—"

"Your Honor," the defense interrupted, "the prosecution maintains the three million dollars is definitive evidence against my client. Mr. Feinstein even did his best to withhold from us evidence that would taint this supposedly definitive evidence. We have the right to contest it."

"Very well, but tread carefully, counselor," warned the judge.

"Kyle, if you'll step up to the computer and do your thing."

He walked up to the computer and brought up a screen. The image was projected onto a screen opposite the jury so everyone could see it.

Kyle said, "By the way, logging in remotely is possible only with a password. The quantum computer is protected by something called quantum cryptography; it's infinitely more secure than the typical standard used to protect digital computers today. It's what I strongly advised the government to consider to protect its files from quantum computers. They chose instead to shut me down."

He stepped through several screens, ending up on the account balances page for a numbered bank account in a Swiss bank. He typed $1,000,000 into a box and was prompted for the password. Kyle instructed his quantum computer to find the password. Within thirty-five seconds, the password was accepted. He then was prompted to fill in the bank account and password of the destination account. He opened another screen and within two minutes had the account number for Mr. Feinstein and pasted it into the destination account box, at which point the prosecutor jumped up to object—but as the judge was sustaining the objection, Kyle instructed his quantum computer to find the password.

Kyle stepped back and, within fifteen seconds, the password was accepted and the deposit made. "You're one million dollars richer, Mr. Feinstein," chuckled Kyle. "And you'd better hope the former owner of the money isn't a hit man or something."

The jury and the few spectators laughed, prompting the judge to bang down his gavel and yell, "Enough! This is not a circus. Mr. Summers, turn off the projector, reverse your transfer, then take your seat." Kyle followed the orders.

With that, the defense rested.

*

The next day the prosecution got its turn with the defendant. Erin was permitted to sit in as long as she remained silent. Mr. Feinstein began, "Mr. Summers, you were charged with attacking Dr. Hugel after you discovered he patented the decoherence component?"

"Yes, but it was withdr—"

"Just answer yes or no," insisted Mr. Feinstein.

"Yes."

"You've admitted breaking the law by selling two quantum computers to Canadian customers?"

"Yes."

"You've admitted financially ruining Special Agent McAdams by using your computer to erase her assets and invent about four hundred thousand dollars in debt?"

"Yes."

"She pleaded with you to reverse the damage you did to her. Did you?"

"She arrested the wrong—"

"Yes or no."

"No."

"Even after she saved your life time and time again," said Mr. Feinstein, looking at the jury and shaking his head.

Turning back to Kyle, he continued, "You pulled a gun on a Royal Canadian Mounted Police officer in an attempt to avoid capture after you fled from Chicago?

"Yes."

"You've admitted tampering with evidence by diverting the three million dollars in your bank account to the accounts of several charities?"

"Yes."

"You attempted to frame the FBI Special Agent in Charge of Counterterrorism by putting one hundred thousand dollars into his account?"

"No."

"We saw you admit this on video, Mr. Summers."

"I never admitted that. I didn't do it to set him up. I did it to show—"

"Stop there. You did it. We know that. Why you did it, we'll leave to the imagination of the jury. What we do know for certain is you are linked to the twelve million dollars."

"I tracked it down."

"Why should we believe you with your track record? Laws don't mean much to you, do they?"

"The law against prosecutors withholding clear evidence of my innocence—"

"Your Honor, non-responsive answer," Mr. Feinstein interrupted, but Kyle kept on talking.

"—from this jury means a hell of a lot to me!"

"Mr. Summers," said the judge, "stop your harangue this instant! Mr. Feinstein has broken no law. Continue, Mr. Feinstein."

"Am I your next target, Mr. Summers? Or maybe this jury?"

"Badgering the witness, Your Honor," objected Ms Csonka.

"I'll sustain that. Get to the point, Mr. Feinstein."

"Your pattern is clear. When you're angry, you strike out in revenge—and we know you were furious with the U.S. government at the time those computers were sold. Did you strike out against the government by selling your computers to customers hostile toward our country?"

"Objection, the question is argumentative," held Ms Csonka.

"I'll allow it. Answer, Mr. Summers."

"Only if you think Canadians are hostile."

"I'll get back to this point in a minute. Jill, display Exhibit 205 please. This is from Special Agent McAdams's case notes. Mr. Summers, please read the highlighted section."

"'Amy Janssen wields total control over Kyle Summers. His all-consuming goal in life is to marry her. She knows this and takes full advantage of her power. He will do anything she says in hopes of marrying her. She orders him around and, like an obedient dog, he obeys and begs for more. His weakness makes him corruptible.'"

He glared at Erin after he finished reading this. She lowered her eyes.

"Is this is a fair characterization, Mr. Summers?"

"Just because Agent McAdams considers me a weak dog doesn't mean I am; she's no psychologist. I did love Amy and I wanted to marry her more than anything else."

"Enough to do anything she said?"

"No."

"We heard testimony from two former employees of Qubit that you were under Amy Janssen's spell. Jill, Exhibit 323, please. Gladys Snyder testified, quote, 'Everyone except Kyle knew Amy and Rick were an item. One night, Charlie, one of our security guards, walked in on the two doing it, you know? Meanwhile, Kyle was waiting for her in a restaurant. She stood him up all the time and treated him like dirt, but he still loved her. It was sad and, I'm sorry, Kyle, kind of pathetic.' Unquote.

"Your employees and two FBI agents said there's nothing you wouldn't do for her. So answer me this, Mr. Summers: Isn't it true that if Amy Janssen decided to sell your computers to the Chinese and Colombians, you would never have dared to object?"

"There were lines I wouldn't cross, even for Amy. When she told me to sell Qubit—"

"Your Honor …" Mr. Feinstein said to object that the witness had answered the question.

"Mr. Summers," instructed the judge, "answer only the question posed."

Mr. Feinstein continued, "If she told you to jump off a cliff, you would. If she told you to sell to the Chinese and Colombians, you would. As long as she held out the prospect of marrying her, you would do anything. Isn't that right?"

"No! Selling to them would've cost me my computer and my chance for Amy."

"Was your company not already on its deathbed?"

"Yes, thanks to the goddamn government!"

"You've made it very clear what you think of the United States government decision that forbids your company to sell its computer."

"And did you expect me to be happy that some modern-day Luddites determined that my computer was too advanced to sell to anyone? That their imbecilic paranoia turned my company's prospects from the next IBM to the next Enron?"

"And your outrage over that decision prompted your decision to betray your country?"

"Objection, Your Honor!" shouted the defense. "Leading question."

"Sustained. Stop coaxing, Mr. Feinstein."

The prosecutor continued, "You knew the company was in deep trouble; you blamed it on the American government. Weren't you dying to strike back at the government?"

"Objection! He's still leading the witness," said Ms Csonka.

"Mr. Feinstein, ask a question that doesn't suggest the answer you want."

"Amy made you an offer you couldn't refuse: agree to the sale to China and Colombia and I'll marry you. With one move, you get revenge on the government and you get the girl. Correct, Mr. Summers?"

"Asked and answered, Your Honor," objected Ms Csonka.

"Overruled. Answer the question, Mr. Summers."

"Incorrect, Feinstein. She never made such an offer, because she knew I would never go along because she knew I would never sacrifice my computer. And we all knew what the computer could do and how easy it would be to detect its use."

"So, you're admitting that the Chinese and Colombians have your computers?"

Kyle looked at Helena as if to say "Help!" but she had no basis to intervene.

"Answer, Mr. Summers," ordered the judge.

"It's pretty damned obvious and it—"

"Thank you clearing that up, Mr. Summers. So we know they have your computers; we know Amy Janssen just took two hundred thousand dollars from the proceeds of that sale, so she must have been in on it; we only need to show you knew about the sale. Now, one of the arguments your defense counsel used to claim you could not have been in on the sale was that you owned forty-one percent of the firm, but three million dollars only amounted to twenty percent of the proceeds from the illegal computers. But you would have if Amy merely told you to, isn't that so?"

"Wrong. I'm not a fool."

"You were a fool for her, Mr. Summers. All she needed to say was take three million dollars and I'll marry you. No more questions of this witness, Your Honor," said Mr. Feinstein, feeling pleased with himself.

"Ms Csonka?" said the judge.

"Yes, thank you, Your Honor. Mr. Summers, what would've happened if Amy told you to go along with the sale to China and Colombia?"

"As I said, I would've refused because we'd have been caught for sure. As soon as the computer was used for what it was apparently used for—breaking into top-secret files—everyone would know how it was done. It would've been the height of folly and arrogance to think we could've gotten away with that. It would've been a sure way to lose the company *and* Amy."

"The prosecution tried to paint you as Amy's slave, but in actuality, there were many times you refused her command, weren't there? What about when she ordered you to sell Qubit to DTC?"

"I absolutely refused because I spent years developing my computer. Selling out to anyone was out of the question, especially to the buggers that led the fight to outlaw my computer. We were told they offered one hundred million dollars for my firm, the price of just twenty of our computers."

"What did Amy say when you refused her command?"

"She said she'd never marry me."

"And you held firm?"

"Yes. I considered their offer robbery and I told Amy I would never do it. I thought with the sale to the Canadians, we could get by until I could set up shop in Canada. Then I'd be successful, and she would marry me."

"There were lines you wouldn't cross. So even if you could have got away with selling to the Chinese and Colombians, would you have done it?"

"No. I feel terrible that my computer was used to identify our agents, and they were killed. They killed little kids, for God's sake." He shook his head. "I could never have lived with the guilt if I was responsible."

"You didn't know Amy and Rick were married until after the sales took place, right?"

"That's right."

"So what could have persuaded you to agree to the division of the fifteen million dollars into two portions of six million, presumably for Amy and Rick?"

"Objection," said Mr. Feinstein. "That has not been proven."

"You started down this road, Mr. Feinstein. Overruled."

"Why would you have ever agreed to two six million dollar portions for your partners and one three million dollar portion for yourself?"

"Accept twenty percent for myself? Give Rick forty percent when I blamed him for the whole mess? Bury the two six million dollar accounts, but leave my three million dollars in an obvious place? I'm not an idiot."

"Even if Amy told you to take twenty percent?"

"Even then."

"Is there any way the division of the fifteen million dollars into the three portions makes sense?"

"Rick and Amy must have known the sales would be detected, so they needed a fall guy. The only way it all makes sense is if the three million dollars was used to frame me, and they hid the rest for themselves. As a bonus, the government shuts us down when the sales are discovered, the company goes bankrupt, and they get thirty-four percent of the proceeds from the auction. Or sell out to DTC when that unexpected opportunity arose, and they get thirty-four million bucks."

"Thank you. No further questions."

"Re-cross, Mr. Feinstein?"

"Just one question, Your Honor. It was predictable you'd be caught, you said, so one way to get away with it would be to set up the three million dollars as a straw man. Obviously a genius like you wouldn't be that stupid, so throw away the three million dollars to protect yourself and split the twelve million with the woman you intended to make your wife.

Remember, we have no proof to link Rick Hugel to the Cayman Islands accounts. When the government confronts you, just point to the three million dollars, and you're free and clear. Right?"

"So you're implying Amy really loved me all along, and we double-crossed Rick? We acted in front of the FBI agent before we knew she was an agent? You make it up as you go, don't you, Feinstein?"

Having planted the idea with the jury, he sat. Helena would save her rebuttal until closing arguments, when she would characterize it as a last desperate ploy to salvage a hopeless case.

Eloquent closing arguments summarized and reinforced each side's major points, and the jury was charged with making its decision. The jury debated for only two-and-a-quarter hours. They caught everyone by surprise, and it took another hour and a quarter to reconvene. It was 5:50 PM.

The defendant was instructed to stand. Awaiting the verdict, he shook so hard, he had to support himself by leaning on the table in front of him. Erin looked almost as nervous. The foreman read the verdict.

"On the count of providing material support to terrorists: not guilty."

Kyle got even more tense as everything came down to the next decision. His legs gave out and he fell onto the chair. Erin stood, apparently wanting to rush to his aid, but the judge glared at her. She sat. Helena helped him to his feet.

"On the count of providing material support or resources to designated foreign terrorist organizations: not guilty."

Kyle whooped and taking Helena in his arms, spun her around saying, "Thank you, thank you, thank you! You saved my life!" He put her down, looked to the jury and expressed his thanks. Erin wept happy tears.

*

On the way out of the courthouse, Erin strolled up to him with a warm smile and said, "Congratulations. I'm happy for you. I told you justice would prevail."

"You arrested the wrong man, then testified against me."

"I drew the obvious conclusions from the evidence at hand in identifying you as the prime suspect. At the trial, I stated the facts, and let the jury do their job. During cross-examination, I freely admitted that Rick or Amy may well have set you up—and, don't forget, I persuaded Helena to represent you, and I risked my job to make sure Amy's link to the money was made in court. All in all, I think I helped you. C'mon, let bygones be bygones. Let me buy you a celebratory drink."

"No, thank you, Agent McAdams. This weak dog isn't interested."

Upset at his coldness, she said, "We went through an awful lot together, Kyle. By the end of our little adventure, I thought we meant something to each other."

"You thought wrong. I never want to see you again. Goodbye."

Her shoulders slumped as he walked away. She walked quickly to her car, got in and fought the tears that were blurring her vision. Unwilling to let him walk out of her life forever, she moved her car so she could see him as he walked down the steps outside the courthouse. He got to the bottom of the steps and paused. He looked left and right, but stood there.

He had nowhere to go, she realized. His apartment must have been rented to someone else long ago. He took out his wallet, which was all he had left other than the clothes he was wearing, looked in it, and shook his head.

He must be broke, too, she knew. When Kyle crossed the street in front of her car, she broke down crying, thinking it was the last she would ever see of him. He went into a bar.

Almost three hours later, Kyle stumbled out of the bar. It was dark by this time. Erin remained in her car, watching out for him; she was afraid he'd end up on the street tonight. He turned left, as if he knew where he was going. After walking two blocks—with Erin creeping slowly behind him in her car a block back—he turned down a side street. She turned the corner and pulled up to the curb. He seemed to be heading to a seedy hotel down the deserted street.

Suddenly, a cargo van rocketed by and screeched to a halt next to Kyle. Two men in ski masks jumped out and set upon Kyle. Erin saw the stun gun, and screamed in her car. He grimaced and fell forward. They caught him and put him in the van, which sped away. Erin took off in pursuit.

There was no use trying to end the kidnapping herself, she knew. She was alone and could not take the chance of shooting at the van with Kyle inside. She took her phone out, but hesitated before dialing. These were probably federal agents; assassins would have killed him immediately. Her call would have to be to the police. But what would calling the police accomplish if the abductors were federal agents? They would show their identification and drive away. Erin elected to tail them. Maybe she could catch them off guard as they took Kyle out of the van.

The van headed toward Midway. *Oh, my God, they're flying him out of the country to a black site*, she deduced. *If they get him out of the country, he might disappear forever.*

She made her 911 call to report a kidnapping. The van pulled to a stop near a hangar at the west end of the airport. Erin stopped outside the fence and watched from her car as three men took Kyle out of the van and walked toward a waiting jet. Two supported the still-dazed Kyle, and one walked ahead to open the jet door.

Where the hell are the cops? Erin wondered. But just then, a police cruiser drove by with lights flashing and stopped abruptly next to the group of men. Two officers hopped out with guns drawn, yelled at them to stop and raise their hands. They lowered Kyle to his knees, and put their hands up. With the police approaching cautiously, Erin could see the men talking to them. One slowly removed his wallet from his pocket and opened it to display his ID. The police relaxed and put their guns away.

While Erin started her car and drove up to group, one of the men pulled Kyle up by the arm and heaved him to the jet. She stopped next to the jet and jumped out with pistol in hand screaming to the man taking Kyle up the steps into the jet, "Hold it right there!" The other four men went for their guns.

"Drop your weapon!" ordered Officer Krupa. Erin kept the gun pointed at the man next to Kyle and explained, "I'm Special Agent Erin McAdams, FBI. I reported this kidnapping."

"Drop your gun," Officer Krupa repeated. With four guns aiming at her, she acquiesced. As soon as her gun hit the ground, the agent with Kyle pulled him up the last two steps into the jet.

"Stop them!" she shrieked as the door closed. The police walked up to her and told her to produce her badge. As she did so, the jet engines started. "These men have kidnapped an innocent man. Do not let that jet take off!" she cried.

"These men are CIA agents. They're taking a terrorist away for interrogation."

"I don't doubt they're CIA, but the man they abducted is no terrorist."

"That dirt bag helped Chinese agents wipe out nearly all our operatives in China," asserted CIA Agent White. "We have orders to arrest him and take him to this jet."

"Kyle Summers, the man they kidnapped, was exonerated of the charges against him in a court of law not four hours ago. The CIA doesn't like the verdict, so they're ignoring it." Agent White looked surprised by that revelation. "Where is this innocent civilian going?" Erin said. "Guantanamo? A black site in Eastern Europe?"

The jet started to move. Turning to the police she pleaded, "Stop that jet!" The police officers looked at each other at a loss about what to do. Erin stooped to pick up her gun.

"Don't!" said Officer Krupa.

She obeyed, but exclaimed, "I have reported a kidnapping. Do your duty and stop this travesty!" The jet taxied toward the runway. "God dammit! If you let these men get away with kidnapping, I'll do everything in my power to see to it you two lose your badges."

Undecided about the correct course of action, they stood there thinking. Erin quickly picked up her gun and pointed it at Agent White. "Call up the pilot and order him to stop!" she roared.

"Calm down, lady," suggested Agent White, as his partner, Agent Neeb, aimed at Erin.

"Both of you, drop your guns!" commanded Officer Krupa, as the two police officers held their guns on the two agents.

"Shoot an FBI agent and you'll spend the next thirty years in prison!" she hollered, still pointing her pistol at Agent White.

"Now, Agent McAdams!" insisted Officer Krupa. She reluctantly lowered her gun. "Call this in and get instructions," Krupa told his partner, Officer Slaght. By the time the order came back, the jet was second in line for takeoff.

"Take them all in," relayed Slaght.

"What about the jet?" Erin screamed. "You're letting them get away with kidnapping, you morons! Get the control tower to stop that jet!"

"Shut the hell up!" said Officer Slaght.

"You'll pay for this!" she continued. The CIA agents laughed. "I'm pressing kidnapping charges against both of you assholes," she said, as the three detainees were put in the back seat of the cruiser. As the police car left the airport, the jet took off.

CHAPTER FIFTEEN

Seeking Justice

The outcome of the imbroglio at the precinct was predictable, Erin's vociferous protestations notwithstanding. Her demands for kidnapping charges against the CIA agents fell on deaf ears. They and she were released with the recommendation to settle their affairs between themselves. She pressed for dereliction of duty charges against the two police officers, but that demand, too, was dismissed.

As she sat, fuming, in a squad car, waiting for a ride back to the airport to pick up her car, she saw the two CIA agents emerge from the station. She put her hand on her gun and mulled over whether to arrest the two on federal kidnapping charges. Before she could decide, Officer Krupa got in the car. She turned her head away from him as he started the car and pulled into traffic. Neither said a word on the ride to the airport.

Finally, as he pulled up to her car, he said, "I don't appreciate your bullshit allegations against us."

"Tough," she replied. "You let them get away with a serious crime."

"We have no business getting involved in your feud."

"The obvious course of action was to stop that plane until you made sure a crime wasn't taking place. It was and you let it happen. You blew it, Krupa," she declared as she got out and slammed the door.

Sitting in her car, waiting for the CIA agents to pick up the van, she phoned Helena to tell her what happened. All she had was her office number. She had to leave a message. When the CIA agents pulled up ten minutes later, she got out, gun in hand, and said, "Hold it right there! You're under arrest for the kidnapping of Kyle Summers."

While Agent Neeb chuckled, Agent White said, "Oh, give it a rest, McAdams. There's nothing you can do about it now."

"Hands in the air, assholes!"

"Go ahead and shoot us," dared the chuckler. She took her Taser gun out of her holster and complied with the request. As Neeb fell to the ground, incapacitated, White went for his gun.

"Don't!" she earnestly suggested, holding her gun on him. "Even through your thick skull you must know I mean business. Now, put your handcuffs on your partner, help him to the car, and put him in the back seat." He obeyed. "Now, on the ground face down, hands behind your back. Come on, you know the drill."

He frowned, but obeyed. She handcuffed him and showed him to the backseat. Off to her field office she sped with her two prisoners.

"You're nuts, McAdams," said Agent White. "You're in way over your head now."

"How does it feel to be taken against your will by a federal agent, jackass?"

"I'll be out within an hour. Your terrorist is out indefinitely."

"You don't get it. I'm pressing kidnapping charges against both of you."

"It'll never stick, McAdams."

"You must know that someone will have to pay for making a farce out of the court's ruling. You're not stupid enough to think it'll be the bastard who ordered this, are you? He'll hang you out to dry."

"Christ, McAdams. All we did was carry out an order to arrest a man and deliver him to the airport. End of story."

"Not quite. As you've no doubt confirmed by now, the man you kidnapped had just been found innocent by a court of law. Whoever gave the order took the law into his own hands when he flouted the court's verdict. Someone's going down for this, White. It's only a matter of who. I'm betting on you two."

"What do you want from me, McAdams? I mean, you're a field agent, too. If you were given an order to arrest a man and deliver him to the airport, you'd obey, right?"

"The FBI isn't in the habit of spiriting people away by jet to some black site. Where is he going, White?"

"Don't know. Don't care."

"Who gave you your orders?"

"Fuck you," said Neeb, as he emerged from his daze.

"Well, I hope you're gay with where you're gonna spend the next twenty years."

"Keep dreaming, McAdams," said White. "There's no way I can be convicted for doing my job."

271

At the FBI field office, the two CIA agents were put in a holding cell. Meanwhile, Erin was embroiled in a heated argument with her boss, who came back to the office to contend with this tempest.

"Jesus, McAdams, what the hell were you thinking? I've got the CIA screaming blue murder at me. We look like a bunch of Keystone Kops here."

"I was thinking this nation and this agency stood for the rule of law. Was I wrong?"

"Don't give me that mom and apple pie bullshit. These guys were just following orders, same as you when you brought Summers in."

"I brought him in to stand trial. They whisked him off to a black site after he'd been found innocent."

"That's the CIA's business, not ours. We don't know what else they may have on him."

"You're not going to let them get away with this?"

"We have enough real criminals to deal with without arresting federal agents for doing their job."

"And does defying the court's ruling not qualify as a real crime? Go after the person who gave the order."

"Drop it, McAdams."

"They made a mockery of the court's ruling," she said. "The CIA can't get away with this!"

"Stop screaming at me, Special Agent."

"I'm not letting this drop."

"You will obey your orders or you're out of this bureau!"

"Is that all that counts anymore? Following orders. Ignoring the Constitution is fine."

"I'm turning them loose. If you do anything to contravene my order, you're fired. Clear?"

Erin stormed out of the office without answering.

She got home that evening so upset that she sat and wept. Afterward, she lay down, exhausted, the emotionally grueling day having taken its toll. A half-hour later she almost hit the ceiling when her phone rang. It was Officer Krupa.

"You didn't hear this from me," he said. "The person the CIA agents named as their boss was Gloria Menendez. She's in Langley." He hung up before she could thank him.

The next morning, Erin flew to Washington DC and took a cab to CIA headquarters. Her FBI ID got her in the front door and to Ms Menendez's gatekeeper. Told she could not see the woman, Erin barged into her office to interrupt what had been an animated discussion between Menendez and Agent White. Erin entered the fray as tempers flared.

"Who the hell are you?" demanded Menendez.

"You certainly are persistent, McAdams," said Agent White.

"So this is the thorn in my side? What is Summers to you, McAdams? Your lover?"

"Just the kind of question I'd expect from the lowlife who ordered the kidnapping."

"Careful, Special Agent. You do fly off the handle."

"What have you done with him?"

"Mr. Summers has been detained as an enemy combatant."

"He was exonerated of the crime. You have no right—"

"We have every right! The damn judge refused to let the jury hear the statement by Janssen that Summers was in on the crime."

"For good reason: she's an inveterate liar. You can't just ignore the court's ruling."

"I don't need to justify myself to you, Agent McAdams."

"How, then, would you feel about justifying yourself to the media?"

"Don't you dare threaten me, Special Agent!"

"What this is really about is your own incompetence in protecting your agents. The entire intelligence community was warned to take extra precautions to protect their data when the hearings were held. Mr. Summers even made some recommendations on how to do that, but you ignored it, and as a result your agents were killed, so to cover up your own incompetence you make this big push to put everything on the inventor."

"Watch out, McAdams."

"Or what? You can't touch me—unless, of course, you get this goon to abduct me, too. What's to stop you?"

"Keep that in mind." She turned to Agent White. "You can go now."

He left, mouthing, "Careful!" to Erin on his way past her.

Erin said to Menendez, "If you're so damned convinced you're in the right here, then you won't mind defending your order to kidnap Mr. Summers before reporters."

"You'll sincerely regret it if you go to the media."

"Release Mr. Summers and I'll let this go."

"If you persist in trying to help this terrorist, you may find yourself in the same boat as he's in."

"And what boat is that? Where do you have this innocent man? What are you doing to this law-abiding American citizen?"

"Stay out of it!"

"I'm in it. And if you dare to kidnap me, too, you should know I've already informed my supervisors that I've come to see you," she lied. "I took that precaution because I know what a filthy scumbag you are. So try it, big shot. Just try to make me disappear, too. Then you'll go to jail, but the difference will be you're the real criminal here. If Kyle Summers isn't released unharmed within twenty-four hours, I go to the media!" With that Erin left the livid woman to consider how to contend with this painful thorn in her side.

While Erin stood by the curb to hail a cab, a grey sedan pulled up. Expecting a kidnap attempt, she jumped back and went for her gun, but nothing happened other than the passenger window gliding down.

"Jumpy, McAdams?" said Agent White.

"Thought maybe I was your next victim," she answered with a titter.

"Get in." She hesitated. "Come on, before someone notices. I want to tell you something." She got in, and he drove away. "It wasn't very nice calling me a goon. I prefer the slur thug." She smiled. He went on, "I wanted to warn you—"

"All I'm hearing is warnings and threats from—"

"Just hold your knee-jerk reaction for once, and listen for a minute. I'm not your enemy. I do my job for the same reasons you do. I assume we're the good guys and we put away the bad guys. Some of the things I do border on immoral, if not illegal, but I accept we have to get a little dirty sometimes in this filthy fight. I looked into what you said about Summers. I had no idea he was just exonerated of the crime. I didn't take this job to be abducting innocent American citizens. You may have overheard me yelling at my boss for getting me involved in this goddamn mess." She nodded. "I found out something you should know before you cross her. This is personal for Menendez."

"What do you mean?"

"Have you seen the names of the DEA agents killed in Colombia?" Erin shook her head. "One of them was Jesus Menendez."

"Her husband?"

"Her son."

"Shit." She gasped. "That's the piece of the puzzle I've been missing. That's why they're so desperate to make him pay. Did you know Summers was a marked man when I was bringing him back to stand trial?"

"I read the file, but there wasn't much detail."

"Then someone in the CIA must have censored it because I swear I wrote a tome on the case for the FBI. Four assassins were sent to kill him, and they didn't care who got in the way. One crippled our jet, and we crashed in the mountains. Summers and I survived, but an FBI pilot was killed. The man who did that was named Jeff Foster, alias Jeff Norris. He claimed to be a CIA agent. Have you heard of him?"

"No."

"He came back to silence me and kill Kyle. An RCMP officer killed him as he was trying to kill me. Kyle had tipped him off. Kyle saved my life more than once trying to get away from them."

"This is personal for you, too, then."

"Yes. The next assassin, whose name was Richard Demeter, killed a Canadian police officer before I killed him. Heard of him?" Agent White shook his head. "The third killed a store attendant. His name was William Veibl."

"Haven't heard his name either. You killed him, too?"

"Yes."

"Christ. Remind me not to piss you off again." She laughed. "And the fourth?"

"Stephen Larkin. The RCMP arrested him, but he's saying nothing; claims he has no idea who hired him."

"Don't know any Larkin," said Agent White.

"Probably all aliases."

"Probably. You think they were CIA?"

"Maybe not. They weren't very good at their job."

"Believe it or not, CIA agents aren't trained for that sort of thing."

"Do you think Menendez would be capable of sending those assassins?"

"She lost her only child, and she was devastated, and I know she blamed 'that quantum computer and the traitors who sold it to the Colombians,' as she put it. So, it's certainly possible, but it had to be off the books. The CIA would never condone these tactics against our own citizens. She would've had to hire independents. I'll look for any evidence of her link to the assassins, but I doubt I'll find anything. She's very smart, and she's been in the game long enough to know how to cover her tracks."

"All right. Thanks."

Agent White dropped Erin off at the airport and went back to the office to start a clandestine look into his boss's activities over the past few months.

Helena got in touch with Erin as she waited at the airport for the flight back to Chicago. She, too, was furious over the outrage. She supported Erin's idea to take this to the media, and undertook to fight for Kyle's release through official channels.

Erin was ordered to attend a disciplinary hearing the next day at the FBI's field office. She was suspended without pay pending further investigation into her conduct on the case.

With no sign of Kyle by the twenty-four-hour deadline, Erin booked a meeting room at a downtown hotel and called every paper, TV station, and radio station in Chicago to invite them to a press conference scheduled for the next morning. She sat to write a speech.

The next morning, with Helena, fourteen reporters, and two CIA agents posing as reporters in the room, Erin took the podium and said: "Thank you for coming. I have a short statement to make, then I'll be pleased to answer your questions." She set her prepared speech in front of her and began reading. "America. Land of the free. We Americans cherish our freedom, but we take it for granted.

"Just imagine living in a country where your freedom can be taken away on the whim of a corrupt government official. Imagine the terror of walking down your street and suddenly a van screeches to a halt next to you, and two men in masks jump out and assault you. You have no chance to fight them off, because before you can even react they've zapped you with a stun gun and dragged you into the van. Imagine you come to your senses a few minutes later. You look around trying to figure out what's going on, and then it dawns on you. 'I've been kidnapped!'

That horrible realization frightens you to the core. You're in the van driving somewhere. You're so scared you don't want to say anything, but you have to know! 'What is this?' you ask. The men don't answer. 'Where are you taking me?' Again no response. 'Are you kidnapping me?' You shudder at that possibility because they're no longer wearing their masks.

"You can identify them—so if they're kidnappers, you're dead. But they still don't answer. 'I've done nothing wrong!' you scream.

"'Shut up' one of the men hollers. You're so scared you start to shake and cry.

"Finally the van stops, and your heart races. 'Are they taking me out to kill me?' The men lug you out, and you see you're at the airport. They're leading you to a small jet. 'Where the hell are you taking me?' you demand to know as your gathering anger overcomes your fear for the moment.

"One of the men hits you hard across the face to re-establish your fear. They drag you onto the plane, close the door, and throw you into a seat. Your heart races again as the jet leaves the ground. You still haven't a clue what's going on.

"Hours later, you land. 'Where are we?' you ask the men sheepishly, but they remain silent. You step out into the heat. You know you're far away from home. They shove you into another van and off it goes, you know not where. You have new guards now and try your luck with them.

"'Where am I? Where are you taking me?' Silence. 'You must have mistaken me for someone else! I've never done anything wrong.' They drive on. A short while later the van drives into a prison of some sort. You're hauled out of the van, led into the prison and stripped naked. They give you an orange uniform and instruct you to put it on. Outraged by this time you refuse and demand your freedom.

"'You can't do this to me! Let me go for God's sake!' This time a guard strikes you with his truncheon, and drags you unconscious to your new home—a six by six cell with no bed, no blanket, no pillow; nothing other than a pail for your bodily functions. You regain consciousness and pray to wake up from this unaccountable nightmare.

"Imagine living in a country where this can happen to you. Well, as you may have guessed by now, you do. You see, this unfortunate American citizen has been deemed an enemy combatant of the United States. On what basis has his country done this? No one will say, because they don't need to say. The government says he is, so he is; there's no debating it. The prisoner can't fight it, because, in the first place, he doesn't know what he's done.

"You see, our government, just like a dictatorship of a Third World backwater, doesn't have to tell him what he's charged with. In fact, our government, just like the prototypical communist totalitarian regime, doesn't even have to charge him. There's no appeal, because there's no trial—not in a civilian court, at least. A military tribunal may hear the case, although they don't need to bother informing him of the charges against him.

"Try defending yourself if you don't even know the charges against you. Conviction is as certain as any show trial in Beijing.

"Should anyone learn what's become of this man, there's still no relief under the law. 'No person may invoke the Geneva Conventions or any protocols thereto in any habeas corpus or other civilian action or proceeding,' says the Military Commissions Act. Thus, according to our government—the same one that continually preaches democracy and tolerance abroad—no court has the authority to challenge its decision. Remarkably, and with remarkably little protest, our government has turned back the clock eight hundred years. The Magna Carta established the right of habeas corpus and it has been a cornerstone of our Constitution since our nation's founding. But no more.

"By the astonishingly simple procedure of labeling him an enemy combatant, our government has made sure this poor man has no rights anymore. He has no right to liberty, happiness, free speech, trial by jury. He has no right to be free from torture. Did you know our government has adopted a policy of torture against enemy combatants? This defies not only our own Constitution, but the Geneva Conventions and U.N. conventions. But that's fine, because the drafters of this law included a prohibition against invoking these laws and conventions.

"Of course, another country could legitimately charge our president, or any other political or military official, with war crimes, but, honestly, who would have the effrontery to do that? I mean, look at what we do to our own citizens.

"This is not merely a theoretical issue, ladies and gentlemen. This has actually happened to a friend of mine. He has been accused of terrorism and labeled an enemy combatant. Who is this man? His name is Kyle Summers. What did he do to earn this label? Well, his troubles began, believe it or not, when he invented the world's most advanced computer—the Qubit quantum computer in fact. Dr. Rick

Hugel was given credit for it, but we now know that Mr. Summers was the true genius behind the machine.

"The government passed a little-known law that forbids the company from selling its computer. Sounds outrageous in a country that prides itself on its capitalist tradition and its knack for inventing trailblazing technology, but the digital computer lobby spooked Congress into its prohibition. In a desperate move to save his fledgling firm from bankruptcy, Mr. Summers decided to ignore the law by selling two computers in Canada; the government elected not to press charges for this.

"Unfortunately, three more computers were sold, one of which went to China, another to a Colombian paramilitary group. Within days, our agents in both countries started turning up dead. Top-secret government computer files with supposedly unbreakable pass codes were breached, and the identities of our agents were found. It had to be the quantum computer, because nothing else out there could've done this.

"The FBI was called in to investigate. I was the lead field agent on the case. I ended up arresting Mr. Summers and charging him. As the person suspected of selling the computers, he was classified as a terrorist. While I was bringing him back from Canada to face charges here, we were beset by four different assassination attempts. Only luck and the help of the RCMP got us through. Mr. Summers saved my life more than once during that ordeal.

"He stood trial, and two days ago was found innocent. The evidence pointed to his partners, Dr. Rick Hugel and Ms Amy Janssen, as the real perpetrators. Dr. Hugel was killed, probably by the person behind the assassins. Ms Janssen is under arrest in Brazil, where she fled.

"Case closed against Mr. Summers, right? Hardly. Someone didn't like the verdict and decided to disregard the court. This person deemed Mr. Summers an enemy combatant, and he has been kidnapped by the CIA. I know this, because I saw the kidnapping take place. I followed the van to the airport and saw them drag him onto a jet. I called the Chicago police, but they refused to intervene when they were shown the CIA identification, and the jet took off. I took it upon myself to arrest the CIA agents on federal kidnapping charges, but the FBI, too, refused to press charges.

"So according to the CIA, the FBI, and the Chicago police, it's just fine to ignore a court ruling, to kidnap an innocent man and to fly him off to a black site somewhere, where he is undoubtedly being tortured as I speak."

Unable to sit silent any further, the reporters started shouting questions. "Who is responsible for this?" a few asked.

"I was getting to that. Angela Menendez of the CIA."

"Why did she do it?"

"She has a personal vendetta against the inventor of the computer. Unfortunately, one of the victims of the slaughter of our agents in Colombia was her son. He and his wife were killed by a Colombian drug lord. This is a tragedy for her, but it does not give her the right to take the law into her own hands. No matter what she thinks, she is not above the law. She committed a serious crime and must be held to account."

"You said Summers also broke the law by selling his computer. Should he not be also be held to account?"

Helena fielded that question. "I'm Helena Csonka, Mr. Summers's court-appointed defense attorney. The charge for selling the quantum computer to Canadian customers was dropped in return for Mr. Summers's agreement to waive his right to an extradition hearing in Canada. This also spared the government an embarrassing loss in court over what is certainly an unconstitutional law.

"Mr. Summers has Canadian and American citizenship. Our government has no right to tell a Canadian citizen he may not sell a computer in Canada. Hell, it has no right to tell an American citizen he can't conduct business in Canada."

Erin added, "What this country—what we—did to Kyle Summers is unconscionable. He did what any reasonable person would do in the face of an outrageous law. I mean, for God's sake, we've destroyed this man, and for what? For inventing the most impressive machine ever invented? Is that what America is about, post-9-11?"

"His machine is useful to enemies of this country," said one of the CIA agents posing as a reporter.

Helena responded, "So are guns, war planes, war ships, tanks, bombs, passenger jets and on and on. If we're consistent, we'd better arrest the people who invent and sell them, too."

"Aren't you concerned you may be jeopardizing yourself with these revelations?" asked a reporter of Erin.

"I am definitely sacrificing my career in the Bureau—a career I loved—because I cannot stand idly by while an innocent man languishes in a black site somewhere, at the mercy of people who think they can get away with whatever they please. I feel I have no choice, because my pleas for justice in this case have been ignored by the FBI.

"This country is supposed to stand for truth, justice and freedom. I became an FBI agent because I believed in those ideals, but if these people get away with this outrage, the obvious deduction is that the United States no longer stands for the rights enshrined in the Constitution. I can't believe we've sunk to that level in a misguided belief that we must sacrifice truth, justice, and freedom to keep terrorism at bay."

"Isn't it illegal to publicly name a CIA agent?"

"Ms Menendez is not an undercover agent, but I may find myself charged as a terrorist for the crime of aiding and abetting a terrorist. All they have to do is define someone as a terrorist to make it so. So they define Kyle Summers as a terrorist, and under the law, if I assist a terrorist, I, too, am a terrorist. Then Kyle's nightmare becomes mine. This is not hyperbole. Ms Menendez warned me against bringing this to the public's attention lest I find myself in the same boat as Mr. Summers—so if you don't hear from me after this, you can presume the CIA is hard at work protecting you from me."

"What do you hope to accomplish with these revelations?" asked another reporter.

"I'm here today to appeal to the fourth estate to do its job. Challenge the government, challenge the CIA to produce Mr. Summers alive and well, challenge the CIA and the FBI to press charges against Ms Menendez. If you let them get away with this, your precious freedom of the press could easily be the next casualty in the battle against terrorism. Any number of laws in post-9-11 America could be used to classify any one of you as a terrorist, and put you away without trial for life. If you think that's impossible, consider all our Constitutionally-guaranteed rights they tossed in the trash in the Kyle Summers case, including the First, Fourth, Fifth, and Eighth Amendments. Why not the ever pesky freedom of the press? So do your job!"

With that declaration, she left, even as reporters hollered more questions. She thanked Helena for the show of support, exited by a side door, and got a cab home.

At her hearing that afternoon, Erin was fired. Even though she had fully expected it, the sentence hit her hard. As she handed in her gun and badge, she began to cry. She was given a few minutes to pack up and she was escorted out of the building.

*

The Chicago media put pressure on the government to explain what became of Kyle Summers. The CIA denied all of Erin's accusations and refused the media's demands for access to Ms Menendez. Agent White got nowhere in his efforts to connect Ms Menendez to the hit men. He backed off when his job was threatened. She quietly retired and left the country for an extended vacation.

The government decided to stonewall reporters by denying any knowledge of the disappearance of Kyle Summers. Most reporters soon gave up, but one young reporter for the Chicago *Tribune* saw this as his big chance; he kept at the CIA and FBI to explain what happened to Mr. Summers. They ignored him for three weeks, but their plan to stall until the reporter got bored went sour when he got a hold of the police file— accidentally copied and left on his desk by Officer Krupa—that confirmed the CIA took Kyle Summers.

"CIA Took Summers: Chicago Police" was the headline in the *Tribune* the next day, and the story went national.

Two days later, CBS radio news reported, "Kyle Summers, the man allegedly kidnapped by CIA agents in Chicago, was found wandering alone along a lonely highway in Idaho late this morning. He showed no evidence of having been tortured, although he seemed to be in a trance. Mr. Summers either could not or would not respond to this reporter's questions. The CIA and FBI denied all along he had been abducted, despite evidence uncovered by a Chicago reporter that police were called out to stop his reported kidnapping at Chicago's Midway Airport, but refused to intervene when shown CIA identification.

"The CIA is now claiming he was temporarily detained for questioning as a material witness and released shortly thereafter. One source within the CIA who declined to be named theorized that Summers and former FBI agent Erin McAdams staged a show to publicize their anti-Patriot Act agenda."

The story was abandoned shortly thereafter.

*

Erin rushed out to Idaho to see Kyle as soon as the report aired. He had been taken to a hospital in Boise, where he had been installed in the psych ward. Seeing him sitting up in his bed in his room, with a look of empty desperation in his eyes, she ran up to him and tried to hug him, but he curled into a ball to protect himself.

"Kyle? Can you hear me?" said Erin. She put her hand on his shoulder and he recoiled. Erin began to cry as a doctor sedated him.

"Come out into the hall," suggested the doctor.

"What did they do to him?" she asked.

"There seems to be no physical problem other than exhaustion and dehydration. We can't find any evidence of physical trauma except for some old bruises. Our best guess at this stage is acute stress disorder."

"Which is?"

"It's usually caused by a terrifying event, maybe the threat of death or serious injury. If he felt helpless or terrified, it could have caused the symptoms we're seeing: being in a daze, depersonalization, inability to remember much about the trauma, flashbacks, a belief that he's reliving the experience, exaggerated startle response, which you witnessed, and avoidance of things and people associated with the traumatic events. His response to you was extreme. You were the FBI agent who made a public case for his release?"

"Yes."

"Would he have reason to fear you?'

"I led the investigation and arrested him."

"I see. I think it would be better if you stayed away from him until he recovers."

"He will recover? What's the prognosis?"

"If the diagnosis is accurate, the symptoms could persist as long as four weeks."

"So it's not permanent?"

"Probably not, but only time will tell. Check back in a week."

Erin left the hospital to look for a cheap hotel. She had no income anymore, and was still dealing with the aftermath of Kyle's attack on her finances. She had been able to straighten out her mortgage, credit cards, and student loan with hard copies and frantic phone calls, but the IRS was on her case and her bank accounts, IRAs, and CDs were gone forever. All she had was the last paycheck from work. After that, she would have to live with her parents until she could find a job.

One week later, she returned to the hospital. She found his doctor, and learned there had been significant improvement in Kyle's case. The two went to Kyle's room. He was reading the newspaper. Erin approached cautiously and said, "Hi." He looked at her, smirked and returned to his paper. "How are you?"

"Messed up. You can go, Doc, I'm not gonna go nuts." He smiled and left. "I understand you got me out."

"I did whatever I could."

"Thanks for that. I'm sorry you lost your job."

"Is that enough to earn your forgiveness?"

"You got me out, but you delivered me to them in the first place. You kept saying everything would be okay if I was innocent, but you were wrong. When I'm awake, I keep my eyes fixed on the door or window, because I'm convinced they'll come to finish me off. When I'm asleep, it's all I dream about."

"What did they do to you?"

"When they weren't interrogating me, I was kept naked in a pen that was absolutely freezing and brightly-lit twenty-four hours a day. There was no bed or blanket or pillow or anything. It was almost impossible to sleep, which was, of course, the point. Two of the guards were ugly women who would stand and laugh at me about how inadequate I am.

"I was interrogated every day, sometimes it seemed to go on forever; other times, it was maybe a couple of hours. They'd make me go for two or three days without water. They never beat me, really, but continually slapped me. Once they brought two vicious dogs in, and had them growling and nipping at me while screaming at me to admit something I never did. Once they held a gun to my head and pulled the trigger; it was unloaded. Jesus, it was horrible."

Tears streamed down Erin's face, but she could find no words of commiseration.

"So much for your justice system."

"I don't think they'd dare abduct you again."

"Me neither. Too risky for them, but I'll die in a horrible car crash or of a heart attack brought on by a pointy umbrella. I have to get the hell out of this country right away."

"I'll go with you."

"No, you won't."

"Please, Kyle. I have nothing! I lost everything because of you."

"And I lost everything because of you. Is that any basis for a relationship?"

"Stop blaming me for doing my job. I am an FBI agent. I had absolutely no choice."

"Stop using your job as an excuse. If you'd done your job, you wouldn't have arrested the wrong guy. If you weren't so taken with very handsome Rick, you wouldn't have been seducing him, so it wouldn't have led to my death threat and I wouldn't have been a murder suspect, and I wouldn't have run, so I wouldn't have been suspect number one. If you weren't so biased against the not-handsome weak dog, you would have seen the obvious—that I had everything to lose by selling to our enemies, and Rick and Amy had everything to gain as long as they could frame me."

Erin cast her rueful eyes down and said softly, "I'm sorry; the evidence against you seemed overwhelming." She looked at him and continued, "God help you, Kyle, you have no idea what love is, do you? It isn't when someone uses and abuses you and tosses you in the trash after you've outlived your usefulness to her. It's when someone is willing to give up everything for you because you mean more to her than her career, her reputation, and even her life!"

As Kyle pondered that weighty notion, an attendant jutted his head in the room and said, "There's a phone call for you. You can take it at the desk."

"It's probably that damn reporter again. Tell him I'm asleep, okay?"

"No, it's a woman and she said it's urgent."

Kyle got up and went out to the desk to take the call. Erin followed. His first word into the phone was "Amy?" Erin's eyes bulged. She knew right away what Amy would try to do. She looked around for another phone to see if she could listen in. She found one in an empty office down the hall, pushed the line that was lit, and picked it up.

Amy was saying, "—… if you'll agree to testify that it had to be Rick. You know I know nothing about the computers, so Rick must have hooked them up. Just say that."

"You're in jail. You know they're listening to this conversation."

"I'm not stupid, Kyle. I'm just asking you to tell the truth."

"They're not stupid either. They know you accessed the numbered account, so you must have known about the sale."

"They know I accessed the account, but they don't know I was in on it, because I wasn't. Rick told me after the fact."

"Uh-huh."

"It's true."

"I thought you had a deal to plead guilty and do ten years in prison."

"It fell through when you were found innocent."

"You lost your leverage. Our whole relationship was a lie from the start. You lied to me to get me into the partnership. You promised to marry me, but you were already married to him."

"I married him, it's true, because I loved him. I did what he told me to do to marry him, not to hurt you. Now he's gone. My husband is dead and no one cares. I'm all alone now and I need you."

"You lied to the police to set me up. You planned to live it up with Rick while I rotted in jail."

"When I went to the police, Rick was dead. I lied to get revenge. At the time, I thought you murdered my husband."

"I was told you were at the police station framing me at the time of Rick's murder."

"That's a lie!"

"Even if that's true, the murder charge was dropped months ago, but still you left me hanging out to dry."

"I never thought they'd find you guilty."

"Come on!"

"I was right, wasn't I? You're free, but now I'm in trouble, and I'm asking for your help."

"Why should I help the person who framed me?"

"Rick framed you. I looked the other way and I'm truly sorry. Help me because you love me—you know you do; you have ever since we met. So do this for the woman you love, and she will marry you and spend the rest of her life making it up to you."

"I don't believe you."

Oh, God, don't fall for this, Kyle! Erin said to herself.

Amy continued, "I'll marry you right away. Come to Brazil. We'll get a priest and get married. Please do this for me, and we'll be together forever."

He paused to think as Erin held her breath. *Don't do it, don't do it!* Erin chanted to herself.

While he considered, Amy added incentives. "When I get out, we'll make love all day, every day. I know how long you've been dreaming about that. You can do whatever you want with me any time you want. If you want, we can have children, or we can just be on our own. Whatever you want, I'll give you. I know you want me, you still love me. Tell me you love me."

"I … I love you."

Erin closed her eyes and felt like crying. *He's actually going to do this*, she thought, but he said, "But, then, I don't have the first clue what love really is. I do know you don't love me and you never will. We both fell in love with the wrong person and it cost us everything. Goodbye, Amy." He hung up and went to his room.

Erin almost screeched for joy, but held back. She ran down the hall, but the doctor stopped her. "Not now," he said. "Something's upset him. Come back tomorrow."

The next day, Erin came back to press her case anew, but he was gone. He'd left of his own accord, but no one knew where he went. Despondent, she flew to Delaware to stay with her parents and figure out her future.

CHAPTER SIXTEEN

Five Months Later

"The rates of increase respectively are six decimal two three, eight decimal nine eight, seventeen decimal six one, twenty-two decimal zero, and thirty-four decimal oh seven," said the rotund, balding, hare-lipped economist.

Why can't you say 'point' like the rest of the world, you pompous ass! screamed Erin to herself. To Erin he struck the highest pitch of irksome.

"So, as we can see," the economist continued, "the incidence of every type of major insurance fraud keeps increasing despite our valiant efforts to halt it."

Valiant, Erin scoffed to herself. *This group is about as valiant as Bozo the Clown.*

"It's now estimated to total eighty billion dollars annually, over eight hundred dollars per American per year."

Erin did some quick math in her head and wondered how he came up with that quotient. Must be per household, she reasoned. The economist droned on, "Yet, as this next chart plainly shows, only a minuscule portion of the crime is successfully prosecuted."

Erin tried to understand the confusing chart through her economist-induced stupor, but could make out nothing.

"On the next chart, my regression analysis—which shows an impressive decimal three two adjusted R-squared—clearly shows that these four factors weigh heavily, and they each reach statistical significance at the decimal oh one level, in leading to fraud …"

Erin went back to sleep with her eyes open.

"Erin? Ms McAdams? Are you still with us?" said her boss twenty-five minutes later. Dour, even hateful, in his bearing, the boss managed to bring out the worst in everyone. Five-foot-three in height and three-foot-five in circumference with a thick skull to match, he did little to inspire Erin's respect, but a lot to inspire her revulsion.

"Uh, yes," she replied, snapping to attention and blushing noticeably.

"I'll repeat what I was saying, since it's clear to me you aren't bothering to pay attention." There was some chuckling from the ass-kissing clique surrounding the boss. Erin glared at them. The homely accountant, whom she had already spurned twice, made eyes at her. She noticed and scowled at the affront.

The boss went on, "Last meeting, the group asked you to come up with some new ideas to combat fraud. What have you come up with so far?"

"The meeting you refer to took place just yesterday afternoon. I've had maybe two working hours to start thinking about this."

"I don't like excuses, Ms McAdams. We brought you in for some fresh ideas, and you've been here a few weeks now. Surely as an experienced *former* FBI agent, you must be able to enlighten us poor hicks?"

More lackey chuckling.

"I have a few ideas, yes, but I'd like a couple of days to flesh them out and to present them properly with slides."

"Tomorrow morning at eight-thirty, then, we'll expect to be impressed. Moving on ..."

Erin sighed to herself and tried her best to look interested for the balance of the three-hour meeting. At 11:14, she shuffled out of the boardroom on the way to her cubicle. As she passed by the boss's office, his twenty-year-old son, who had been puzzling over an Archie comic, hopped up to watch her walk by. She noticed and shuddered inside.

"I'll be boss around here some day," he boasted.

"I'm sure you'll richly deserve it," she replied as she picked up her pace. He smiled.

She got to her cubicle, chanting to herself, *I hate this. Oh, God, how I hate my life!* But her depressed and bored expression immediately altered into one of mingled shock and delight upon seeing Kyle sitting in her chair. "Kyle!" she said, as he stood to hug her. "What are you doing here?"

"I'm touring shit holes of the Great Plains. Omaha is the highlight." Erin smirked. "I came to see you, of course."

"Why?"

"I'll get to that. First, tell me what in the name of God you're doing in Nebraska."

"I wasn't exactly employable after being fired by the FBI, and I didn't have the luxury of looking long for work since you

297

bankrupted me." He lowered his eyes. "So, after a fruitless search for three months while I mooched off my parents, I took a job here investigating insurance fraud."

"How do you like it?"

"Well, I just made it through another three-hour meeting without dying of boredom … I'm seriously contemplating suicide. What are you doing here?"

"Have you heard about Qubit's launch in Canada?"

"Of course. I hear it's off to an enormously successful start. Congratulations. What are you doing here?"

"Can we go somewhere to discuss something very important?" he said with a smile.

"Sure. Let's go to the café downstairs. It shouldn't be busy at this hour." They walked toward the elevators. "Uh, I assume you know two police types are following us?"

"Sharp as always, Miss McAdams. They're my bodyguards."

"Aren't you special? Is our important discussion to include them? And what are we discussing anyway?"

"Patience," he urged, as the four got into the elevator.

She smiled at Kyle on the way down. "You look really nice," she said. He smiled, but said nothing. "Politeness would demand you return the compliment," she pointed out.

"Oh, uh, nice lookie ball thingies," he said, looking into her eyes. She jabbed her elbow into him. "Careful," he warned. "My bodyguards will rough you up."

The male bodyguard held Erin and Kyle back until his female partner checked out the main lobby and waved them forward. "It's a bit of a pain," Kyle explained, "but I don't take chances anymore, especially in this country. These two are husband and wife. They're among the best in the field, I'm told."

*

The bodyguards led them to the safest table in the café, and left them alone at the table while they took up posts on either side. "So, why are you here?" Erin asked.

Kyle's confident visage changed as nerves took over. "Erin, the way I left things between us … my only excuse is I was really muddled. It was so unfair of me to blame you for everything I went through." He took her hand in his. "I know I left you in a real predicament. After everything you did for me, giving up your job to get me freed from that awful place, I just left you alone. Can you ever forgive me?"

"So you're here to apologize?"

"Yes." Her face showed disappointment. "But not just that." He hesitated.

She helped him. She smiled and said, "Don't be nervous, Kyle. What are you trying to say?"

"Erin, I, uh, I think I'm, uh, in—"

The waitress came by at that instant to ask for their order. "Not now!" yelped Erin. The waitress turned up her nose and left. "Now, what were you saying?" she said with a tremor in her voice.

"I want to tell you you're the most amazing person I've ever met." Her face fell. He saw her disappointment, which made him more anxious. "Oh, who am I kidding?" he said in frustration. "Why would you ever be interested in me?"

She said, "For God's sake, Kyle, you're the most amazing man I've ever met. *I love you!*"

"That's the first time anyone has ever said that to me," he declared. With tears in his eyes, he took her hand and added, "I can't tell you how happy it makes me feel."

"Good. Now make me happy."

"You told me I had no idea what love is, and you were right. I still don't. What I do know is you're the finest person I have ever met. I know you're the only person on Earth I can trust without hesitation. I know you gave up everything for me and that means everything to someone who's been so cruelly used by so many people. And I know I want to be with you—I think forever. If that's love, then I love you, Erin McAdams." She stood, pulled him up out his chair, hugged him and kissed him. He resumed, "So you'll come with me?"

"I'd love to. Where are we going?"

"Qubit is in Kamloops, B.C. I find it pleasant in B.C. when I'm not dodging bullets."

"What would I be doing?"

"A lot: lobbying to open the U.S. market, which I think will happen soon with all the foreign competitors buying our computer." She nodded. "And I want you to help Helena to get our computers back from the damn government. I hired her; she couldn't resist the constitutional fight or the money I offered. She'll also help defend us against lawsuits by Amy and Rick's family for a huge share of the firm, nervy pricks. She'll beat them, I'm sure.

"But, most importantly, I want you to help me run the company. I want you to manage the firm, help me make important decisions, second-guess me, and watch my back—

I'm naïve, you know." She nodded with a grin. "I want you by my side every day. If you say yes, I'll make you ten percent owner of Qubit."

Her eyes opened wide. "Kyle, that's too generous."

"I hope some day soon we'll be equal owners."

She smiled and kissed him. The bodyguards came over to congratulate her. Kyle said, "I got a husband and wife team for a reason. Erin, this is Ruth and she'll be your boon companion from here on. Her husband Shawn looks after me." They shook hands.

Erin, looking up and down the muscular Shawn, said, "Can't I have him to guard me instead?" with a sly smile.

Kyle smirked and Ruth frowned. "She has a unique sense of humor, Ruth," explained Kyle.

Erin reassured Ruth, "I'm only kidding. I'm sure I'm in great hands."

"Miss McAdams!" interrupted her boss, who had come downstairs for a coffee. "This is not break time. I suggest you get back to your office this minute if—"

"Oh, go join a troupe of munchkins, why don't you, you shitty little blob," suggested Erin, as she took Kyle's hand to lead him outside.

"You're … you're fired!" shouted the blob as he shook his pudgy fist at her. Ruth stepped between him and her charge as Erin and Kyle followed Shawn out of the building.

Erin and Kyle walked to the waiting car hand in hand to face an exciting and dangerous future together.

END

ABOUT THE AUTHOR

Novelist ROBERT POWER was born in Canada, but raised and educated in the United States. He stayed in university so long, Berkeley eventually gave him a PhD to get rid of him. Working as a consultant from home, he drove his wife crazy until he took up writing fiction in his too-ample spare time. Neither he nor his wife know what they were thinking when they decided to have four children, but they're happy they do—most days. They live in southern Ontario. Visit his website: rdpower.ca.

ALSO BY R.D. POWER

2020

For Power or Love

For Power or Love 2

Forbidden

Taylor Made Owens

Thank Sophia for Sam

FICTION-ADVENTURE/ESPIONAGE

Is America's national security apparatus out of control?

KYLE SUMMERS NEVER IMAGINED THAT INVENTING THE WORLD'S FIRST VIABLE QUANTUM COMPUTER WOULD LEAD TO BANKRUPTCY, BETRAYAL AND A DESPERATE FLIGHT FOR HIS VERY LIFE.

ACCUSED OF TERRORISM AGAINST HIS COUNTRY, HE IS PURSUED BY FEDERAL AGENTS AND HUNTED BY ASSASSINS BENT ON REVENGE FOR THE BLOODY HAVOC UNLEASHED BY HIS COMPUTER.

HIS ONLY HOPE IS THE FBI AGENT SENT TO BRING HIM TO JUSTICE.

WILL HER UNSHAKEABLE FAITH THAT TRUTH AND JUSTICE WILL TRIUMPH OVER MORAL MYOPIA LEAD TO HIS SALVATION OR HIS UNDOING?

ISBN 9780991798384

90000

9 780991 798384